# COWBOY, IT'S CHRISTMAS

## A MEN OF STONE RIDGE NOVEL

### HEATHERLY BELL

# PROLOGUE

$\mathcal{G}$ather up, everyone, because the ladies of SORROW have news! After last year's mess, I had a brilliant idea, if I do say so myself.

You'll remember that last year, Winona James, the country music star, fell in love with one of *our* men, Riggs Henderson (can't say anyone blames her). Well, that means another woman in town, for which we are eternally grateful. Another man of Stone Ridge, settled and happy.

Yet, there are so many more. Even though not all seem ready to settle down (Beau Stephens, I'm looking at you) their *mothers* are anxious for grandchildren, lickety-split! And since we *ladies* do take care of everything that needs doing around here (by the way, some help would be welcome) we've tackled this latest issue, too. The work around here never ends!

But now, with the help of Winona, and all the many connections she has to show-business folk, we have interest from one of them Hollywood studios. The setting of a new reality dating show will be Stone Ridge itself and we will be interviewing women to vie for the heart of "Mr. Cowboy." I personally have my eye on Wade Cruz, who has recently been permanently sidelined from the rodeo circuit. He's been injured but he'll get over that right quick. His lovely mother raised him to be a proper man of Stone Ridge and helpful in every way. Rose died not long ago, poor lamb, and all of us ladies of SORROW have been delivering casseroles and motherly love to Wade.

Frankly, it's time "Wild Wade" settle down and we want to help him. Yes, we do. He could be our first *Mr. Cowboy*, and with those smoldering rodeo-cowboy good looks, help bring truckloads of women into town.

Because I'll let you in on a little secret: only one woman will win *this* contest, but we have *plenty* of men for them to stick around for.


~ BEULAH HAYES, President of SORROW (Society of Reasonable, Respectable, Orderly Women) and keeper of the *Men of Stone Ridge* bible, tenth edition. ~

*D*aisy Carver loved Christmas, but in her opinion, the Christmas décor at the Shady Grind bar and grill had gone a tad overkill this year. The tinsel seemed to be everywhere, bright blinking red and green lights draped across the stage in the back, and bundles of mistletoe hung from the ceiling at approximately every two feet. This had likely been done by a desperate man looking to hook up. There were so many lonely men in their women-scarce town.

And still, no one was even trying to kiss *her*. She'd purposely sat under this mistletoe all night.

The bane of her existence was that Daisy had two older brothers. Two big, brawny cowboys that could take care of themselves in a dark alley. One of them, Jackson, owned this bar and was here tonight. And in case *he* wasn't, there was always her oldest brother, Lincoln. At some point in time, and without her approval, he'd assigned himself as her guardian and protector. Between her brothers and their tattletale wives, Eve and Sadie, it seemed that no man alive

3

would ever dare to approach Daisy unless he was ready to get married to her the next day.

But all she needed was one *brave* man.

She'd dated a little here and there, but every kiss was a dud. Granted, she had a high standard to meet. When she was eighteen, a cowboy had kissed her within an inch of her life. Nothing had ever compared. Though she did get asked out a lot, she was often accused of being too much of a "good girl" and "not fun." That was all going to change. Though marriage, pregnancy, and babies were winding through their town like a virus, Daisy wasn't interested in any of that. Still, when it came to sex, she'd recently decided that she would like to find out what all the fuss was about.

But tonight, she was here simply to forget her troubles and enjoy the show from a seat on the barstool. Her brother Jackson was on the stage playing guitar and singing "It's Christmas, Cowboy," one of his latest country music chart hits. Singing harmony with him was a hugely pregnant Winona James. She'd just had twins seven months ago and must have gotten herself pregnant again the next day. She honestly looked like she'd swallowed a pumpkin. The kind that they sold at the pumpkin patch in nearby Kerrville. This October they'd gone for a personal best with a pumpkin that weighed in at close to two hundred pounds. It won the county contest.

Daisy would never tell her so, but well, Winona looked like she'd swallowed half of that pumpkin. And this time, she wasn't carrying twins. Just one baby. One!

As the song ended and Winona was helped off the stage, Lenny called out, "Hey there, Winona! You think they forgot to take a baby out?"

There was raucous laughter, including from Winona, who shot back, "So I got knocked up again. But I have it on good authority that this one is a *girl*."

A roar of approval at that, because there hadn't been a girl born in Stone Ridge, Texas, for around ten years or so.

"She sings, plays guitar, *and* is having a girl," Jackson said from the stage. "Ladies and gentlemen, let's hear it for Winona James!"

Winona waddled to the bar where her handsome rancher husband, Riggs Henderson, sat on a stool next to Daisy.

"Hey there, Winona," Daisy said.

"Hi, sugar." Winona threw her arms around Daisy. "How are you these days?"

"Oh, you know." Daisy threw a look at the mistletoe hanging above her head. "About the same."

"Ah, I see." Winona caught Riggs's eyes, and waved her hand. "Riggs?"

"Oh, yeah." Riggs leaned forward and bussed Daisy's cheek. "Merry Christmas."

Lord, he smelled good. If he wasn't in his forties *and* married, Daisy would be all over that. Best of all, he didn't scare easily.

Daisy sighed. "Thanks."

"Levi?" Winona called out to the bartender.

"Huh?" When the part-time bartender/horse wrangler turned to Winona, she was pointing to the mistletoe above Daisy's head. He nodded, then leaned across the bar to kiss her cheek. "Merry Christmas, Daisy."

Gee, how exciting. Practically an air kiss. But this would be about as good as it would get for Daisy Carver in Stone Ridge. And it wasn't as if scandalous things didn't happen here, they just happened to other people.

Not *Daisy*.

She was the good girl, as far from her mother's reputation as a girl could get.

It wasn't that she wanted a scandal, but a little excitement would be nice.

Over a year ago, Winona had moved from Nashville to find herself a baby daddy. She'd had a long line of suitors, sure, Daisy heard all about it. But in the end, she'd given up on the idea. Then she wound up accidentally pregnant by Riggs. Some thought Winona would be going back to Nashville eventually, but Daisy didn't see *that* happening. She watched Riggs hold out his hand, and when Winona took it, he smiled and led her out the door.

Jeremy Pine slid into the stool next to Daisy vacated by Riggs.

"Boy, I sure dodged a bullet with that one. Whew." He made a mock swipe of his brow. "Poor Riggs. Got himself saddled with a wife and twins, and another already on the way."

"What do you care about it?" Daisy took a pull of her beer.

"Riggs is a good guy. He should be enjoying his twilight years or some such thing, not bringing up babies."

Daisy snorted. "*Twilight* years? Face it, you're jealous it isn't you. I heard you auditioned for the part as her 'personal assistant.'"

"I wouldn't have taken the job."

"You're too young for her anyway. Winona wanted a *real* man."

Jeremy straightened. "I am a real man, sweetheart. I'm twenty-five now, don't forget."

Jeremy wasn't bad looking and he had a sexy cowboy air about him. Tight Wranglers, tipped Stetson, beard stubble. He was no Wade Cruz, but he had a nice smile and an interesting face.

"So, you want to get out of here or something?"

"Hell, no." He bristled. "Jackson's here. He'll see us leave."

"Coward."

"I'm no coward, just smart as a whip. I don't want to get married yet."

Daisy scowled. "Who said anything about marriage?"

"C'mon, Daisy." He gently put his arm around her shoulder and squeezed lightly, as if giving her sympathy. "It isn't just your brothers. You're a nice girl. And we all know you're a...a...you know..."

"A *what?*"

"A tease," he whispered.

"That's a vicious lie," Daisy lied.

"Why would anyone lie about that?"

"I have no idea! That's my personal business, so how would anyone know whether it's true?"

"I guess it's the way you...act. Plus, your two brothers. No one's turned up dead, so we just assumed—"

"And made an ass of yourself!"

"Well, if it's not true, then." Jeremy removed his arm from her shoulder as Jackson headed toward the bar. "Maybe no one has the guts to find out."

"That's the first thing you've said tonight that makes any sense. There sure are a lot of gutless men in Stone Ridge."

She would correct herself, but she was just too mad. As she'd been taught from the time she was a little girl, the men of Stone Ridge were above reproach. Honest and hard-working ranchers. Traditional. They banded together in times of trouble, helped each other out with broken fences, stuck cattle, emergencies of any kind, and even construction of the new school and clinic.

And they took care of their women. Who were "their" women? Every female from birth to death. As a consequence, a man knew that if he didn't take care of *his* woman, there would be someone else ready and more than willing to take his place. And God help the man who ever raised a hand in anger toward his woman. He'd be run out of town and probably tarred and feathered.

Those were the *good* parts about Stone Ridge and Daisy appreciate them as much as the next woman. The bad parts were unfortunately conjoined with the good ones. All this tradition and protection grated on a young woman who wanted a little adventure. Daisy might have played it safe her whole life, but it was time to broaden her horizons. She was tired of waiting around for something to happen. She would *make* something happen!

A little less protection and a lot more freedom was in order. Though probably neither one would happen tonight.

Jackson joined Daisy and fist-bumped with her. "Hey, Shortie."

"You were good up there tonight," Daisy said. "Are you and Eve comin' over for Sunday dinner this week?"

"I'll have to ask Eve."

"*Please* don't leave me alone with Lincoln and Sadie. The whole night will be about Sammy and how wonderful he is. I hate to tell them, but though I adore Sammy, his ears are too big for his head. So, he's not perfect."

Jackson burst into laughter. "Boy, you sure are easy to rattle these days. We'll be there."

"Thank you!"

"Hey, so how's Wade doing these days?"

"*Wade?*"

Wade Cruz was Daisy's longtime crush and Lincoln's best friend. A rodeo cowboy, he was rarely in town, though he'd made an appearance at his mother's funeral a few months ago only to leave again.

"Lincoln told me that he's back. He got injured and came home. Didn't you hear? Thought you of all people would know."

It felt like the floor had given way beneath Daisy. All the blood rushed to her head.

*Wade. Wade Cruz. Injured? When? How? Why?*

"Lincoln didn't tell me. No one told me."

"Probably figured you already knew."

"It's not like I keep tabs on him."

Jackson cocked his head and grinned. *"Really?"*

Daisy took one last pull of her beer, set it down, and climbed off the stool. "I'm tired of you teasin' me."

"What? I just got started. Okay, okay." He went palms up. "Shortie, c'mon. Don't go."

She shoved his shoulder, and kept walking, waving him away. When she stepped outside, the sky had darkened to a purplish hue. A chill snapped through the air and she tugged her jacket close. They'd had a strange and early winter, ice storms and snow blanketing areas that rarely saw any. In Hill Country, a foot of snow had fallen not long ago, and temperatures dropped to the thirties.

But some folks knew how to keep warm.

Here and there, couples were kissing in the cabs of their trucks, on the tailgates, and in little quiet corners. Jolette Marie Trueheart was in a clinch with some cowboy. Sigh. It had been so long since Daisy had been really and properly kissed. Too long since a certain man had pushed her up against the wall, crashed his lips over hers, sunk his fingers into her hair, and pulled her against him. She remembered well the day and time because it may as well have been written on her heart. She'd been eighteen, and Wade Cruz had kissed her in the bedroom of her family home. Then, as if shocked he'd done it, he ran out of the room so fast he nearly fell on his way out.

Even so, she might not have taken it so personally if he hadn't left town a couple of days later.

She'd called him out on it the next time she'd seen him,

weeks later, working as a ranch hand for her father between rodeos.

"I thought *you* of all people weren't afraid of my brothers. You can hold your own."

Wade threw a stack of hay down and wiped his brow. "Who the hell said I'm afraid of 'em?"

"Um, you ran out on me so fast I thought your ass was on fire."

"Listen, Daisy." Wade tipped his hat and gazed at her from under hooded lids. "You need to understand a few things."

She crossed her arms. "And I suppose you're going to tell me these things."

"Now, I can't tell you *everything*. That's something your husband's going to have to do." He slid her a wicked grin and cocked his head. "But the thing is, men and women need to be on an even and equal playing field. It's only right. Both should have the same amount of…experience. Know-how. Catch my drift?"

"I think I do." She suddenly "got" that she was apparently a bad kisser. Humiliation thrummed through her. "But I can learn."

"I'm sure you will, sweetheart. Just not with me." Then he'd walked away and climbed back in the pickup to shove out another bale of hay.

And nearly ten years later, Daisy still hadn't found anyone that came close to that kiss, all thanks to one man.

*Wade Cruz.*

## CHAPTER 2

*W*ade's arm hurt like a son of a gun.

This morning, he'd rolled out of bed, and in a hazy fog of sleep he'd forgotten about the compound fracture he'd earned when he'd fallen off a bull in the last qualifying round of the National Rodeo. He'd paid dearly for that memory slip when he put too much weight on his left shoulder. His arm now ached and throbbed, reminding him of the moment the injury had occurred. But no pain had ever been quite like that one. None of his prior concussions, scrapes, cuts, aches and pains. That had been raw, sweltering, bone-grafting, screaming pain.

He'd simply stayed flat on his back where he'd landed while around him everyone ran to help. The sky had been particularly blue that day and he remembered that a bird landed on a stall and a horse nickered. Other than that, Wade couldn't process anything. Not the pain, nor the fact that he'd been so close to another win only to lose it all. And he'd sacrificed far too much to the rodeo already.

But all this knowledge would come later.

Then, he'd noticed the blood, and the bone jutting out of

his skin. Another cowboy passed out at the sight. Wade was simply numb, possibly protected by his body's endorphins. Too bad the relief was temporary. The numbness had worn off soon enough.

Even after surgery, casting, and physical therapy his arm might never be the same.

"This is a career-ending injury," the announcer had said at the time, predicting the future.

Now, Wade staggered to the shower, dressed, and made coffee. He massaged the tightness in his left shoulder caused by the nagging soreness in his arm.

"You won't win," he told his arm.

Last night, when he'd reached for the pain-killing meds the doctor had prescribed, he'd knocked the entire bottle off his nightstand. They'd scattered all over the hardwood floor since he'd not tightened the cap after his last dosage. He wandered back into his bedroom and slowly picked up every last pill and shoved them back in the bottle. Squatting, he swallowed one with his coffee. Sooner or later, he'd wean himself off these, but for now they did the trick of numbing the pain so he could get through his day.

The doorbell rang, and Wade fervently hoped it wasn't someone with another damn casserole for his freezer. A betting man, Wade would stake his life on this being yet another casserole dish.

"Two to one odds," he muttered as he walked to the door.

There, on the other side of his front door was Beulah Hayes herself, carrying another dish.

"Good morning, Wade." Beulah held out the covered plate. "Breakfast."

"You didn't have to do that, Miss Beulah." He took the casserole, using his good arm, and stepped aside. "Come on in. Coffee?"

"Don't mind if I do."

She followed him into the kitchen, no doubt surveying it all. Beulah was president of the ladies of SORROW (Society of Reasonable, Respectable, Orderly Women) and worried far too much about Wade. Unfortunately, she and the ladies thought it was their personal, God-given duty to look out for every man of Stone Ridge. Now that Wade was without a mother, they'd ramped it up.

"I see some progress has been made."

But not enough and she didn't have to say so. Yesterday, Wade had started going through his father's ledgers. Then he'd walked to the north pasture to survey the land. Unfortunately, there was so much to be done, he didn't know where to begin. He mucked the stable belonging to his horse, Dante, and checked in on his old bull, Satan. Before the end of the day, he'd run out of steam. So, he'd watched several hours of film of his last winning season. That was enough to send him to bed early.

Lincoln had been over earlier this week, trying to talk Wade into allowing him to help get the cattle ranch back in business. To do that, he either needed an influx of cash or to use up the last of his savings because his father had left him and his mother with close to nothing.

He scratched his chin. "Ran into a little problem with the barn yesterday. I'll get to it."

"That barn is about to fall in on itself. You need to allow the men to help. That's what we do around here, after all."

"Yum, smells good. What is this?" Wade pulled the tin foil back to peek and change the subject.

"My French toast casserole." She puffed up with pride.

"I had no idea you could make a casserole out of French toast."

"You can make a casserole out of anything."

"I'm beginning to see that." He grabbed a cup from the top cupboard, ignoring the pain in his arm at the stretch.

Beulah had taken a seat at the small white farmer's table in the nook. "I'm worried about you."

"Don't waste your time. I'm fine." He poured and set her coffee down.

"You're not *fine*. Rose hasn't even been gone six months."

"But it was a long time coming." Wade pushed back the memory, ignoring a different kind of ache.

He didn't sit, hoping not to encourage too long of a visit. He leaned a hip against the counter and sipped his coffee.

"I've been thinkin'..." Beulah began.

"Uh-oh."

"I have just the solution to your troubles."

"Really? Have you got a new arm in there for me?" Wade eyed the big brown tote bag she carried.

She narrowed her eyes. "Your arm still aching you much?"

"Nah, it's all healed up," he lied. He was not in the habit of worrying anyone. "Pastor June was by earlier with a casserole. She says the answer to my problems is attending church."

"That never hurts."

"Those wooden pews are hell on a rancher's back."

Beulah shook her head. "You've always been strong as a bull. I do hope you're not as stubborn as one."

"Don't worry, I've quit the rodeo. Or it quit me. Either way."

"That's wise, but it's not entirely what I meant by *stubborn*."

"What did you mean?"

"Wade Cruz, when's the last time you were in a *serious relationship* with a woman?"

"Why, Miss Beulah. I had no idea you cared. And here I thought you were happily married." He winked.

"I'm serious, child. Listen up. Winona has us interest from one of them Hollywood studios. But we have to act fast.

Don't you know, we're goin' to have us a reality TV show right here in Stone Ridge, Texas!"

"Did you nominate my house for one of those fixer-upper shows?" He'd been telling everyone who would listen that he would do the work around here himself.

"Why would I do that when we have all the manpower we need, free of charge?"

"But why else would anyone make a reality show here? Does it have to do with a cattle competition?"

Beulah straightened and smiled. "It's a love competition."

"I thought that was against the law."

She squinted. "A *dating* show: *Mr. Cowboy.*"

Wade snorted and nearly spit out his coffee. He could just picture it now. A cowboy smiling into the camera, holding a rope instead of a red rose.

He laughed, a full belly laugh, and damn it all, that felt good. "That's…that's pretty funny."

"I don't know what on earth is so *funny*!"

"You're serious?"

"The studio is going to start weeding through the women soon. Interviews, photo shoots, the whole shebang. But it will help pique their interest once we choose a man. They'll pay for a photo shoot of our cowboy, right here in town, no need to go anywhere. Then the studio will select a large group of women and eventually move them to a location right here in town. Probably sometime next summer. They'll stay for weeks while they compete for the heart of a cowboy. A man of Stone Ridge."

"I see, and so you think maybe my house could serve as the location where they'll all stay? It depends on how much time I have." He waved his hand around the kitchen.

He'd quite by accident once watched a preview of one of those dating shows, and the homes provided for the contestants were lavish and large. They'd probably expect a little

15

rustic ambience in Hill Country, but Wade worried he had a little too much rust in *his* mansion.

"No, sugar. I want *you* to be our first Mr. Cowboy."

"See, that's *really* not funny."

"We all just want you to be happy. And a good woman would do that for you. I know we don't have enough of them here, so that's why I've gone out of my way to arrange this for you."

"Well, quickly go out of your way to un-arrange it."

"You don't mean that."

The hell he didn't. He'd lasted thirty-three years without getting hitched, and he didn't see the point anymore. Children would have been the point, according to his mother. But it was too late to make her happy.

Drawing on the manners his sainted mother taught him, Wade forced his voice to be gentle. "I know you mean well, but I'm not interested. And I'm sure there's a lot of men you could approach who would be. Jeremy Pine, for instance. Why not him? He's a looker."

"Jeremy is twenty-five and acts like he's twelve. If we're going to put our best face on this contest, we need a grown man."

"I'm flattered, but still not interested." He uncovered the casserole, found a fork, and took a bite. "Mmm, Miss Beulah, you sure can bake. Come over anytime."

Beulah shook a finger. "Wade Cruz, do not distract me with talk of my superior baking skills!"

At that precise moment, there was another knock on the door. "That's probably Lincoln."

He threw the fork in the sink and opened the door to Daisy Carver.

His heart hopped and started racing as it always did for no apparent reason other than Daisy always had him feeling off balance.

Kind of comical that she would say that, since Daisy was about the only woman in town he'd never dated. It had to do with her age, since she was a good seven years younger. It had to do with her brother, who was Wade's best friend in the world. It also had to do with the fact that Daisy confounded him on every level. He'd never fooled himself into thinking he understood women, but Daisy took his confusion to a stratospheric level.

She was at once Scarlett O'Hara and Daisy Duke. Beauty queen and auto mechanic. Overalls and lipstick. Sweet and ornery. Innocent. Sexy. He could go on, but why bother. She was off-limits. He'd kissed her once in a moment of sheer madness, when he was young and stupid, full of piss and vinegar. The intensity of that kiss had scared him off for good.

And for someone who faced off angry bulls for a career, that said something. It wasn't that he feared Lincoln or Jackson, with whom he could hold his own, thank you very much. But he loved the Carvers, had spent half his life with them, and he couldn't see ruining that by disappointing Daisy as he no doubt would eventually.

He was forever stunned to see her, and forever making efforts to avoid her.

Then she opened her Cupid's bow lips and spoke, shattering the quiet, and reminding him that he was staring. "You're back."

TWO WORDS.

That's all Daisy had to say as she tried to collect her thoughts. As she tried to control the slow roll of her heart and the sense of utter chaos of emotions. She was at once thrilled to see him, while a rope of fear uncoiled inside her telling her to step lively. Guard her heart. Wade was undoubtedly the best-looking man in all of Stone Ridge. Despite that, he was famously single and had been for as long as Daisy could remember. Rumor went he was a bit of a player, but Daisy didn't listen to rumors.

Wade had dark, wavy hair and sensual lips with a smile that always tipped slightly at the corner. And the way he filled out a pair of Wranglers was almost criminal. But Wade didn't *look* injured even if she had it on good authority that he was.

"Hiya, Squirt. Come on in, it's welcome-back-Wade week, apparently." He waved her inside and led her to the kitchen.

Daisy saw Miss Beulah and stopped midwalk. "Hi, Miss Beulah."

"Hello there, young lady," Beulah said. "Will I see you at church tomorrow morning?"

"Of course."

"I'll see you and your grandmother then." Beulah stood and gathered her tote bag. "Now, Wade, just think. You could be happily married in six weeks' time."

*Married in six weeks' time?*

Oh Lord, he was engaged! Another thing no one had thought to tell her.

*I knew this would happen one day.* Wade was seven years older than she was, the same age as Lincoln. She shouldn't be at all surprised he was finally settling down. If the thought made her gut roil, it was her own damn fault. She should have stopped thinking about Wade long ago.

Wade walked Beulah outside. "Thank you for the casserole."

"Think about it. I only want you to be happy."

"Sure." Wade shut the door and turned to Daisy. "What's up? Want some French toast casserole? Say what you will about her, but Miss Beulah can bake."

Daisy just stared at him. She couldn't believe this moment

had finally come. Wild Wade Cruz was getting married. Although she didn't understand the rush. Six weeks? Was he madly in love or was the woman pregnant?

He glanced at Daisy and went palms up. *"What?"*

"You look good, all recovered." She took a deep breath, sucked in all her regrets. "Well, I'm very happy for you."

"Um, thanks?"

"No one told me. I didn't know."

"Well, that's because I didn't exactly want it broadcast all over town. I asked Lincoln not to say anything."

"Why not?"

"It happened. Not my proudest moment, Twerp."

Getting engaged was not his proudest moment. At this point, she almost felt sorry for the *woman.*

Daisy swallowed hard. "Just...h-happened?"

"It's to be expected, and though I managed to avoid it for years, it finally happened to me."

"I wish you wouldn't make it sound like a death sentence."

"Sometimes it feels that way. But I've got the ranch, and I'm going to bring it back to what it was before. It's just going to take some work."

Good grief. "Wade, I'm sorry, but I don't think anyone should go into a marriage that makes them feel like they're riding out a death sentence."

Wade narrowed his eyes. "Huh? What are you talkin' about?"

"You're getting married, right? Isn't that what Beulah was doin' here, congratulating you?"

"Wait." He held up a palm. "You thought I was getting married? *That's* why you're happy for me?"

"Why else?"

"I thought you were happy I'm fully recovered from the injury."

"Well, that too, of course." She swept her damp palms

across the top of her jeans. "You're *not* getting married, then?"

"No." He chuckled.

"But…you said you'd avoided it for years, and it finally happened to you."

"You thought I meant I was getting married."

"What *did* you mean?"

"The injury. I was lucky, for years, but my luck ran out. No more rodeo for me."

"I'm sorry." But she wasn't sorry that Wade wouldn't be on the road any longer.

"Don't waste your time feeling sorry for me."

"I'm not. I hate that you can't do what you love anymore."

"I'll find something else to love."

"Does that mean that you'll be stayin' in Stone Ridge from now on? No more traveling?"

"That's right."

A moment passed between them. They were both quiet enough for Daisy to hear the sound of her own breathing.

"What did Beulah mean? You could be married in six weeks? I heard her say it."

"I see your confusion now. It's some contest she's dreamed up with Winona. They're going to bring more women into town for our *very* lonesome bachelors." He scooped some of the casserole into a bowl.

"But what does that have to do with you?"

He shrugged. "I'm single. She seems to think I'd be interested in being Mr. Cowboy and having women fight for my attention."

"Why would *you* of all people need any help finding a wife? That's ridiculous! What did you say to her?" Daisy ignored the bowl he set in front of her. "Are you going to do it?"

"Mr. Cowboy? I told her I'd think about it but aw, hell, no."

She accepted the bowl and sat at the table even if she had no intention of eating at a time like this. "Good, because surely one of our Stone Ridge women is good enough to be your wife."

There weren't all that many eligible women in their women-scarce town, but there was Daisy. And Eve's business partner, veterinarian Annabeth. Jolette Marie, and Lucy, a waitress at the Shady Grind. There *were* women available and they'd probably all arm wrestle to get a chance with Wade.

"I'm not *lookin'* for a wife. Beulah and the biddies are just worried about me. They're trying to take up the slack in the nagging department. Doing a good job, too."

Daisy didn't touch the casserole even after he'd handed her a fork. With all the talk of marriage, she'd lost her appetite.

"I'm sorry you were hurt."

"I'm alright."

He seemed to be, at least outwardly, but Daisy didn't believe him for a second. The rodeo had been Wade's life for years. Being sidelined for the rest of his life had to be excruciating.

"You *look* fine."

"Still got all my limbs as you can see. Just a compound fracture." He flexed his left arm and grimaced. "The association took care of the surgery and medical bills, so I stayed in California for a while to recover."

"Linc told me you're going to be working on bringing back the ranch."

"Trying to be a rancher, just like my daddy."

"You're staying...for good?"

She almost couldn't believe this. For half of her life, she'd watched as Wade came back to town and left again. Some said he would sell the ranch after his mother died, and probably never return.

"It's not like I have a choice. This ranch is all I have left in the world."

"Don't make it sound like you're being *punished.*"

"Sorry. You know what I mean. I'm used to a little more excitement than mucking stalls and herding cattle."

"You'll have plenty of excitement now because Beulah will be on you until you agree to be Mr. Cowboy. You know she's never giving up on you. Does she ever give up?"

"You have a point. She'll get the message eventually."

"You're not going to want to hurt her feelings and that's what you're going to have to do to get her to stop."

He winked. "Sweetheart, I have a way with ladies. I can figure out how to say no and not hurt her feelings."

"Yeah, I guess you're pretty good at that, aren't you?"

He ignored her comment. "Do you want coffee?"

"I had coffee before I came over. I need it to open my eyes."

He stopped halfway to the cupboard. "Water? Milk? I think I have milk."

"Wade, I'm not here to eat!" She pushed her bowl away.

"You sure are ornery today, Twerp." He came close and tweaked her nose.

Her anger flashed. "I'm not a kid, Wade."

This is what he did with Daisy. He called her nicknames and tweaked her nose. Tousled her hair.

"Hey, I know that." He patted her head.

"I have an idea. A really good one."

"Uh-oh. Now I'm sinking deep in manure. Two ideas in one morning. I hope at least one of them is good."

"There's only one way Beulah will leave you alone and that's if she thinks you're already serious about a woman."

"Good point." He set his coffee mug down. "But I've been

away for a while, so I haven't really dated anyone. I suppose there's always Jolette Marie…"

"No, not *her*. Actually, all you have to do is pretend to date someone."

He crossed his arms and frowned. "Sounds…complicated."

"It doesn't have to be. Like, for instance, I could tell Beulah that we're dating. You…and me."

"No one's going to believe that, least of all Beulah."

"Why wouldn't she?" Daisy stood. "I've dated a lot since you've been gone, and it would just make sense that I'm ready to settle down."

He hooked a thumb to his chest. "And me? Does it make sense that *I'm* ready to settle down?"

"You're going to have to work with me here. At least *try* to follow along. Look, I'm trying to help you. I'm different than all the buckle bunnies you've dated. That means I'm settling-down material. And I'm right here!" She stuck out her arms.

"I see you." He chuckled.

"There's no need to find you a woman from a reality TV show. Those women would be afraid to break a nail and I'm guessing they wouldn't appreciate the natural smell of a cattle ranch. I fix cars for a living and I'm not afraid of a little crap." She straightened. "Or a lot of it."

"You would make any rancher a good wife, true enough."

"So, it's a good idea?"

"Who would know this thing is fake and who would know it's real?"

"We'd have to tell my family the truth, of course."

"Yeah. I could never lie to Lincoln."

"He'd see right through you." She smiled. "But everyone else can believe it. Right? And that will solve your problem."

"Tell you what. I'll think about it."

23

# CHAPTER 3

*Dear Albert,*

*I'm writing this note with a short update.*

*Not only did my amazing matchmaking skills bring Lincoln and Sadie together, they also reunited Jackson and Eve. I do hope you're watching from wherever you are in heaven, now that you finally found the light.*

Lillian "Mima" Carver assumed that her dearly departed husband had found said light because he'd stopped visiting her. Oh, she wasn't crazy, not according to the doctor anyway. When she'd first started writing these letters to Albert and he'd appear, boots, spurs and all, she'd thought life on the range had finally driven her out of her mind. But the doctor said that as long as she understood Albert wasn't really *there*, and if he brought her comfort, there was no harm done. Although the jury was still out on comfort.

Now in her late seventies, and having raised one son and three grandchildren, Lillian worried she might not have much time left. And she still had one grandchild's happiness to secure.

Her precious Daisy.

She continued writing to Albert:

*Not only are Lincoln and Jackson both married and happy, there's a new Carver baby, and another one on the way! Eve is pregnant, too, and although Sadie had a boy, little Sammy, there's still hope for Eve. Of course, I love them anyway, boy or girl. But we could use some girls for the future generation. We don't want this problem happening all over again twenty-five years from now. If you could do something about that and assist me down here, it would be much appreciated. I'm obviously doing all the heavy lifting.*

*Next up is Daisy, of course, and I will need all the help I can get. She seems bound and determined to fly in the face of everything I've taught her and go after "that Wade." She can't see the rodeo cowboy is a womanizer and a flirt. Still single at thirty-three. His poor sainted mother, God rest her soul. Rose had her own ideas about the two of them. Claimed Daisy and Wade were fated, and she'd seen it in the tea leaves or some such thing. Anyway, he's always been too handsome for his own good, that Wade. Quite a charmer, he is, and not right for my Daisy.*

*I want someone else for Daisy. Someone closer to her age, like Jeremy Pine, or maybe Maybelle's grandson. There are so many choices for her. Why she insists on this crush she's had on Wade for years is beyond me. Infuriating, really. I blame Hank for foolishly indulging her every whim. I don't blame our son entirely, though, as he'd had a lot to make up for over the years. But perhaps he could have kept his daughter away from the ranch hands better than he managed. Wade worked for Hank when he was off the tour, and now and then I'd catch him flirting and smiling at Daisy.*

Lillian set her pen down and stretched. She glanced at her wristwatch and noticed it was nearly time to leave for church. She'd finish this letter to Albert later. It wasn't as if he was waiting for it.

She started down the hall to remind Daisy that it was time to go, when she saw her sitting at the breakfast table.

Fully dressed and drinking the coffee she claimed necessary to life.

"What on earth? I usually have to pull you out of bed to make it on time!"

"You're exaggerating. Don't I always go, every Sunday?"

"We're usually late."

"We won't be today."

Well, wasn't this working out to be a beautiful Sunday morning. Lillian grabbed her coat and off they both went to Trinity Church. Pastor June preached about family and home, two of Lillian's favorite subjects. She sat proudly between Daisy and Eve. Sadie was helping out in the nursery as she couldn't bear to leave Sammy alone yet. Naturally, her grandsons weren't here as they didn't attend often, using the ranch as an excuse. And, she noticed, neither was Wade. No surprise there.

But there sat Jeremy Pine, right next to his mother. Lillian waved. He waved back, the sweet boy. No doubt about it, he and Daisy would make beautiful babies. Her, with the blond hair she'd inherited from her mother. Say what you will about the woman, she was the town's beauty before she high-tailed it out of here and left Hank and their three small children.

Yes, *Jeremy*, with matching blondish hair to Daisy's, but a slightly darker shade. Both had green eyes. Lillian could almost see their adorable babies.

The pastor wrapped up the sermon and then mentioned the Nativity play and the need for a few more last-minute volunteers.

Sadie caught up with them as they were all filing out. "Sammy is going to be baby Jesus!"

"He's a little big, isn't he?" Daisy said.

And while Sammy had looked more like a three-month-old at birth, weighing in at a strapping nine pounds, ten ounces, he was still a baby, for crying out loud.

"Do you think they're actually going to use a *newborn*, sugar?" Lillian nudged Daisy. "Sammy is perfect for the part."

"If y'all say so."

Lillian patted Sadie's back. "Best of all, we'll get Lincoln inside the church again. Last time he was here y'all got married."

"Oh, he'll be here." Sadie beamed and cooed at Sammy. "He's so proud. And Sammy just adores Lincoln. Every time he walks in the door, Sammy squeals in delight."

Eve elbowed Sadie. "He's just like his mama."

"Ha, ha." Sadie hip-checked Eve.

Outside, the air was clear and bright with a cold snap coming. Lillian felt it in every one of her arthritic bones. "Let's get on home, Daisy. I have some baking to do."

But they hadn't reached the truck when Beulah accosted them. "Lillian, a word?"

Bless her heart, Beulah meant well with the Mr. Cowboy contest. Lillian was of the mind that she didn't want any of these women being carted in from out of town. She worried they wouldn't be screened carefully enough. They might wind up with some women who didn't mean well, like those simply looking for a so-called sperm donor. Ahem. But now that her men were hitched, she didn't much care if they brought in more women. It might help their future generations, too.

"How can I help you, dear?"

"I just visited Wade yesterday, poor lamb. He's not too keen on the idea of being our first Mr. Cowboy. I'll need your help to convince him." She gave Lillian a conspiratorial smirk. "I know you have a vested interest."

Lillian didn't much want to have this conversation with Daisy present, but Beulah did seem clueless to the predicament. "Can I call on you later? We'll work something out, I'm sure."

"Sorry, Beulah," Daisy piped in. "Wade told me that he isn't going to do it."

"Well, now, I wouldn't jump to that conclusion so fast." Beulah held up a palm. "I don't give up easily. A few more visits from the ladies of SORROW, a few more casseroles, maybe some photos of whom he'd be dating might be of some assistance."

"You have photos of these women?" Daisy asked, sounding a little agitated.

"Not the actual ones, no. I have examples. How can I expect them to sign up without knowing something about the rancher they'll be dating? This is a brand-new reality show, and they'll have no idea who it could be. Only that he'll be a real cowboy."

"That should be enough, for now. Women love their cowboys," Lillian added and met Beulah's gaze, trying to clue her in this conversation should take place out of Daisy's presence. "Daisy, let's go."

"Well, I hate to be the one to give you the bad news, but Wade isn't going to do it because he's already dating someone. She'd be upset."

"Why, he didn't say anything to me yesterday. That little weasel," Beulah said. "Wasting my time like that."

"Maybe it isn't serious," Lillian said, though she hoped it was. She chose to be encouraged that Daisy didn't sound at all upset by the fact.

Lillian didn't much care who Mr. Cowboy would be. Sadie's brother, Beau, would be a fine choice.

"I think it is. Serious enough," Daisy said.

"Who is she?" Beulah leaned in. "Some buckle bunny? Surely not Jolette Marie."

"N-no. It's a nice girl, someone really stable, and ready to settle down. You'd like her."

"I still don't hear a name." Beulah sniffed.

"It's me." Daisy straightened. "*I'm* his woman."

"MIMA! MIMA, ARE YOU ALRIGHT?" Daisy fanned the church bulletin in front of her grandmother's nose.

She knew that Mima wouldn't like the idea of her and Wade, but she didn't think she'd sway and nearly fall down. Mima acted like Daisy had just announced she'd started dating the devil himself. Daisy and Beulah slowly lowered her to the bench seat right outside the church, and a small crowd gathered around them. Good thing Sadie and Eve had already left, or they'd be having fits.

"Let's give her some air," Winona said.

Delores, Winona's housekeeper and nanny, used the double stroller as a weapon to push people back.

"Get out of my way, child." Beulah elbowed in. "I've got the smelling salts."

"She doesn't need *smelling salts*," Daisy protested. "She's going to be fine."

"Fine? She hardly looks fine. What on earth do you expect when you drop a bomb like that?" Beulah got the smelling salts out of her tote bag.

Mima brushed her away. "Bless your heart. Get that ammonia away from me. I'm fine. I just mistakenly heard Daisy say she was Wade's woman. But I'm old and I've had flights of fancy before."

Daisy chewed on her lower lip and fanned harder while everyone else exchanged worried glances. As soon as she got Mima in the truck, she'd explain the ruse. She should have waited to take Mima into her confidence, but Beulah got so pushy. Suggesting that women would decide whether or not to join the show based on Wade's good looks! Suddenly all Daisy could picture was Victoria's Secret models arriving by the truckload, all for Wade. No, she had to put a stop to this, and the sooner the better. Wade would thank her as soon as he heard. No more casseroles or nagging from the old biddies.

He could remain happily single, as long as he pretended not to be.

"I did *hear* wrong?" Mima pushed the church program out of her face.

"Let's go home where we can talk about this." Daisy offered her hand to help her up.

"That's a good idea," Winona said, now holding one of her twins on her hip. "Go home and take a nap. That's what I'm going to do."

"You and I need to talk, Winona." Beulah waved her hands in the air. "This news puts a monkey wrench in my plans. We need to confer on who will be our Mr. Cowboy. Lots to think about."

"I'll call you." Winona waddled away, Delores following her with the stroller.

On the drive home to the ranch, Daisy tried to explain. "Honestly, Mima, don't you think you'd know it if Wade and I were serious? I'm not *really* dating Wade."

"Well, butter my biscuit, why would you lie to your poor old granny? A shock like that could kill me!" Mima fanned herself using the same now rumpled bulletin.

"I don't know why you hate Wade so much. He's Lincoln's best friend. They grew up together. If you like Lincoln, and I think you do, then you should like Wade just fine."

"Sugar, I don't *hate* anyone. You ought to know better than that. He's just not right for you, that's all."

"Oh yeah? And who is?"

"Someone wonderful. You're beautiful, sugar. Look just like your mama. Everybody says so."

The words sliced through Daisy. She didn't want to be compared to a woman who'd left her husband and three children. For years, she'd tried to be as different from her as possible. Choosing to be a tomboy and picking an untraditional profession to go into. An ugly rumor occasionally drifted through town that Daisy wasn't even Hank's daughter because Maggie Mae had an affair and cheated on her husband. No one believed it anymore, because Daisy was a Carver through and through, but it still burned to think of her mother as an unfaithful woman. Her daddy had never deserved that.

Mima was still talking. "You deserve the best man of all. I think it might just be Jeremy Pine."

It wasn't just the comparison to her mama that spiked hot anger in Daisy, but the suggestion that *Jeremy* was the right one for her. He was a friend, and Daisy liked him, but she wasn't going to marry him. Not in a million years. He didn't even like Daisy.

"What's so great about *him?*"

"Did you see him today at church, sitting right there next to his mama? What a sweet, sweet boy."

Daisy groaned. "I love you, Mima, but you're not going to pick who I date *or* marry. Sorry."

"But why would you lie to Beulah? Did Wade ask you to do this for him?"

"He's too busy recovering from his injury and trying to get a cattle ranch back in business. So, he's not interested in that silly reality show. Beulah came by yesterday, and we could both tell she wasn't going to let it go. He doesn't even know I'm doing this. He's probably going to be upset when I tell him."

Wade wouldn't like it, but they'd probably have to do a

few public things to throw others off. He couldn't, for instance, hang out at the Shady Grind and flirt with every other woman, or no one would believe the lie. And they should probably do some of the holiday events in town. It would just be a fun time, for a little while, and in the end, Wade would thank her someday. Probably.

"And what were you doing there *yesterday*, young lady?"

*Reminding myself of what a real man looked like? Wondering why Wade still didn't see me as a woman?*

In other words, torturing herself.

"I didn't know he'd quit the rodeo and is back home for good. No one told me. I thought he was just home and getting ready to leave again, just as always."

"I didn't tell you because I didn't want you rushing right over there to comfort him. The ladies of SORROW are taking real good care of him."

"He's a friend, and I wanted to see him."

"He should kiss your feet for pretending to date the likes of him. He's a womanizer, that's what. A terrible flirt. Honey, you're too young to know this, but sometimes it's best to settle for a man that isn't *quite* as good-looking. Not as popular with the ladies."

"What about Lincoln and Jackson? The women all think they're gorgeous. Not me, of course, that's disgusting. But you make it sound like they're homely."

"They're *Carver* men, sugar. That's a distinction you must always make. Sadly, not every woman is fortunate enough to marry a Carver man." She shook her head.

Daisy sighed deeply. "You'll need to help me tell the rest of the family, so no one else has a panic attack. I'll tell Lincoln, and you can tell Jackson and them."

"And your father?"

"I'll tell Daddy, too. But he's always *liked* Wade."

"Hank likes everyone and everything since he got

engaged to Brenda. Still, don't take advantage of this new and easy nature of his when you tell him."

Later that day, Daisy wondered if she should go up the hill to the large cabin where her father always stayed and tell him first. Not far from the large family home where Daisy still lived with Mima, his cabin was closer to all the cattle operations. But Brenda Iglesias, who was a constant presence in her father's life these days, would probably be there with him. They'd practically moved in together, and Brenda had quit her job as the live-in maid for the Truehearts. She now did Mima's previous job of feeding the cowboys three squares a day.

Daisy liked Brenda, but after all these years, it was plain weird to see Daddy with a woman. Her father had always been such a hard and fierce man. She was painfully aware to be his favorite, and he demanded a lot more from her brothers than he ever did from her. She'd always believed it unfair. Daisy had been allowed to make the decision to go to school to be an auto mechanic, whereas for both of her brothers, they were expected to be ranchers.

She'd never even questioned the fact that she'd been fortunate to be born a girl in Stone Ridge. Over the years, a few men had left town to find a bride, but that still hadn't fixed the men-to-women ratio. Of course, like most women, Daisy saw this as an advantage, and now Beulah and the biddies were trying to change all that.

Well, now she had a timeline. Because even if Wade *didn't* get chosen as Mr. Cowboy, if they brought this show to town odds were one or more of the runner-ups would be after him.

And she couldn't let that happen until she finally had a chance for Wade to see *her* as a choice.

# CHAPTER 4

*W*hen Sadie got home from church, she realized Sammy had fallen asleep during the car ride. She carefully unstrapped him from the car seat and lugged him inside, hoping he'd stay down for at least an hour. But the minute she crossed the threshold of their cabin, Sammy woke up as if completely rejuvenated from a fifteen-minute snooze.

Predictably, the moment he saw Lincoln, Sammy squealed in delight and kicked his legs.

"Your son just got the part of baby Jesus in the Nativity play!"

The moment Lincoln turned to her, Sadie knew something was horribly wrong. He gave Sammy a half-hearted smile, not his usual, *look out, I'm-about-to-throw-you-up-in-the-air* look.

"Congratulations, Sammy." Lincoln rose and took Sammy from her, then kissed Sadie's temple. "Hiya, bride."

She went into his arms, and he used his free arm to pull her in tight. Her cowboy's arms were so strong and warm that she nuzzled into the deep embrace. She'd loved Lincoln Carver since she was a girl, and still couldn't believe they were married. Sometimes the happiness was so strong that she could almost feel it in the air around them, sparkling and snapping like a live wire, wrapping around her heart.

All three of them stood in the expansive entryway of their large cabin for a few minutes until Sammy squirmed.

"I'll make lunch." Holding Lincoln's hand, she pulled him into the kitchen.

The cabin Lincoln had built, with help from his daddy and brother, was so new that Sadie could smell the fresh scent of pine wafting all around them. She was still getting accustomed to all the room they now had, too, when for almost a year they'd lived in her cramped cabin on Lupine Lake. Now, they had a two-story "cabin" with a large dining room, kitchen, and three bedrooms upstairs. They were far enough from Jackson and Eve's cabin and the main house down the hill to have their privacy, but still close to family.

Sadie made turkey sandwiches with all the fixings and opened a bag of potato chips as Lincoln played with Sammy. She'd been worried that Lincoln wouldn't be happy about them having a baby this soon, since they were still practically newlyweds. Sammy hadn't been planned, but as Linc promised, they had adjusted their plans, and he didn't seem at all burdened by Sammy. He was the light of Lincoln's life.

She watched out of the corner of her eye as he threw Sammy up in the air a few times, each time easily catching him. The first time he'd done that she'd nearly had a heart attack. But Lincoln would never fail to catch his son. He would, however, sometimes fail to tell Sadie when he was burdened with a problem, because he claimed he didn't want her to worry.

Sadie set Sammy in his high chair and let him pummel a

couple of chips with his fist, occasionally taking a bite or two.

Next to her at the large farmhouse table, Lincoln ate his sandwich quietly. The silence between them was thick with worry. She could almost hear his thoughts.

Finally, Sadie was able to take no more of this. She reached for his hand. "What's wrong?"

"Nothing." He squeezed her hand as if to reassure her.

"*Something's* wrong. You need to tell me."

"I don't want you to worry if nothing comes of it."

"I promise I won't worry."

He snorted. "You won't keep that promise."

"Alright, I lied, because I'm already worried. So, it won't make a difference once I know *why* I'm worried."

"Gah! Bee!" Sammy said, having smashed all his chips into dust.

Sadie gave him another chip. "Here you go."

"Is that good, buddy?" Lincoln asked Sammy.

"Cooscoo!" Sammy replied with his drooly smile.

"Stop avoiding the subject. Remember, you said on the day we got married there was nothing we couldn't get through together?"

"And we'll get through this, too. I just don't know if everyone else will."

That sounded ominous and Sadie immediately knew. "Rusty."

Lincoln slowly nodded. "Yeah."

Before she and Lincoln were married, an old rodeo cowboy had started sending Hank emails. They'd thrown her father-in-law into such a funk that Lincoln had taken over, as he so often did. Rusty claimed to have had an affair with Lincoln's mother, Maggie, and that she'd told him Daisy might be his daughter.

Sadie now lost her appetite. Tension coiled through her

stomach like a snake. This had to be killing Lincoln. How long had he kept this to himself?

"What's happened?"

"He's very ill, supposedly dying, and would like to see Daisy again just once before he goes. He's leaving everything he has to her."

Sadie swallowed hard. "Even if...even if he's not one hundred percent sure?"

Lincoln met her eyes, his eyes hooded and unreadable. "He must be sure."

"Well, he can't be. Daisy has at least a fifty percent chance of being Hank's daughter."

Daisy was so close to her daddy. She would be devastated to know she wasn't his biological daughter. Devastated to know the ugly rumor she'd refused to believe was true.

"I'm going to have to tell her." Lincoln took her hand and squeezed it. "Soon."

The words lay between them like little bombs.

A while ago, Lincoln had personally met Rusty, even driven him by Daisy's auto shop, so he could take a look at her from a distance. But Rusty had violated that agreement and hopped out of the truck. He'd talked shop with her, without letting her know who he might be. It was the last agreement he'd made with Lincoln and he'd honored it so far.

But Lincoln had wondered if he should have told Daisy the truth instead of shielding her and protecting her.

"She'll forgive you."

"For keeping this from her? I'm not sure that she will. Maybe the right thing to do was to bring it all out in the open, have the DNA tests, be done with it all."

"You were worried of what it would do to Daisy if she wasn't Hank's daughter. She still had a fifty-fifty chance and no matter what, she *is* Hank's daughter. You meant well and Daisy will understand."

"I don't know." Lincoln ran a palm down his face, and even Sammy couldn't make him smile. "I've got to talk with my father this afternoon."

"Are you going to tell him?"

"Maybe. But we have cattle business to discuss anyway."

Sadie spent the day playing with Sammy, grading papers, and planning the last week of lessons before Christmas break. The kids were so excited about the holidays that she didn't think they'd accomplish much, but she still had to try to keep their attention. But Lincoln wasn't home for dinner, probably off brooding. This protectiveness of his sometimes went too far. She wanted to be his soft place to fall, always, and that involved knowing what was eating at him. Now she knew, at least, but still had no idea how to comfort him if he wanted to brood.

Sadie gave Sammy a bath and put him to bed in his crib. He took few naps, but the one redeeming grace was that he'd slept through the night early on. When she put him to bed at seven o'clock, chances were good he wouldn't wake up until six the next morning. That meant she and Lincoln always had the evenings to themselves, making love and behaving like they did before they'd had Sammy.

"Good night, honey." Sadie shut the light off and left the door ajar.

She'd just washed her face and brushed her teeth when Lincoln got home. She ran down the steps to meet him.

He stood in the foyer, Stetson tipped, eyes weary.

"I told Hank," he said, closing his eyes and pinching the bridge of his nose. "He didn't take it well."

Sadie went into his arms.

"Where were you? I wish you'd come home earlier, maybe to give Sammy a bath."

At least it would distract him if nothing else.

"I'm sorry." He crushed her against him, so tightly that for a moment she couldn't breathe. "I love you. More than you'll ever know."

"And I love you, but I don't like it when you brood." She tweaked his chin.

"Point taken."

Then he kissed her, the way only Lincoln could. Warm, deep, with a passion that always made her knees liquid.

"You're forgiven," she said breathlessly when he broke the kiss.

"Let's go to bed," Lincoln said, tugging her up the steps.

He wore the same wicked smile he did when he wanted to tear all her clothes off. This was *her* Lincoln, the one she'd loved for half her life.

She followed him upstairs, where she took his mind off everything else but her.

On Monday, at work, Daisy decided she'd practice this new dating-Wade thing even if she still hadn't told him it was happening. Because she worked forty-five minutes away in Kerrville, there wasn't much of a chance anyone here would tell him before she did. So, when Bob, the tire specialist, asked her to go on a date for what had to be the hundredth time, she didn't just say no because she didn't date coworkers who were twenty years her senior.

"I'm sorry, but I'm dating someone." She wiped motor oil off her hands. "We're pretty serious."

"Figures." He shook his head in disgust. "Who's the lucky guy?"

"Wade Cruz."

"The rodeo star?"

"That's him."

She let the idea sink in, letting it roll around her mind like melted chocolate.

*Daisy and Wade are dating.*

*Did you hear Daisy and Wade are a thing?*

*I thought Wade would never settle down, and now along comes Daisy.*

*They make a cute couple.*

She wasn't going to lie. It was a nice feeling.

"Man, that was a heartbreaker of a ride. I watched when he went down. He had a real chance at being the best in the world, and now his career is over. What a tough break."

Daisy never watched the rodeo. Too scary. Lincoln had also done some rodeoing in his day and that's about the time Daisy stopped watching. It was terrifying to watch her big brother put himself in danger, not to mention Wade.

"He's recovering nicely."

This was another lie as she wasn't quite sure that he *was* recovering well. But if he wasn't, he'd certainly put on a good act.

Daisy went about her day, fixing a few sets of brakes and taking out and replacing an old alternator with a new one. Lou was planning on closing down for two weeks during the holidays, which meant that Daisy had to earn all she could in the next several days.

On her lunch break, she crossed the street to her favorite coffee shop and ordered a hot mocha latte and an egg bite. Even Lou was getting into the spirit of the holidays, dragging out the sad, greased-stained artificial tree in his office and setting out garland haphazardly inside the shop. All in all, it was a normal Monday on the job.

Until she recognized the man. Again, he sat in his truck across the street from Lou's Auto Shop. Short, graying hair, goatee. Every time she glanced in his direction, he made it a point to look away. He was obviously casing the shop, though she wondered what he found valuable at Lou's. Lou rarely carried cash in the register, and everyone paid with plastic these days. Sure, tires and alternators could be expensive, but he'd be better off robbing the coffee shop.

"Lou, that man is here again," Daisy said, hooking her thumb.

"What is it with that guy?" Lou scratched his temple, leaving a streak of engine oil. "Last week he told me he was having lunch with his girlfriend. I've never even seen him with a woman."

"He's obviously lying. I think he's hoping to break in, maybe while you're gone."

"Well, there won't be anything left to steal. If he wants this old desk and chair, he's welcome to them. Heck, I'll do fine with the insurance claim. Get everything around here new again. The missus would be happy."

Daisy had hoped Lou would take this more seriously, because the dude bothered her. There was something very suspicious about him. Like he was sitting there collecting everyone's secrets.

"Did you test the alarm system anyway?"

"Sure, sure. Don't worry so much!" Lou waved her away. "Back to work with you."

Daisy did get back to it, working her butt off for the rest of the day. Three more brake jobs. Those always took so long. She put in some overtime and after work resisted the temptation to stop in for a cold beer at the Shady Grind to give Jackson the fake news. But she wasn't sure he'd be there tonight, and she had to stop telling everyone before she actually told *Wade*. There were two of them in this fake relationship, after all. And he had yet to be informed.

It was true that she'd never known Wade to be serious with a woman, though his high school girlfriend cheated on him and ruined him for all women. Daisy, of course, didn't want to believe that even if all evidence seemed to support it. All she'd ever known of Wade was a good guy who looked after her when her brothers weren't around. He'd been Lincoln's best friend since grade school, and they'd toured the rodeo together for several years. Eventually Lincoln gave up the dangerous bull-riding events to focus on lassoing, but Wade stuck with dangerous bulls for years.

Driving home, she crossed the entrance into Stone Ridge with the weathered sign:

*Welcome to Stone Ridge, established 1806 by Titus Ridge*
*Population 5,010*
*\*Women eat free every ~~night~~ Tuesday at the Shady Grind\**

Now that Jackson owned the bar and grill, things weren't quite as loosey-goosey around here. But Daisy nearly drove off the road when she noticed a new, and large, billboard at the entrance to town:

*Mr. Cowboy, a new reality dating show*
*Coming soon to Stone Ridge*

It must have gone up after she'd driven to work this morning. Hideous, it blocked some of the skyline. A giant-sized photo of a handsome man Daisy didn't recognize smiled down on all the "little people." He had sparkling white teeth. But sparkling wasn't a strong enough word. How about blinding?

Well, she'd have to speak to someone at the chamber of commerce about this. She would, too, if they had a chamber. Unfortunately, they didn't, so she'd have to take this up with the biddies of SORROW. They'd gone too far this time, and surely Jackson, and Mr. Lloyd from the General Store, not to mention Pastor June from Trinity Church wouldn't like this, either.

When she got home, Daisy found Mima knitting on the couch in front of the fireplace.

"Did you see that billboard? It's taking up half the skyline! It's hideous. What an eyesore! Why hasn't anyone complained yet? I'm going to file a complaint. That's what I'm going to do."

Mima scowled. "What is this mess? I don't know what you're gnawing on about."

After Daisy explained, Mima chuckled and shook her head. "Oh, that Beulah. I heard that would be going up but didn't know it would be this soon. She thought that might encourage a lucky man to step up."

"Lucky man? *Lucky man?* How would you like to be surrounded by beautiful women, all perfectly lovely, and then have to pick just *one?*"

"Well, sugar, that's how it's done. We're not going to encourage a *harem.*"

"These dating shows are ridiculous. No way anyone chooses his life mate with all that pressure. They have a few weeks to get to know each other and make a lifetime commitment. I can't even decide on a dress in a few weeks."

"That's because you don't like dresses. Speaking of which, sugar, maybe if you wore them more often, like Sadie does…"

Daisy blew out a frustrated breath. "Not this again."

She was far more like Eve, comfortable in her jeans, boots, and a T-shirt most of the time. Sometimes paired with a flannel shirt if it was cold outside. But Mima didn't seem to understand that Daisy would have plenty of men to choose from if only she didn't have big brothers.

"I wish you'd settle down and not just with your fake boyfriend. If you don't like Jeremy, I'll think of someone else."

"You better find a brave one. Did it ever occur to you that I might actually really *have* a boyfriend if only Lincoln and

Jackson didn't scare every one of them off?" Daisy went hands on hips.

"I'm sure they don't do that," Mima muttered.

"Speaking of my fake boyfriend, I have to go over there tonight and tell Wade."

"Oh, wonder how he'll take the news?" Mima's voice sounded deceptively mild.

She didn't fool Daisy. Mima hoped this would all blow up in Daisy's face and that Wade wouldn't go along with it. And while Daisy wouldn't be too surprised if that happened, she hoped he'd at least hear her out while she made her case.

She took a shower and dressed in her new jeans and flannel shirt. At the last minute, she decided on a peace offering in case this didn't go as well as she'd hoped. She grabbed one of the apple pies Mima had baked yesterday and was out the door.

"You too?" Wade said several minutes later when he took the pie from Daisy. "Well, at least it's not a casserole."

She shrugged. "I remembered you like apple pie."

"That's right, Peanut. It's my favorite."

Wow, he hadn't called her Peanut since she was *twelve*. This was going from bad to worse. She followed him into the kitchen, unable to take her eyes off his behind. Wade wore those Wranglers of his extremely well. Tight in all the right places. What would he do right now if she grabbed him and kissed him the way he had planted one on her all those years ago? She was better at kissing now than she'd been back then, the first time she'd ever been kissed. Wade had been her first real kiss and she could still feel the way her ears had buzzed and her brain stopped processing thoughts.

"Um, so, did you do any more thinking about what I suggested?"

He set the pie down and quirked a brow. "You were serious about that."

"Of course. This idea will work."

"I don't think it's such a good plan."

"Why not?"

At the moment, he seemed to be struggling to form words, and she worried he was in pain. Then he grimaced and rubbed his elbow, proving it. "Just…take my word for it, okay?"

"Well, it's too late. I already told Beulah at church, and it worked. Everyone thinks we're dating and they're already looking for someone *else* to be Mr. Cowboy." The words came out in a rush and, boy, did she feel stupid when his eyes grew wide, then narrowed. "So, you're welcome."

"I wish you hadn't."

But she wasn't scared. Instead, she was gall-darned mad. Fury spiked through her and her heart raced as fast as a cornered rabbit's.

"Really, Wade? I'm so awful that you can't even *pretend* that you're mine?"

He flinched, and she realized he couldn't stand the thought of hurting her. She bit her lower lip to keep from crying.

"That's…that's not the problem."

"Then, what is it? If it's my family, I already told you we won't lie to them."

"I wish that were it, but that's not it, either." He rubbed the stubble on his jaw.

"Are you going to *tell* me? Do you already have a girlfriend?"

"No, but I wish I'd thought of that."

"Huh?"

"I'm not fast enough on my feet or I would have thought to tell you that I already have a girlfriend. Another fake girlfriend, so I can't have you be my fake girlfriend as that might offend her. Maybe that would have worked."

She felt dizzy with the lies. "Gosh, you lost me."

"That makes two of us."

He took several steps toward her, so close she could smell the leather of his boots and see the gold specks in his caramel-brown eyes. It didn't escape her fondest memories that he'd only been a little closer than this the time he'd kissed her. He reached to tug on a lock of her hair, further enhancing that memory. Now she could almost smell the peaches that had been ripe that September. If she dared to close her eyes right now, she might also remember the taste of his lips on hers, his warm tongue exploring.

But she didn't dare close her eyes because she didn't want to miss a thing.

"This is playing with fire. If we spend too much time pretending, I'm going to fool myself. And then we're going to wind up in bed. Which wouldn't be a good idea."

This sounded like a fine idea to her. It sounded like an adventure and she was ripe for one of those.

When his thumb lowered to trace her bottom lip, she nearly lost her balance. "Wh-why not?"

He took a step back, breaking the spell. "Because I'm too old for you."

"No, you're not. Maybe when I was eighteen you were, but not now. That age difference has a way of not being quite as important anymore."

"I'm also a broke-down cowboy, in case you hadn't noticed." He held his left arm out.

"I don't care about any of that."

"Maybe I do."

"I don't think that's fair. You should let me decide."

His gaze slid appreciatively down her breasts, to her legs. "Damn, Peanut, you're all grown up, aren't you?"

She was glad she'd worn her new jeans tonight that were a size too small.

"Well, I'm glad you noticed."

"Oh, I noticed." He sent her a slow and easy smile. "Okay, look. If we're going to do this, we'll damn well do it my way."

# CHAPTER 5

*W*ade was already exhausted. Maybe it was the meds. They made his brain fuzzy while they simultaneously took care of the pain. He would need a full night's sleep to find a way out of this mess.

Pretending to be anything more than friends would be playing with fire.

Daisy Carver was beautiful. To Wade, she always had been. He didn't care that she dressed casually and never made an effort to look particularly feminine. No long and manicured nails on her. No hair extensions or false lashes. Just long, natural blond hair and equally long legs. She usually kept her hair in a high ponytail which gave her a perpetually girlish look. But tonight, the second time he'd seen her in as many days, she'd let her hair down. And he was a goner. He pictured fisting a handful of that hair while he kissed her until she begged him to stop. Or asked him to never stop.

A thick layer of sexual tension had always flickered between them, one that, try as Wade might want to deny, had never gone away. He could tell himself this heap of desire and lust was happening to him now because he hadn't been with a woman in so long. But although accurate, that wasn't the reason he now stared at Daisy like he wanted to take her to bed and keep her there for days.

The point was, he'd like to think he was a better man than that. She of all women deserved better than a dried-up rodeo cowboy with a practically lame arm. If he felt this way at thirty-three, what would he be like at fifty? He didn't want to saddle her with an older man and his orthopedic problems, all due to his lifestyle choices. All due to wanting to be the best in the rodeo and to indulging an addiction to adrenaline rushes.

When he'd had to start over and pick a new career, ranching was his only option. Stone Ridge was home, even if he didn't have quite the same attachment that some of the ranching families had to the land itself. Too many memories of his mother here. She'd held on to this land so tightly Wade wondered if in the end it had killed her. To Wade, land was just dirt, and he didn't know why people were willing to die over it.

Daisy was a rancher's daughter through and through and she loved this town with the same reverence that his mother had. She deserved a man who wouldn't slowly die stuck in this small town.

He was off-limits, too old for her, too experienced. It didn't matter that she made his heart switch like a kitten's tail. They were never going to happen.

But he supposed, if she wanted to pretend for a while, it might help him out.

"Okay, Peanut."

This is what he did with Daisy. He called her nicknames and tweaked her nose. Tousled her hair. Kept it affectionately tender and nonsexual. Safe. But his skills with women were sorely rusty as he hadn't even been with a woman in one long year. He seemed to remember being a whole lot more charming than this.

"But if we're going to do this, I have a few rules of my own."

"Okay." She took a seat on his living room couch, tucking one luscious leg under. "Tell me."

Those jeans she wore were so tight he half wondered if she'd painted them on. He tried hard to focus. Parameters. Boundaries. He needed them before he lost his fool head. Again.

"Light PDA. Hand-holding, kisses on the cheek, that kind of thing."

"Are you *kiddin'* me? No one's going to believe we're for real. Not with your reputation."

He used to be proud of that reputation, had been when he was younger, but now it stung to think even Daisy categorized him there.

"I'll make it look real. Don't you worry about that."

"What about a light kiss on the lips? No tongue."

"Tongue is out of the question."

"In public, sure. I agree."

"Correct me if I'm wrong, but that's all this is. In public fake dating."

"Sure, but we should spend a little time in private practicing all this or it's sure going to look ridiculous."

He squinted. "Ridiculous?"

"Fake."

"Uh-huh. Which it is."

"Wow, I can't believe you're being this thick. Work with me here!"

The problem was he wanted to work her. He wanted to work her so good she'd have trouble walking the next day. Oh, crap. *No.* Those thoughts weren't allowed in his head. Okay, maybe just in his head where they could do no harm.

He was enjoying the fantasy and didn't realize Daisy was staring at him.

"Does that make sense?" she asked.

While indulging himself, he must have missed something. "Does *what* make sense?"

"The Riverwalk this weekend? Our first out-in-public date. Everyone will be there."

He hadn't planned on the Riverwalk. In fact, he hadn't been out of the house much. Once in a while he dropped by the Shady Grind, but with Lincoln MIA these days, Wade had begun to grow sick of all the rodeo questions.

*How many concussions have you had, in total?*

*How many bones have you broken?*

*What happened? Did you lose your focus?*

*Did you hear the bone crack?*

*How much blood?*

He wished he could claim a lack of focus on the day he'd broken his arm. Instead, everything had gone perfectly that day. He'd been enjoying the attentions of a buckle bunny just minutes before, but no one took his focus off the ring. His focus had always been key in his success. The problem was his age, and a body breaking down from all the beating it took over the years. And unlike Lincoln, Wade had failed to quit while ahead. Now he was the focus of commentary on what could go wrong on the way to the top. How close one could come and still lose it all.

Yeah, that was him. A cautionary tale.

"Sure, yeah. The Riverwalk. That sounds okay." He ran a hand through his hair. "You keep everyone away from me that wants to talk about the rodeo. Deal?"

"You don't want to talk about the rodeo?"

"It's all anyone ever asks me about. I'm sick of talking about the accident. Tired of talking about this arm." He touched it lightly.

"Does it hurt much?"

"Only if I breathe." When she winced, he chuckled. "Just kiddin', Peanut. I'm good."

"Also, stop calling me *Peanut*. I'm not twelve."

He cleared his throat. "Alright. What other pet name is good?"

"It's a pet name?"

"Sure, what else would it be?"

"I think it's that name you call me when you want to put some distance between us." She crossed her arms. "Like Squirt and Twerp."

Okay, he was officially out of his league here. Daisy wasn't just gorgeous, she was smart as a whip, and nobody's fool. For years, he'd had a steady diet of women who wanted only one thing from him. He gave that away easily enough.

He tried a smile. "You might be right about that."

"I know I am." She sent him a conspiratorial wink. "Since I'm helping you with this, maybe you could help me with something, too."

"Yeah, name it, Pe—uh, name it."

"Well, here's the thing. You might have noticed that I haven't had a serious relationship. Like, ever."

"Hadn't noticed."

"Of course you haven't." She untucked her leg and repositioned herself on the couch, knees pointed toward him. "It's not like I have trouble finding men who are interested in me."

"No doubt."

"It's just that most of them aren't as brave as you are."

He scratched his temple. "How's that, now?"

"I have two big brothers who are overly protective."

"And me. You've got me." He thumped his chest.

"Right. But you're not my brother, don't forget."

"I'll still kill anyone who tries to hurt you."

"Anyway, that's why I'm not all that experienced, you know, at being someone's *girlfriend*."

"Okay. I understand."

"You do?" She brightened.

Now he wasn't sure that he *did*, because the fact that he understood seemed to greatly encourage her. He must have missed something. "Um, do I?"

"Geez, do I have to spell it out for you?"

"Apparently."

She covered her face. "Don't make me do that. It's too embarrassing."

"C'mon, you can tell me anything. I've kept all your secrets. I have no clue what—"

And then he stopped talking. Because he suddenly knew exactly what Daisy was referring to and it hit him square in the solar plexus. Nearly knocked all the air out of him, just like that time Satan threw him during practice and nearly impaled him on a post.

And he found himself wishing he was in that situation right now instead of this one.

"You figured it out," she said quietly, lowering her gaze.

"Daisy, are you a virgin? Is that what you're trying to tell me?"

"Yeah, kind of. A little bit. Mostly."

He ran a hand down his face. Poor Daisy. "*Why* are you telling me this?"

"First, I trust you. You won't tattle, even if everybody probably already knows. But it's nobody's business."

"I'll take it to my grave, sweetheart." He made a motion to sweep his finger across his heart.

"Second, because you should know why I might act a little awkward on our dates together. Why I might not know all the right moves."

"What part of fake don't you understand? Don't worry about any of that."

"And third, and this is the tough one. Because I thought you might help me with my moves."

All the blood rushed out of his head. It was as if someone had hit him with a baseball bat.

"Moves?"

"How to turn a guy on, that kind of thing. I've waited too long for the right man and this is the year I have a little adventure."

"Why do you want to do that? It's nice…being a virgin." He lowered his voice even if they could only be heard by Dante and Satan.

He could not believe they were having *this* conversation.

"Nice? Are you kiddin' me? It makes me…weird. I'm too old to be a virgin."

"Maybe you should get married. That will take care of it."

"Right, because 'nice girls' get married first." She held up air quotes. "Don't give me that eighteenth-century stuff. I'm a modern woman. I have to be sure I don't marry a man who likes to tie his wife up for sexy times."

Oh, now there went an image he'd never be able to wash out of his brain.

He wanted to tear his hair out. "You are driving me nuts. Look, I don't want to be the guy who 'teaches' you." Now *he* held up air quotes.

This could get complicated. Playing with fire wasn't the right term here. They were fooling around with a nuclear bomb.

Maybe he should have hightailed it out of town the day after Daisy appeared on his doorstep. Hell, he could still get out now while the gettin' was good. He'd leave a note, escape the biddies, *Mr. Cowboy*, and the woman who was single-handedly trying to kill him.

*Coward.*

*See? You won't win,* he told his arm. *I'm still young. I can have a life and fool around with a beautiful woman.*

No, this was Daisy, for crying out loud. *Peanut.* But his Peanut was all grown up, and when he wasn't looking, she'd turned into a sexpot.

*Gulp.* He pulled at the neckline of his shirt. Was it hot in here?

"You did the right thing waiting. You should be in love your first time," he said.

"Were you in love your first time?"

Hell no. In fact, someone older had initiated him, which made him wonder if he was playing the double-standard card. He'd been sixteen, and granted, tall for his age. She'd been twenty-five or so, visiting her cousins when she found him in the barn one night. Wade thought she'd been looking for Lincoln, whom she'd flirted with all night, but she shook her head and said "no." She'd straddled him, lifted up her skirt, and that was all she wrote.

He didn't even remember her name.

"Okay. I think it's time for you to go home. My head hurts."

She rose, a look of concern in her eyes that immediately made him sorry he'd said anything. "Not your arm?"

"My arm is fine compared to my brain. It's about to explode."

She blinked. "Are you mad at me?"

"No, I'm not mad. Just very…"

*Torn and confused.*

*Weary. Injured. You name it.*

"It's okay. I've given you a lot to think about." She walked toward the front door. "But remember this weekend. The Riverwalk."

Then she turned and sashayed her cute behind out of his

55

home. Slowly, he closed the door. The framed photo of his mother on the fireplace mantel smiled back at him.

And if she could see him now from heaven, she was laughing and saying: "I told you so."

SOMEHOW, Wade made it through the rest of the week without seeing Daisy. Thank the sweet baby Jesus, the casseroles stopped coming every day, and he had few interruptions. No more mention of Mr. Cowboy or how important it was that he settle down with a good woman. Maybe he could actually get some work done around here.

Lincoln came by a few times, to check in, and yell at him to take care of his arm and do his physical therapy. Then he'd offer to do some of Wade's chores and only leave when Wade kicked him out.

Wade's arm hurt every day, but especially after a long day of ranch work. He found himself taking several pain pills a day, hating that he needed them. Someday this would get better. His arm would be fully healed and with any luck no residual pain. But the pain made him feel old, lame, and useless. Still, being permanently sidelined from the rodeo meant he had to find another way to make a living. For the rest of his life.

When he went into the barn for feed or equipment, he glared at the Model T that sat there like a relic of times gone by. An antique, a gift from his father. Mocking him.

On Tuesday and Wednesday, Wade worked on the fence line. He was so bored that he nearly fell asleep standing up. Safe to say, ranching was nothing like the rodeo. He imagined the only adrenaline shot he might have was if the barn fell down, which at this point looked like three to one odds. He'd take that bet.

Dante and Satan were the only animals left on a formerly

large cattle ranch. Once, they'd had thirty head of cattle, two bulls, a stable of horses, pigs, and goats. He might not be much of a rancher, but his father had been, and *his* father before him. Wade might have been a rancher, too, but early on Jorge Cruz saw something special in Wade.

He noticed that his only son was fearless. When Wade was ten, he'd walked across the top of the wood pigpen fence, fallen in, and nearly been lunch. He'd tried to explain to his father that he thought he'd clear it and only missed it by an inch. He'd do better next time.

"There won't be a next time! Boy, don't you got any good sense? If you get hurt, your mother will kill me."

But despite that threat, Wade was always getting hurt. He fell from trees, which he climbed because it would be crazy not to.

But he'd never fallen off a horse. He'd been riding since age five, and they'd never owned anything but well-behaved, docile, and trained quarter horses. Then, when Wade was about twelve, he'd mounted a horse his father was considering purchasing. Something spooked the paint, and he bucked, trying to throw Wade off. The owner yelled. Wade's father cursed. His mother cried, but the horse bucked for several seconds before anyone was able to control him.

It had been the time of Wade's life. He never fell off, no matter how hard that horse had bucked.

And his father saw gold.

From that day on, Wade started training for the rodeo.

"What would you think if you could see me now, Dad?" Wade muttered now as he pounded another nail in the fence.

Things had gone well for several years. His father supported Wade's training, sometimes selling off cattle to pay for expenses. Once Wade started touring and earning money, he put it right back into the ranch. For a while, the cattle operation thrived. His mother was happy, and Wade loved that he had a part. The part he enjoyed. Not the fence repairs, hay bales, pulling cattle out of ditches, tagging, and mucking.

He enjoyed flying on the backs of horses, lassoing steer, the crowds cheering. He sat on bucking bulls. He got to listen as the announcers talked about him. They called him cocky but gifted. Bold. Daring. "Wild Wade" became his nickname early on as he racked up the wins. He hadn't known what an adrenaline junkie was at the age of sixteen, but he did now. And Wade had simply been born that way.

He didn't blame his father for making the most of Wade's talents. He did, however, blame him for ruining what might have been.

A truck came up his driveway, kicking up gravel. The red, long-bed truck was familiar, and Wade immediately recognized his closest neighbor, Riggs Henderson. Their lands abutted each other.

Wade met him, fist-bumping when Riggs climbed out of his truck.

"You know, you could hire some help around here," Riggs said, eyeing Wade's boots. Probably also eyeing the state of Wade's ranch. "Just call me or Sean over anytime. Free of charge."

"You're busy enough with the twins."

"Between Winona and Delores, I'm lucky if I get to hold one of them for longer than a few minutes," he chuckled.

"Don't forget I worked for Hank between tournaments."

"I'm sure it will all come back to you." Riggs nodded. "Again, I'm sorry about your mother."

"It had been coming for some time."

"Still isn't easy."

"No. Guess not."

It was, however, easier when he didn't have to think about it. When he didn't have to live in the same house where she'd died. When he could ride bulls and forget his pain. Now, he was here and every day felt like a struggle, and not just because of his arm.

They walked quietly for a few minutes, their boots kicking up gravel. "There's a cattle auction coming up. Sean and I are going. You got a plan?"

Here was the thing. Everyone seemed to think Wade Cruz should be rolling in the money. All those winnings over the years. Hundreds of thousands of dollars. Compounded interest. He *could* have been well-off had he always been in control. Unfortunately, he'd made the mistake of trusting his father. His own flesh and blood. He hadn't known that Jorge Cruz liked the casinos. When he'd died suddenly, Wade and his mother learned the truth.

Eventually, Wade managed to bring back possibly half of what he should have had in a lifetime of earnings. He'd done that by entering every tournament he could for years. By working for Lincoln's father during off-season. Saving and socking everything away. Then he'd been sucker punched by his mother's cancer and a truckload of medical bills Wade slowly paid off.

What he had left of his savings would have to do because he had no options left. No more competitions, no more so-called "easy" money.

"The plan is to make this a working cattle ranch again."

# CHAPTER 6

*D*aisy had been waiting for the Riverwalk all week long. After her last week of work at the auto shop before they closed for the holidays, generous Lou gave everyone a bonus. After work, Daisy went to buy a new pair of boots with her bounty.

She'd decided on a pair of low heels with blue inlays, her typical style, when Jolette Marie came up beside her. Since there were no shoe stores in Stone Ridge (or hair and nail salons or much of anything else) everyone came to Kerrville to shop. Either that or they ordered online and waited. And waited.

"Oh, those are *cute*," Jolette Marie said.

"Thanks. I need a new pair for the Riverwalk."

These were practical but also pretty. And the price was right.

"Same reason I'm here." Jolette Marie held up a kickass pair of boots with a killer heel. They were black with red inlays.

Daisy reconsidered. She should get boots with a heel. Much sexier. If she didn't buy a sexy boot, was there any point to this at all? Picking up a similar boot with heels, Daisy gasped at the price. This would be almost her entire bonus.

"What's the matter? Don't have your size?" Jolette Marie, daughter of the wealthiest man in Stone Ridge, didn't have to worry about price tags. "I'll help you look."

For several minutes, Daisy pretended this was the issue. They looked for a size eight, when Daisy was a size seven.

"You know what? I'm going to buy these." She held up the first pair of boots. Damn the torpedoes.

"Suffer for fashion, I always say."

"Smart." Daisy didn't like to suffer, though, for fashion or anything else.

She paid, waving goodbye to half her bonus. It would be worth it if Wade found her feet sexy.

"Are you going with anyone to the Riverwalk?" Daisy asked, making conversation as they walked outside with their packages.

"Several someones." Jolette Marie winked.

She was one of the women who didn't want to settle down with just one guy when there were so many to choose from. It occurred to Daisy that she might find a kindred spirit in Jolette Marie but for a different reason.

"Hey, did you see that billboard they put up?"

"Hilarious."

"I think it's ugly. An eyesore."

"So does my daddy. He claims he's going to sue." Jolette Marie snorted.

Daisy didn't think her kindred spirit would be an old multimillionaire, but so be it. "Good for him."

"Well, Daddy says he's going to do a lot of things that he never does."

"Aren't you worried about all these women they're going to be bringing into town? To take *our* men?"

But then again, why would Jolette Marie be worried? She was beautiful and had the attention of every single man in town. Even Lincoln had dated her for a while before he and Sadie fell in love. The most unfair part of all this to Daisy was that Jolette Marie had older brothers who didn't seem to give a hoot what she did with her life. Or whom she dated. Lucky stiff.

"Don't worry." She waved her hand dismissively. "Those women won't stick around for long."

Daisy hoped not. She thought about it as she drove back into town, once more having to pass by the giant man with the blinding smile. Hopefully she and Wade would be able to pull off this fake-dating thing. From time to time, a news story would come out about the handsome rodeo star who was forced to cut his promising career short. Daisy was no fool. This was precisely the kind of man those reality dating shows wanted. Former football and baseball players. What if the producers came into town and got wind of the fact that a retired rodeo star lived in Stone Ridge, still famously single?

Maybe then even Beulah wouldn't be able to stop them from coming after Wade Cruz.

THE STONE RIDGE Riverwalk was a pale imitation of the larger San Antonio Christmas Riverwalk to the north. But in a rare show of collaboration, every holiday season Stone Ridge and their sister town, Nothing, put on their own much-smaller version. This had been going on for several decades, since before Daisy was born. Because Nothing, Texas was known for...well, nothing. The Riverwalk had become their claim to fame. Even if it was held along the riverbanks that ran through Stone Ridge.

Stone Ridge had Titus Ridge, and Founder's Day, but Nothing had no clue who had founded them. Or why.

Booths were always set along the banks of the Guadalupe River which curled through Kerrville, Stone Ridge, and down to Nothing. A show of bright-colored blinking lights lit up the night sky, with holiday lights hung between the trees. Every few feet had fresh Christmas trees decorated by the children of both towns. The effect was scenic, but Daisy had never been able to capture or do it justice with a photograph.

"Are you ready, Miss Daisy?" Wade's slow smile was knowing and conspiratorial as he'd held out his good arm.

He'd dropped by to pick her up at the ranch, good manners on display to the point that Mima scowled only once. Dressed in a pair of jeans tight in all the right places, he wore a long-sleeved white button-down and a black Stetson.

She now strolled alongside Wade, holding his warm hand. They'd walked by a few booths, Daisy's feet already hurting.

Wade noticed. "Everything okay?"

"New boots." She should have broken them in first.

His gaze had lowered to check out her, yes, *sexy* feet. "Nice. But they look uncomfortable."

"Come right on over here, Daisy Mae," Lenny called out from his booth. "Take a load off."

Lenny was a retired postal worker who never met a job he didn't like. Since retiring, he'd been a part of Stone Ridge's volunteer fire department. He also played a clown at birthday parties and had recently purchased a broken-down golf cart which he used to drive folks around downtown. Now that they had a medical clinic in town, he'd park himself outside and wait for the pregnant ladies. Of course, he didn't charge for any of these services, as that was not the Stone Ridge way. He simply liked to keep busy.

Today, he'd fashioned a massage table into one like the kind found at malls in bigger cities. The chair was an office-style one on wheels that he'd probably borrowed from Eve's veterinarian office.

"Need a massage?" He wiggled his fingers.

"Um…"

"You seem to be having a little trouble walking," Lenny said, throwing a small towel over his shoulder. "I studied the five-point system for stress relief."

"Lenny," Wade said, voice thick with humor, "I think you're pushing decency boundaries here."

"Son, I firmly doubt that."

"You're not touching my feet," Daisy said, though they hurt like she'd stepped on a nail.

Earlier, Jolette Marie had been walking in her new boots as if on a cloud. Wonder how long it would take Daisy's feet to get numb enough to where she'd stop feeling them.

"Oh good! Lenny, please. My shoulders," came Winona's voice. She waddled to his booth.

Riggs followed her, pushing the double stroller with their twin boys.

"Right this way, Mrs. Henderson." Lenny made a big sweep of his arm.

"This pregnancy has been hell on my back," Winona said, and smiled at both Daisy and Wade. "Hiya, guys. I'm sorry, did I cut ahead of you?"

"No, we're just…trying to decide." Wade cocked his head and fought a smile.

Winona began to moan as Lenny massaged her shoulders. Oh, geez. Daisy flushed a little. Winona must be one of those screamers she'd read about and seen in the kind of movies she wasn't supposed to have watched.

"Should I be jealous?" Riggs asked, parking the stroller next to the booth.

"Oh, baby, it's just that your massages never last long enough," Winona said.

"Try wearing some clothes next time." Wade chuckled, and he and Riggs fist-bumped.

"How do you think we got in this mess?" Winona laughed, patting her belly. "I can't stay away from the man."

All this moaning and talk about making babies and not wearing any clothes was making Daisy a little hot. And with Wade standing right next to her, his warm body and large hand holding hers...she almost forgot she *had* feet.

"I think I'm going to take my girl to get some roasted chestnuts or some hot chocolate," Wade said. He smiled as Beulah and her husband, Lloyd, walked by.

A couple of women wandered over to them as they waited at the hot cocoa booth run by Pastor June. Daisy recognized them as some of the women who barrel raced in local and regional tournaments. She had a lot more in common with these women, who weren't afraid to break a nail or find a split end. They eyed Wade with something close to resembling hero worship.

"Hey, Wade," Belinda said. "I heard you were back."

"In the flesh," Wade said.

"I'm sorry about your arm," Kari Lynn said. "Tough break."

Wade stiffened noticeably. "Part of the gig."

"It shouldn't have happened to you." Kari Lynn reached to touch his arm. Not his bad one, which possibly meant she didn't even know which arm he'd injured.

Wade put an arm around Daisy. "Yeah, well. It did happen."

"Is it getting any better?" Belinda asked, ignoring the arm he'd draped on Daisy.

"June, is that cocoa ready yet?" Wade asked, clearing his throat.

He was the only one who got away with calling Pastor June by her first name, but she and Wade's mother had been the best of friends. Every Sunday, Wade and Rose used to have dinner with Pastor June and her family.

"Hold your horses." Pastor June handed over the cups and everyone chuckled.

"That's hilarious." Wade took his arm off Daisy's shoulder and accepted the cups.

"Do you think you'd ever give lessons?" Belinda asked. "Because I want to take my racing to the next level."

"Me too, and I'd love some tips."

Both women flanked him at which point something strange happened. Wade slid right into flirtatious mode, like a toggle had been switched.

"Why, ladies, I don't think I'd be the best teacher for pretty women like yourselves. I don't know if I could concentrate on the job at hand."

They giggled, and Daisy fumed. It was a sort of unwritten rule in Stone Ridge that women didn't fight over a man. There were too many of them. But of course, some men were different. Special. Men like her brothers and Riggs Henderson. Beau Stephens. *Wade Cruz.*

She stepped back and left Wade to his fan club because not two feet away from her was Beulah. She would be getting a piece of Daisy's mind in about three…two…one…

"Miss Beulah, I saw the billboard y'all put up and it's a real eyesore." Daisy crossed her arms and tried to look mean.

"Well, hello to you, too, Daisy. And why should our billboard bother you?"

"It's hideous, and I'm a concerned, tax-paying citizen."

Beulah pursed her lips. "It was decided long ago, child. Maybe if you got your nose out of car engines and looked around, you'd notice something. This town is changing."

"Because you're tryin' to change it!"

"Sugar, maybe you haven't considered this, but it's unfair that there aren't enough women for our single men.

And I'm attempting to correct that, with the help of Winona."

"What *I've* noticed is that this project is headed by two women who already have their husbands. So, why should y'all care?"

"I thought you and Wade were together. Why do *you* care?"

"Um, yeah. We are together. But I still care."

She tossed her hair back and looked behind but didn't see Wade where she'd left him. At least Beulah wouldn't be a witness to her fake boyfriend flirting with other women. He had a reputation for being a womanizer and a category-five flirt. Daisy had never believed that, but she'd just seen Exhibit A.

She hated that he was proving Mima's theory about him to be correct. Maybe he hadn't changed at all. Maybe Daisy was fooling herself that he ever could.

"Excuse me, Miss Beulah." This was said by an older gentleman Daisy didn't recognize "But the young lady has a point. Do we really need the billboard to be the size of a jumbo jet?"

"It is not the size of a jet!"

"I beg to differ," someone else said. "Yesterday I swear I saw it all the way from Nothing."

"Y'all always thought you were better than us, just because you're closer to Kerrville."

"Stupid idea, you ask me. Just watch Nothing rise from the ashes and clobber your *Mr. Cowboy* contest."

Daisy smiled. Apparently, she'd started a brand-new rivalry between Stone Ridge and Nothing. Maybe they could have the contest in Nothing.

It's not like they had anything else going on.

She left Beulah to fend for herself. As she strolled, she saw no sign of Wade. Regret pulsed through her. She was never going to be able to compete for his attentions the way other women did. This fake-dating thing would never work. In the back of her mind, yes, she'd hoped that maybe this would lead to a little reality of her own. He could teach her how to behave, how to give signals that she wanted a man, and she'd try it all out on him.

Sadie walked up to Daisy, pushing her stroller with Sammy in it, all drooly faced and gurgling.

"Hey, puddin'." Daisy bent and tweaked her nephew's nose.

"Can you come over for dinner tomorrow night?" Sadie asked, and she looked so worried that Daisy wondered if something could be seriously wrong.

"Sure. Why? Are you okay?"

"Why wouldn't I be?" Sadie laughed it off, rolling her shoulders. "We just miss you, that's all."

"We had Sunday dinner together just the other night."

Sadie held up a palm. "But not at *our* house."

Lincoln caught up to Sadie then, tugging her close. "You coming to dinner, Shortie?"

"Sure."

She saw these two all the time. They sounded so excited about dinner. Weird.

"Um, can I bring Wade?"

"*Wade?*" Lincoln narrowed his eyes. "You don't need to pretend with us."

Daisy shrugged. "He needs a home cooked meal, too."

"Of course he can come. We haven't had him over since he got back," Sadie said.

"But this is kind of a family thing," Lincoln said.

"Oh, it is?" Daisy was even more confused now.

"I think it's okay." Sadie threw him the look that turned her big brother into a piece of marshmallow.

He rolled his shoulders. "Sure. It's fine."

"Have y'all seen Wade?" Daisy turned in a slow circle.

"Look for the women," Lincoln said with a snort.

Eve and Jackson were standing under the long branches of a weeping willow not so discreetly making out. Daisy thought it useless to ask them if they'd seen *anyone*.

She walked a few more steps, looking for the single women as Lincoln suggested. No Wade anywhere. Kari Lynn and Belinda were now chatting with some other men. Had he just left her here? How would she explain that to Mima? Daisy was going to have a serious talk with him because she didn't want him to keep filling the stereotype that had been created for him. He was feeding right into it and he was far better than that.

Then she found him, half hidden in the darkness under a willow tree. He stood, his back against the tree trunk. "Hey."

"Wade? What are you doin' there?"

"C'mere." He beckoned her.

She hesitated, then walked slowly toward him, unsure of why this moment seemed markedly different. Maybe it was the darkness of the night or that he cut such a lonely figure. But she was a type of nervous she'd never been around Wade. Heat pulsed through her. Excitement thrummed. Something new and scary.

*This is what you've been waiting for. Don't be afraid. Step out of your comfort zone.*

She walked under the branches toward him.

"I thought I asked you to keep me away from people who want to talk about the rodeo. How dare you leave me alone with those piranhas?" He slid her a slow smile.

"Kari Lynn? You seemed to be doing just fine."

"I wasn't."

"Could have fooled me."

"I fool a lot of people. Just didn't think you'd ever be one of them."

That simple statement shocked her because he'd never been so open. But it was true that Wade had never been able to fool her. This was the reason she didn't listen to the rumors. She understood him. She knew the one thing he'd feared the most.

And she knew who had hurt him because she'd seen it happen.

"They just admire you for everything you've done. Your accomplishments."

Even if they'd been a little too flirtatious for Daisy's taste, she also saw that they meant to gain some knowledge from an expert.

"All they want to talk about is the rodeo. I'm done with all that."

"Maybe with tournaments, but they made a good point. You could teach others."

He shook his head. "Not doin' any of that. I'm a rancher now. That's what I need to be."

"No one *needs* to be a rancher."

"When all I have left is a broke-down ranch, yeah. I kind of need to be a rancher."

*All I have left.*

Daisy didn't like to hear those words coming out of "Wild Wade's" lips. Did he really feel like he had nothing else left in his life? His mother was gone, sure, and he'd been close to her. His father had been dead for a few years and Wade never talked about him anymore. But Wade had friends, admirers, and the entire town of Stone Ridge behind him.

Daisy opened her mouth to tell him the ranch was not all he had left, when he put a finger to her lips.

"First lesson, Peanut. When a man you're interested in beckons you, don't hesitate. Hesitating sends the wrong message."

"Right. You just…surprised me, standing over here in the dark."

"Surprises can be a fun part of a relationship."

She nodded. "And…what else should I do? If…if I'm interested."

"You can always lean close, like this."

"Okay." She stepped closer.

He tugged on a lock of her hair. "If you want a man to kiss you, and you're too shy to do it yourself? Stare at his mouth."

She studied his lips, which as it happened, she'd done many times before. Just not when he was *watching*. Now she felt as if time had stopped and they were the only two people in the world. A low breeze kicked up from the river, sending a shiver down her back. The scent of hot cocoa and rain lingered in the air all around them.

"Just like that," he said, and his voice was low, a soft growl. "It's an invitation."

She couldn't tear her eyes away, hypnotized. The anticipation was killing her. He was going to kiss her. Yes. Maybe? Oh, please. Desire rolled through her with a tiny slice of apprehension. This was the moment she'd been waiting for. For years, she'd wanted to compare. She'd wanted to see if the one time had been a fluke. Because she'd been eighteen, half in love with him for most of her life. Now, she'd kissed a few men since that first time with Wade. Not many, to be sure, but enough to know that nothing had ever met that threshold.

She'd told herself it was her imagination, her memory simply enhancing the moment to far more than it had been.

Wade tipped her chin to meet his eyes, and in a slow and luscious move, he lowered his lips to hers. The kiss was slow. Sweet. And delicious. He tasted like a mix of cocoa and mint. It made her think he'd actually prepared for this moment and that more than anything sent tiny tingles of awareness thrumming through her body. She reacted to him, to the heat of his long and lean body. She reached to thread her hands around his neck and draw him closer. His breathing shifted and he deepened the kiss.

Strong hands pulled her close, hip to hip, enough that she could feel his arousal.

They were both breathing heavy when she heard the distinctive voices of Sadie and Lincoln drawing closer, carrying along with the sounds of children laughing and holiday music playing.

"No, baby, he can't have honey," Sadie said. "Not until he's one."

"Sorry, Sammy." Lincoln chuckled. "You don't know what you're missin'."

Daisy broke the kiss, worried they'd be caught. She slid her hands down Wade's arms. "Should we stop now?"

"Only if you want to." Then he took her hand and led her a bit farther into the darkness.

She proved that she did not want to stop, by once again studying his lips. Damn, it was a good mouth. Sensual lips, the top slightly fuller than the bottom.

"You are a quick study, Peanut."

He kissed her again, this time decidedly *not* sweet. There was an urgency in that kiss, one that pushed her heartbeat into a wild race. She drank him in, unable to get enough.

"Okay, now we're stopping." Wade pulled back.

"Why?"

"I need to take a step back before I do something I regret."

"*Regret?* Like what?"

He met her gaze. "You don't want to know. I need to stop now before I lose control. Before I forget the code I live by."

Her breath hitched. Oh Lord. He was losing control. With *her.* "Wade…"

"I mean it, Peanut." He took a step back. "Not now."

"Did I do something wrong?"

He chuckled. "Not at all."

"Because you said we stop only if I want to."

"Yeah, but now I need to."

She stared at the bulge in his jeans, understanding dawning. Momentarily, she was robbed of the power of speech.

"And it would also help if you don't stare," he snorted.

"Oh gosh, I'm sorry!" She clapped a hand over her mouth.
"Don't be."

Daisy was trying to think of something to say when over Wade's shoulder she spotted the man who'd been hanging around the auto shop for weeks.

*Here* at the Riverwalk. He seemed determined, his stride filled with purpose and hostility.

Coming straight for her.

# CHAPTER 7

*W*ade hadn't done this kind of necking since he was a teenager, back in the days when kissing was the main event.

Sure, there was a certain adrenaline rush from kissing a woman he should *not* be kissing. A few feet away from people who might want to kill him for doing so. But that certainly wasn't the reason his heart raced like it did just before the chute opened. He'd just discovered, quite by accident, that he thoroughly enjoyed the way Peanut, uh, *Daisy* kissed.

Then suddenly Daisy looked over his shoulder, her mouth a small circle, her eyes wide as twin circles. The fear in her eyes had a sobering effect on Wade. It had the effect of ice-cold water being dumped over his head.

"It's…it's *him*."

Wade followed the direction of her gaze and saw a man coming toward them. Out of instinct, he stepped in front of Daisy, meeting the man halfway.

"I need Daisy Mae Carver." The man pointed past Wade to Daisy. "That's her right behind you."

"Who wants her?"

The man pulled a rolled-up manila envelope from inside his windbreaker. "I'm Jeff with Wilson Investigations out of San Antonio. You lose 'em, we find 'em."

"You're that man at the auto shop. I've seen you," Daisy said from behind Wade, then stepped beside him. "And I'm not afraid of you."

The man blinked. "You shouldn't be. Actually, I'm trying to help you."

"I'll take that, thanks." Wade held out his hand.

Jeff hesitated but Wade gave him the look he gave steer he was about to hog-tie and the man handed it over.

Wade accepted the envelope. "How are you trying to help Daisy?"

"She could come into some money."

"Ha! That's a likely story," Daisy said.

"Quiet, Peanut. Let's hear the man out."

"Actually, the man who hired us has known where you are for quite some time. But it was only last week that my firm was dispatched to locate you, make sure we had the right person, and deliver this envelope to you."

"You couldn't use the old-fashioned post-office method?" Wade turned the envelope over in his hands and read the return address. It was from a law firm. He handed it to Daisy.

"I get paid to make sure this gets into *her* hands. Leaving no chance that some well-meaning person will intervene."

"I don't understand." Daisy opened the envelope.

"What the hell is going on here?" came Lincoln's voice as he joined them.

"This man claims he has something for Daisy and that she could come into some money." Wade gestured to the man.

"Oh God," Sadie said, but it wasn't a happy sound. More of a strangled one.

"What's happenin'?" Jackson joined them, and together he and Lincoln flanked Daisy and Wade.

"Nothing good," Lincoln muttered.

Only then did Wade realize that all the color had drained out of his best friend's face. For a former rodeo cowboy often called "lucky" for avoiding any serious injuries, Lincoln had never looked so scared to Wade.

"Is Rusty dead?" Lincoln asked.

"*Rusty?* Who's Rusty?" Daisy said.

Suddenly Jeff didn't look so certain of himself. "No, he's not dead, and I think I should just leave y'all alone. There's a lot to discuss."

"Not so fast." Lincoln grabbed the man's jacket and pulled him back. "If Rusty isn't dead, why are you here?"

"It's a tricky matter. A family matter."

"Since you just dropped a bomb on *my* family and left me to diffuse it, I suggest you start talking and explain." Lincoln's tone and body language suggested the man wasn't going anywhere.

Wade felt the snap and crackle in the air surround him and he welcomed it. He smelled fear.

But not his own. Lincoln's.

Jeff smoothed down his jacket, scowling. "My client is Rusty's brother. He won't contest Rusty's last will and testament. But if Daisy is going to be the beneficiary of Rusty's estate, then she needs to submit to a DNA test to prove she's his biological daughter."


DAISY FROZE. She must have heard wrong. For a moment, she didn't understand. When Wade reached for her hand and squeezed it, she pulled out of her daze. She wished she understood why this "Rusty" thought she was his daughter. She was *Hank's* daughter. Then a thick sense of dread pulsed through her as she tried to think of reasons this idea would even occur to the man. And only one of them came through as painful as a slap.

*Her mother.*

"The rumor about my mother...it's t-true?"

"I have no idea what you're talking about," Jeff said, throwing his palms up.

"Thank you for your help. We'll take it from here." Lincoln did everything but use his boot on the man's behind.

"Let's go home." Lincoln turned to Daisy. "We have a lot to talk about."

But Daisy was too busy trying to make sense out of legalese. "Wait. Rusty thinks I'm his daughter?"

"He's *wrong*," Lincoln said.

"What the hell," said Jackson. "Why didn't I know about this?"

"Let's go back to our cabin," Sadie echoed Lincoln. "We need some privacy to talk this through."

People were already staring. Riggs, with that worried look of his, wanting to help but reading the room.

"Well, I'm coming," Jackson said. "This is a load of bull hockey."

"Of course you're comin'," Lincoln said. "Everyone is."

"And so am I," Wade said, quirking his brow. His tone brooked no argument. "We're on a date."

As if he needed an excuse. Daisy wanted him there, too. He was practically family.

Lincoln rolled his eyes, then went palms up. "You too, of course."

Not long after, they were all gathered in front of the fireplace in the great room of Lincoln and Sadie's cabin. The fire roared, easing the chill in the air, both of temperature and mood.

Sadie returned from putting Sammy down for the night

and sat on the arm of Lincoln's chair, curling her arm around him. "Sammy's asleep."

Jackson and Eve were seated nearby on the leather couch, holding hands. Eve was biting her lower lip and Jackson had the same scowl on his face that Lincoln did.

And Wade? He was simply holding Daisy's hand and quietly listening.

Lincoln explained how last year Hank had been contacted by a man who claimed he could be Daisy's father. When even the possibility that Daisy might not be his daughter became too much for Hank to deal with, Lincoln took over.

"Remember the old bowlegged man that came into the shop over a year ago to talk engines with you?"

There had been an older man, but that was so long ago, and she talked to a lot of people at the auto shop. She did remember this older man being about her father's age, and seemingly incredibly gratified that she knew her engines. Because of his enthusiasm, it did seem strange that he'd never come back for the tune-up he claimed his truck needed. But she figured he'd found another shop and never thought about it again.

"I think so."

"That was Rusty Jones." Lincoln took off his hat and dragged a hand through his hair. "He talked me into driving him by your work, so he could just catch a glimpse of you. It was part of an agreement I made with him."

"Agreement...you made with him? *What* agreement?"

"Lincoln was trying to protect you," Sadie said.

"It's okay, baby." Lincoln rested his palm on Sadie's leg. "This is for me to explain."

Lincoln went on to tell Daisy that he'd never intended for Rusty to meet her but had simply agreed for him to watch her from a distance. The old man had violated their agreement and climbed out of the truck before Lincoln could stop him.

"I had a feeling then that wasn't the end of it," Lincoln said. "Unfortunately, our mother contacted him just after she left us and told him that you...you might be his daughter. A product of their one-night stand."

Daisy swallowed hard. Her mother, the buckle bunny. The memories of her were almost nonexistent. But there were some random photos here and there, pictures of Daddy with a beautiful blonde, two boys, and a baby in her arms. Daisy imagined they'd been kept simply to prove that someone had given birth to them. A biological connection.

But Maggie was not her family. Her family was in this room, plus Hank, and Mima, who'd been more of a mother to her than anyone else. Even Eve and Sadie had mothered her from time to time. Daisy had never lacked nurturing. And until now, she'd thought numerous times, at least I have my daddy.

"That might be true." Wade squeezed her hand. "But she could also be Hank's daughter."

"Right. There's a fifty-fifty chance anyway, and it's not like Daisy looks like anyone but..." Lincoln didn't finish his sentence.

"Our mother." And how she hated that.

Maggie had been a beauty queen in her hometown of San Antonio, but clearly heartless.

Until now, Daisy believed she hadn't had any intimate relationships with men because of big brothers who were a little too protective. But she'd been ignoring one blatant and obvious fact. The thought occurred that Daisy had distanced herself from Maggie in every way she could.

She couldn't do anything about her blond hair and green eyes. Instinctively, she hadn't wanted Hank to look at her and think of Maggie. To look at Daisy and be reminded of pain and loss. She'd wanted to be as different from Maggie as she could, and she'd succeeded.

Daisy had been a tomboy, having an affinity for and choosing to work in a male-dominated profession. She'd never been overly concerned about her appearance. Mostly, she dressed for practicality and comfort, not fashion. She'd believed it was due to being brought up on a ranch with two older brothers, cattle, and horses. But Eve and Sadie were brought up similarly and yet eased into that part of their lives that involved hairstyles, makeup, and falling in love with the boy next door. Not Daisy.

And at least one of her dates had referred to her as "uptight," a "cold fish," and the worst of them, a tease.

So, here she was, a twenty-six-year-old virgin, and daughter of a buckle bunny. *Please don't let me also be the daughter of a rodeo cowboy.* A living and breathing, walking cliché.

"Daddy knows about this?"

"He does," Lincoln said. "All except for this latest development. See, Rusty is sick, and he's kept in contact. It's true that he wants to leave everything to you. But he doesn't have any other children. For him, a DNA test isn't necessary. He's willing to take that chance and…I guess you won him over that day when you chatted mechanics. Rusty is also a mechanic. Somehow, he's fooled himself into believing that was in your nature. His influence."

"Do I have to do this DNA test?"

"No," Jackson said. "You don't have to do anything you don't want to do."

"That's right," Lincoln said. "Entirely up to you."

"It won't change anything." Sadie reached for Daisy's hand and squeezed.

"I don't see why I should take the test. I don't want or need his money. His brother should have it."

"This is more about whether you want to know," Eve said gently. "In case you want reassurance."

"No need. I already know I'm Hank's daughter."

"Of course you are," Sadie said.

"Damn straight," Lincoln added.

"No question," Jackson said.

Wade had stayed quiet all this time and Daisy wondered what he thought. She would ask him later, privately. If Wade had a differing opinion, she wouldn't want him to be forced to go against her brothers. But she could almost see the wheels spinning. He had opinions. No doubt about it. When she looked at him, he simply gave her a small smile.

She turned to Lincoln. "You *should* have told me this sooner."

Daisy could already see the worry had been eating at her brother. Sadie sucked in a breath, but otherwise the only sound in the room was the snapping of the wood as the fire consumed it.

"I know."

He hung his head, looking like a whipped dog. Her eldest brother, always taking care of everyone and sometimes neglecting himself. Until Sadie came along. It was the first time she'd ever seen him truly happy.

"Listen, Tiny," Daisy said, using an old pet name for her tall big brother. Always broad shouldered enough to take on the family's worries and his own. "You protected me, as you always do. Thank you."


EVEN IF HE didn't have to drive Daisy home, Wade insisted on walking with her down the hill to the family home where she and Mima now lived alone. After dusk, the evening temps had lowered by at least ten degrees. Nearby, she heard a cow lowing and thought of Daddy. She'd have to see him soon and reassure him that she didn't care what this Rusty man had to say. Hank was her father and always would be.

She and Wade walked side by side in the quiet, his easy gait next to her painful hitch.

"You shouldn't have worn those boots." Wade broke the silence.

Yes, that's just what she expected him to contribute after tonight's bombshell. He'd sat right next to her, heard that she might not be a Carver, and he had nothing more to say than her boots were inappropriate footwear.

"Um, yeah. Well, they're pretty."

"I didn't think you cared about that sort of thing."

"Maybe I do."

"This is ridiculous." He stopped on a dime in front of her. "Get on my back."

"What are you *talkin'* about?"

"Your feet are killin' you and that's enough pride on your part. I can't take any more of this."

"I'll be damned if I climb on your back like I can't walk. That's just humiliating."

"More so than having blisters on your feet for days?"

"Look, I'm not some *buckle bunny* that's got to be weak so that her strong cowboy can take care of her."

Oh *man.* Where had that come from? She hadn't meant to sound so defensive.

Wade stared her down. "No, you're a pain in the ass is what you are."

"You take that back!"

"I will if you climb on my back. We have several more yards to go and your grandmother will kill me twice if you walk inside the house limping." He cleared his throat. "I'm afraid she's going to think...other things."

"What other...? Oh. Oh," Daisy said as it slowly dawned on her.

"Yeah, if I'd had sex with you behind that tree, or in my truck, believe me, you would be limping."

Her face must have flushed and darkened to the red color of a stop sign. It was surely hot enough to fry a flapjack on it.

"Fine, then."

He lowered his body enough that she could climb on him, then straightened, tucking his arms under her knees. And it actually wasn't all bad, this piggyback ride. Kind of fun. She remembered how once, just after Eve and Jackson started dating as teenagers, she saw them fooling around in a similar fashion. Back then she'd thought both of them a couple of idiots but now it made a whole lot more sense. It was simply an excuse to touch.

And she appreciated having a reason to tighten her arms around Wade's shoulders and plaster her body against his. Lowering her head to an inch from the crook of his neck, she inhaled his fresh clean scent. It would be like this if they made love, she imagined. Flesh against flesh, their bodies sliding against each other...

Wade's bad arm seemed to be trembling which yanked her right out of her happy place. This couldn't be good. "Is carrying me hurting your bad arm?"

"No, but thanks for asking."

She was quite familiar with the quiet stoicism of a stubborn cowboy, so she shifted her weight as best she could and repositioned herself. Unfortunately, that made her slide down some, and Wade used his back to pull her up.

"Stay still," he ordered.

Weren't they a pair? Her with her dumb feet and him with an injured arm. He still hadn't mentioned anything about it tonight.

They walked a few more steps before she couldn't take it anymore. "Aren't you going to tell me what you think?"

"About *what?*"

"You know what! The stupid DNA test."

"Yeah? What of it?"

Oh, so he was going to pull this slowpoke cowboy thing on her. "Would *you* do it?"

He was quiet for several seconds. "What I would do doesn't matter. You have to do what's right for you."

She jumped off his back when they were a short distance from the house. "And what if I don't know what's right for me?"

He shoved his hands in his jacket and gazed at her from under hooded lids. "I take it this isn't about the money."

"Of course not." She crossed her arms and shook her head. "I'm afraid."

"You're not afraid of anything except maybe getting kissed. And I think we took care of that tonight." He tweaked her chin. "But me? I'm a risk-taker, so if you're asking what I'd do, then I'd want to do it."

"You'd take the test?"

"Not for the money, of course. The old man can keep it. But I'd want to prove it to myself. Prove that I'm right."

"You'd do something scary because you think you'll get the answer you want?"

"Yeah, guess I'd be betting on myself. That's the only kind of bets I've ever made. But you're talkin' to someone who thrives on a good adrenaline rush. Guess I'd be nervous for a while until I found out. You might call that scared. I would just call it the anticipation of a sweet moment of victory. Every time I got on a bull I didn't know if he'd throw me into next week or if somehow, through skill and good luck, I'd hang on. Maybe I'd be killed, or maybe I'd live."

"You did that every time?"

"That's half the fun of it for me." He snorted. "Was."

In the past few minutes, Daisy's thoughts had run the gamut. On the one hand, she needed to know. She craved reassurance. Safety. That had always been important to her. The other side of her was too afraid to know because if she didn't get the right answer, it could change everything. It would be devastating.

"I don't think I'll ever be able to stop thinking about this if I don't take the damn test."

"Don't let that happen. You could let this go. Forget it."

"But I'm not like you. I don't like the anticipation. Not knowing. Maybe I want it to be over with. I want to prove what I already know."

"You do what you want, and no one will judge you for it." He took her hand and led her to the door. "Good night, fake girlfriend. I had a good time."

"Sure, me too. Until that man showed up, I was enjoying everything about the night."

"Yeah. Me too." He gave her a wicked smile.

Hand on the front door, she turned once more to see him walking back to Lincoln's cabin, where he'd parked his truck.

"Wade," she called out and he turned. A thin sliver of moonlight glinted off his dark Stetson, making it appear almost gray.

He slid her an easy smile and cocked his head. "Yeah?"

"I...I want you to go with me. To take the test."

"You're going to do it."

She nodded.

"If you need me, I'm there."

She cracked the door open, then watched him hike slowly back the way they came before she shut it.

Mima was sitting at the kitchen table, a skein of yarn in a basket, her needles whipping away. "Well, *someone* is finally home."

When she glanced up, she must have read Daisy's mind, because her eyes narrowed, and she threw her knitting down. "What's wrong?"

Everything Daisy had learned tonight and every doubt she'd ever had that the rumors about her mother were true rose like bile in her throat. The ugliness of it all threatened to cut off her air supply.

Her mother wasn't sure *who* her father was. What kind of a woman…

"It's…it's…I'm…not…"

"Oh, baby girl!" Mima threw her arms open wide.

And Daisy went into the arms of the woman who'd raised her and cried her heart out like she hadn't done since she was a little girl.

# CHAPTER 8

*D*ear Albert,

  *Well, the worst has happened. I thought I'd dealt with enough pain for two lifetimes or more. Watching my daughter-in-law walk out on her three children was enough to shatter this poor, old heart. My poor lamb Lincoln, the oldest, feeling responsible for everyone. Jackson, his mother's pet, completely lost and wondering what he'd done to chase her away. But the worst of them was my baby girl, Daisy.*

  *The precious child was only three and cried every single night for her mother. Those wails and cries of pain were enough to kill most old ladies. Fortunately, I'm stronger than Texas dirt. Well, you remember all this. You were there. Trying to help, usually going out in the barn or out in the fields to hide. I don't completely blame you for that. Hank did the same and they were his children, after all. But no one knows what to do with grieving children.*

  *I didn't much like Maggie to begin with, but after she left her children, I hated someone for the first time in my life. Hank was of no use, as he had his own demons to handle after Maggie left him.*

  *But now this.*

*And I thought I'd already had the lowest opinion of Maggie I could possibly have!*

*Wherever you are, I imagine you already know that Daisy might not be Hank's daughter. I don't believe it, naturally. Of course, she's Hank's daughter! Any other thought is just too terrible to think. Daisy has always been closest to her daddy. He was big enough not to punish her for looking just like her mama. And he would never abandon any of his children, our Hank, but least of all his Daisy.*

*After all that mess that Maggie left in her wake, Daisy became her daddy's shadow. There was no question in my mind that she wanted to make sure he wouldn't also leave her. And to think all this time I've been worried about "that Wade" taking her away from us. Now I'm worried that circumstance will. If Daisy takes the DNA test, and she isn't Hank's daughter, will she want to do that "I gotta go find myself" thing all the young'uns do? That could take her out of Texas, let alone Stone Ridge!*

*Worse, will she think there's no hope she won't turn out just like her mother?*

*She's a Carver through and through. It isn't just that we raised her to be a kind young lady, completely different from her heartless mother. If nothing else, we know for a daggum fact that she's Maggie's daughter. But look how different she is from her! Biology doesn't matter, anyway, only family does. The family that raised you, and I think Daisy must realize this.*

"If she doesn't realize it, then you're goin' to have to show her." Out of the blue came Albert's familiar deep drawl.

Lillian jumped. Albert sat on their bed, leaning back on a pillow, legs crossed at the ankles. The old man's ghost hadn't visited her in over a year.

"Albert! This is a fine how-dee-do! Where have you been, old man?"

"Busy. There are a lot of interestin' things to do over here."

Lillian didn't bother asking. He wasn't real. This was just her imagination, after all.

"Sounds like there's another mess goin' on down here. Makes me almost glad I'm dead."

"What do you think I should do?"

"Stay out of it."

"How can I stay out of it when there's a chance my Daisy could fall apart? I can see it in her eyes, she's tempted to take that DNA test!"

"Let her."

*Let her.* Well, it was a thought. After all, fear itself shouldn't be a reason to hold back from learning the truth. From *confirming* the truth.

"Anything else, old man? You seem to be dripping with advice today."

"You're goin' to need to talk to her about Maggie. We never talked about her. Daisy deserves to know the truth about her mother. It's not all black and white and I can see that now."

*Talk to Daisy about Maggie.*

Why didn't she think of that? Oh, wait. She just did. "Right. She should know that Maggie wasn't *always* terrible."

"This is what I'm sayin'."

Maggie did have some good qualities, after all, or Hank wouldn't have married her. Yes, Lillian realized, he'd still been reeling over losing Brenda. But for a time, he and Maggie had been happy. It was important that if on the long odds Daisy wasn't Hank's biological daughter, she'd find some connection to the goodness in Maggie, however small.

"What if we're all wrong and Daisy isn't Hank's daughter?"

"We will deal with it when we cross that bridge."

"Yes, thank you, Albert. I've decided. I will neither

encourage nor be against this testing thing. I'll be neutral. Like Switzerland."

"Woman, if you manage that, I'll come back from the dead and eat my daggum hat."

DAISY ROLLED out of bed the next morning, her thoughts a jumble. She'd stayed up too late last night, reading and re-reading the request for a DNA paternity test from Rusty's brother. He wanted it to be done at a reputable center he'd chosen and wanted to be present when it was done. Apparently, the man was seriously worried. Or maybe he simply thought Daisy to be a gold-digger type after some poor old man's fortune.

These DNA tests could be done with kits anyone could order online, though they weren't as accurate. And anyway, how could she get Rusty's DNA? She didn't want to see the man again after he'd talked to her just like she was anyone else he'd meet on the street. *He* could have told her the truth then and saved her poor father and brother from dealing with this secret.

Of course, she could get Daddy's DNA to compare it to hers, but then *he'd* find out.

She didn't want him to know that she was even consid-ering this. It might hurt his feelings to think she had any doubts. And he had enough on his plate with calving season coming up. He was finally happy again, in a relationship with Brenda, whom Daisy had recently learned was his high school sweetheart. She'd never asked many questions about Maggie, and certainly no one ever talked about her. Daisy didn't realize until recently that her mother hadn't been Daddy's first love even if they'd married young.

That was Brenda Iglesias, Eve's mother. Had Maggie somehow stolen Hank away from Brenda? Another thought too terrible to process. Because no matter who her father was, Daisy couldn't get away from the fact that Maggie was her *mother*. Daisy was even named after her. She made sure never to use her middle name and hated when she'd been called on as "Daisy Mae" in school until she corrected everyone.

"Just *Daisy*," she'd say. "Daisy Carver."

Daisy picked up the landline phone in her bedroom and dialed the number of the establishment listed in the papers.

"I'd like to, um, make an appointment. Please."

"Mornings or afternoon better?"

"Either. The soonest you have."

The receptionist asked a few more questions, and Daisy made the appointment. Just a few days away. Soon, she'd have her answer. And then came that feeling Wade loved. Anticipation. It made Daisy sick with fear. She'd have made the appointment for tomorrow if one had been available. She wanted to stop feeling like she was standing on the edge of a precipice, bracing herself for a fall.

Last night had been a catharsis. Crying until she didn't think there were any tears left took a lot out of her and she'd slept solid all night long. It was also clear that Mima didn't want Daisy to take the test. So, she'd be one more person she wouldn't tell. Eve and Sadie were the worst snitches, and she wouldn't tell them, either. Her brothers were out of the question.

That pretty much left Wade and she found she didn't mind that at all.

Walking into the kitchen, Daisy found Mima already awake. She'd made her usual king-sized breakfast of grits, waffles, bacon, eggs, and hash browns.

"Good mornin', sugar. Feeling better today?"

*Nope, I'm feeling like a truck ran over my heart. The prairie dogs are currently feasting on the leftovers.*

"So much better! Thanks for listenin' to me bawl last night. I'm sorry about that." Daisy helped herself to a cup of coffee.

"That's a lot to get off your mind."

"Well, I'm not going to worry about it anymore," Daisy lied. "I don't need a test to prove I'm Daisy Carver."

Mima's eyes widened in surprise. "You mean it?"

"You thought you were going to have to worry about me moping around the house for days until we got the results?"

"I think that's for the best. No good can come out of it, and that man will get his brother's inheritance. As it should be. He's family."

"Should I go see Daddy today?"

"He and Brenda are going to get a Christmas tree, I believe."

"I just worry about him."

"You know Hank. Tough as a rock. He has no doubts you're his so I'm sure he's relaxing."

Daisy doubted that. *Lincoln* hadn't been relaxing. "I should talk to him about all this."

"Eventually you will." Mima patted Daisy's hand.

She and Mima ate breakfast in silence. Normally, Daisy didn't mind. But this morning the quiet closed in on her. Not long ago, this house was filled with Jackson and Eve living here, too. Now, both of her brothers had homes they'd built on their land. A few years ago, Daddy had moved up the hill into the smaller house closer to the cattle operations.

It was just Mima and Daisy in this big house now, except for Sunday dinners. Daisy had some freedom with her bedroom on the other side of the house, and she used a separate entryway so that she didn't wake Mima on the rare nights when Daisy came home late. But she sometimes thought it would be nice to rent a cabin on Lupine Lake for a little more privacy.

"What will you do once I move out of this house?"

"Why? You planning on goin' somewhere?"

"No, but maybe…someday. I should get married, I guess." Daisy shrugged.

She did want to get married, naturally. The right man hadn't come along just yet, or maybe that had been her keeping men away. Remaining pure as the driven snow for all the wrong reasons.

"When that time comes, I guess I'll just roam around this big house by myself. Y'all will visit, I'm sure. It's not like you'll be far, anyway. And I guess Albert will show up more then."

"Huh?" Her grandfather had been dead for years.

Mima waved her hand dismissively. "I like writing letters to him. Then I imagine that he's sitting right there with me, listening."

"That's sweet…I think."

"The man was ornery as all get-out, and not my first choice in a husband. But funny how love works out. Your grandpa was the great love of my life."

Daisy nearly spit out her grits. What was it about this family and all the secrets?

"You never told me that before. Why was Grandpa not your *first* choice?"

"Well, of course, he was. But before we dated, there was someone brighter and shinier. I had my head turned. Luckily, Albert waited for me." Mima shoved some more bacon on Daisy's plate. "All this mess has got me to thinkin'. We should really talk some about your mother. Don't you think?"

As much as Daisy did not want to discuss her mother, she had become front and center in their lives. "Was *she* the reason that Daddy and Brenda broke up? They were high school sweethearts, but my mother was the one who got knocked up. Did she take him away from Brenda?"

"Oh, no. Nothing like that. Much as I wish, can't blame that one on your mother. See, Hank wanted to marry Brenda, but her family didn't approve of him."

"*Excuse* me?" Daisy dropped her fork. "Didn't approve of my daddy?"

"We don't talk about the painful past much around here." Mima chuckled. "Hank is a good man now, but he wasn't quite settled as a teenager. Had a little bit of a wild hair about him."

She couldn't see that in her father. Ever since she could remember, he'd seemed sad and defeated. Lonely. Until Brenda.

"Shows you how wrong you can be about someone," Daisy said, hoping Mima caught a hint about Wade.

He wasn't the man Mima thought he was, either. He'd been hiding from those women and Daisy figured his flirting might have been simply force of habit. Almost like putting on a show. Rodeo cowboys were used to that sort of thing and he hadn't gotten it out of his system yet. She'd love to dig deep and find out what made Wade Cruz tick, but she had her own problems now.

"Her family wanted her to marry Ricardo, and Brenda always did as she was told." Mima put her cup down and stared off into the distance. "A good girl and wonderful daughter and mother. And she and Ricardo were happy for a while. Just as your father and mother were."

"I can't believe how Daddy could have ever loved *that woman*."

"That woman is your mother," Mima said slowly. "And with all her faults, and there were many, she gave all three of you life. She didn't have to do that."

"Sorry if I'm not feeling grateful for that today but I'm just...not."

"I don't blame you. We should really talk about her more, but maybe another time."

"What's wrong with right now?"

"Did you forget? Today, we're going to the church to help Pastor June set up. It's the tree lighting ceremony tonight. She got a huge tree from Oregon, came in on a long-bed truck, several feet sticking out, I heard. Plenty of complaints as they drove through Nothing. Anyway, the men have to be there early to help get the tree up. And I signed you up to help Sadie entertain the children. Arts and crafts."

It was the last thing Daisy felt like doing today, but she supposed that she and Wade should be at the event together. Otherwise, Beulah would be sniffing around, asking questions. A few days ago, Beau Stephens had reportedly refused to even consider being Mr. Cowboy. He, too, said he was serious about a woman, but now Daisy wondered if he was lying, as well.

Now Beulah was after Sean Henderson, and Daisy was more than certain Sean would say no, too. Eventually, this would all circle back to Wade, the perfect choice for Mr. Cowboy. Surely Daisy and Beulah were not the only ones who could see that.

An hour later, Daisy watched with fascination as the fresh pine tree was hauled up using heavy farm equipment. It took ten big men to do it, among them her brothers, as well as Riggs and Wade. Wade wore his black hat and jean jacket and when he caught her eye, he smiled and winked.

"Did you know Wade's arm still hurts?" Daisy asked Beulah. "He's certainly not going to say no to helping."

"He seems fine to me. Why don't you go give him a massage later, like a good girlfriend would?" Beulah gave her the side-eye.

"That's exactly what I plan to do." Daisy coughed and cleared her throat.

"Winona said the producers have asked for a cowboy who was a former sports star, or a rodeo star. Do you know anyone like that?"

"I do, but he's taken." Daisy crossed her arms. "Would they want a multimillionaire instead? What about one of Jolette Marie's brothers?"

"Hmm. Well, they're all mean as the devil but one of them is fairly handsome. I'll suggest it."

Once the tree was straightened and bolted to the church, the men took a break. Daisy noticed that Eve, Sadie, and Winona had joined their men, so she ran over to be with Wade.

"Hi, Wade." She rubbed his arm, then went on tiptoes for a quick kiss on the lips.

"Hey." Under the brim of his hat, his caramel-brown eyes were soft and warm. "Are you okay?"

"Yes, sure," she said, then loudly, "I'll have to give you a massage later, rub out all the kinks."

Wade sent her a slow smile. Uh-huh."

"We have to make this look good," Daisy hissed. "The producers want a former rodeo star and obviously Lincoln is taken." She put her arm around his waist, encouraging him to do the same, which he did.

"Sure, baby, of course I'll cook dinner for you tonight. Why, your wish is my command," Wade said loudly enough that Beulah turned.

"Don't be silly. I'll cook dinner for you! I just love takin' care of my man."

"Somebody have our volunteer fire department ready," Lincoln joked.

Everyone cackled with laughter over that one. Burn a few meals and suddenly she was toxic in the kitchen.

"Let's get back to work now," Riggs ordered, always the one to keep everyone in line. "This tree isn't going to light itself."

As with every year since they'd started the tree lighting tradition in Stone Ridge, the inside of the church had been decorated as a winter wonderland. Lights were hung from the beams, green garland and fake snow accenting the large room. Booths were meant to entertain children. Arts and crafts were usually ornament making. Lenny had a booth where he created shapes out of balloons. This year, a lot of reindeers with lopsided ears. Sadie had a booth where she read holiday stories to the children.

Eve and Annabeth brought in cats and dogs that were being considered for adoption. But they always made the parents wait until after Christmas to finalize adoptions. Of course, Mima was always at the knitting booth with Delores and most of the ladies of SORROW. They were selling scarves and caps, and the proceeds would be put in a fund for further town projects.

This year, the new medical clinic had a booth, too. Trixie, the midwife, was giving out lollipops to the children. Dr. Grant was walking around with a stethoscope around his neck, clearly not knowing what else to do with himself.

It was always a marathon day of an event, culminating in the tree lighting. People came and went during the day, always returning in the evening for the real action.

"Okay, Jimmy Ray," Daisy said now. "No *more* glitter."

"Just a little bit more," he said, shaking the jar.

He was on Daisy's last nerve. By the third hour, she'd wanted to go home and collapse in her bed. She hoped to last long enough to see the lights go up. The men had been outside working on that for hours.

"Hey, sweetheart. Is this boy bothering you?" came Wade's smooth drawl, a hint of humor in it.

Daisy's heart surged to see him, and when he looked at her as if he was seeing her for the first time, her knees got weak.

Jimmy Ray scrunched up his nose. *"Sweetheart? Who's your sweetheart?"*

"Do you know what a sweetheart is?" Wade tipped his hat.

"That's what my daddy calls my mommy."

"I call my girlfriend sweetheart," Wade said.

"Is Miss Daisy your girlfriend?" This was from Ellie, one of the few grade-school girls.

"Duh," Jimmy Ray said, shaking out enough glitter to cover a small town.

"Miss Sadie used to be Mr. Carver's girlfriend but now she's his wife," Ellie said. "And I helped."

"It was my idea," Jimmy Ray said.

"How did you help, darlin'?" Wade ignored Jimmy Ray and tousled Ellie's hair, earning a smile.

"I helped write the sign."

"There was a sign?"

"Lincoln had all the children write 'Will you marry me' on a big sign and they were all there when he asked her," Daisy explained.

It was the most romantic thing she'd ever heard of, and coming from her lame-about-romance brother, it clinched the deal. Lincoln was in love and he didn't care who knew it.

"Wow." Wade winked at Ellie. "You might be able to call yourself a matchmaker now."

Ellie straightened. *"Really?"*

"Me too!" said Jimmy Ray. "I'm a matchmaker."

Daisy took the jar of glitter from his hand. "Matchmakers don't like glitter."

A choir of voices sounded like angels, and Daisy turned to see Winona near the entrance leading a group of Christmas carolers. Among them were all the ladies of SORROW, including Beulah, right behind Winona. "O Little Town of Bethlehem" brought quiet to the noisy room.

This song, especially, stopped time for Daisy. The ladies, dressed in gowns reminiscent of the Old West, sashayed through the church. Winona occasionally reached out and ruffled a child's hair or tweaked a nose.

It wasn't until they'd circled the room once that Daisy realized Wade was holding her hand. Here was the only *person* she'd ever known who could stop time for her. Her heart hammered away as his warm, big hand held hers.

Something so simple. Not the first time for her, a handsome guy holding her hand.

But somehow, it did feel very much like the first time, and like a private, sacred moment.

# CHAPTER 9

When the lights were plugged in, the town's Christmas tree lit up the entire town square.

Wade had almost forgotten about all the small-town holiday celebrations. For the past few years, he hadn't been home for much of the holiday, usually getting back in time to celebrate the day with his mother and be off again shortly after, chasing the next tournament win. She understood. Her mounting medical bills were overwhelming, and they were all on Wade.

But his mother used to love this kind of thing. She was always right in the thick of it, helping the ladies of SORROW, volunteering her services wherever needed. Even now, he could almost feel her presence. Everywhere.

He and Daisy were sitting on the tailgate of his truck, watching the lights blink in their random patterns. That tree had been hell on wheels to yank up and he was happy not to have had to do it on his own. His arm had lit up like a coal of fire and he promised himself to take it easy for the next few days. He'd stopped restricting himself from the pain pills and taken them as needed. If he didn't do his physical therapy routine on a regular basis, he wouldn't be able to manage all the chores on his ranch. Or give up the ghost by noon.

Earlier today he'd spent the day looking through the old books his father kept on the ranch operations back in the days when it had been, if not profitable, at least sustainable. The possibilities existed, and if he made a few changes from the way his father did business, he might actually do better. Eventually. Of course, he was a long way from there. He had plans to attend the cattle auction with Riggs, which would require the bulk of his savings.

But sitting here next to Daisy had seriously taken his mind off his problems.

"What are you thinking, Peanut? You're so quiet."

She swung her sweet long legs. "I made the appointment."

He nodded, worrying he'd encouraged her to do this when he'd simply shared what he would have done. For someone who didn't like danger or uncertainty, this had to be killing her.

"Name the time and place."

"Rusty's brother will be there, too. The place had all the instructions and knew to contact him. I didn't have to do anything but call."

"He thought of everything."

"I wonder if he hates me."

The thought unnerved Wade. "He has no reason to *hate* you."

"Well, maybe he thinks I want the money and that's why I'm taking the dumb test. He doesn't know I hope to prove that I *can't* take Rusty's money."

"You don't need to care what he thinks. He's got his agenda. You have yours."

She was silent for several more minutes, and the quiet calm of the evening descended on them. All of the families with young children had left long ago. Only a few stragglers remained.

"Wade, do you remember my mother?"

Wade had a clear recollection of Maggie Carver. In particular, he remembered the days after she'd left Stone Ridge. Rumors ran rampant. Maggie had been kidnapped by her family, who'd never approved of her moving to the Podunk town. Maggie had emptied their checking account and taken off for the Bahamas. Or Maggie had left town with a rodeo cowboy. He figured that in the end no one must have believed she'd been kidnapped because the law was never involved. Which always made Wade think that she must have left a note or said something...to *someone.*

His mother, along with the ladies of SORROW and others, descended on the Carver household with casseroles and offers to babysit little Daisy. Often, Wade was in tow simply to hang out with his best friend, who didn't talk about his missing mother. This was more than okay with Wade. But for a while, Jackson went everywhere with them as a little tagalong because Lincoln wouldn't leave him behind.

"I remember her as a nice lady, believe it or not." He honestly didn't know whether that would help or hurt but he couldn't lie to Daisy.

Daisy's head jerked back. "How so?"

"She was, well, very pretty, of course." He crossed his arms and cleared his throat, feeling odd describing Lincoln's mother this way. Truth be told, he'd had a tiny crush on the younger Mrs. Carver, just as he'd had on his first-grade teacher. "Nice, too. She made cookies for us kids and to my knowledge was never mean to anyone."

"I don't remember her. At all."

"You were little, so I'm not surprised. But you were her shadow, her mini-me. Always clinging to her leg and never letting her get too far out of your sight."

Daisy snorted. "Imagine that. And still she made a clean getaway *somehow*."

"For what it's worth, I think she loved you all." Wade reached for Daisy's hand, knowing this might be tough to hear but he would want to know this, were it the other way around. "I think everything is a whole lot more complicated than we can know."

"I just wish I knew *why* she left."

"She didn't leave a note?"

"Don't think so." Daisy took in a deep breath. "But I never asked. Since I can't remember her anymore, it's almost like I can't hurt for what I don't remember losing. The pain is all in theory. In the past. And now…it's less pain than anger. I'm the daughter of a woman who abandoned her family. Her *children*."

Wade understood far too well. He remembered the exact day and time he'd discovered how fond his father was of the blackjack tables. And how he'd used Wade to fund his obsession. In some ways, Wade was a gambler, too, but he'd sworn never to fall down the same rabbit hole that his father had. Every now and then, he feared that he was far too much his father's son. The addiction to gambling, he'd heard, gave the gambler a rush of adrenaline.

Wade wanted to believe that he only bet on himself, but sometimes the similarities between father and son were unnerving.

"I'm not excusing what she did, because there's no reason that makes it okay. But I'm guessing that with everything she left behind, she must have thought she had to leave for whatever reason."

"I'm sure she justified it somehow. I never asked enough questions about her, but now, with all this happening…it's brought her up again."

"That's only natural."

"There's so much I didn't know. When Daddy started dating Brenda, that's when I found out that *she* was his first love. Not my mother."

This was news to Wade. "Seriously?"

"But I asked Mima, and my mother didn't break them up. They imploded on their own. So, there is that."

"She can't have been all bad," Wade continued. "Nobody is."

"No, obviously. She must have loved us at some point."

"There you are," came Lillian Carver's voice. After a quick appraisal of Wade, she nodded. "Well, hello there, *Wade*."

"Mrs. Carver." He hopped off the tailgate and held his hand out for Daisy. "You look very lovely tonight."

"Why, you charmer."

Funny, it didn't sound as if she believed it. Wade wasn't too surprised. He hadn't been the older Mrs. Carver's favorite person for some time now. She'd always been kind and courteous enough, but she blamed Wade for being the influence on Lincoln's rodeo career. He supposed that was easier than believing that Lincoln had a mind of his own when it came to such things. Mrs. Carver was a loyal sort and he appreciated that more than most.

Besides, he was certain that without Lillian Carver, Daisy would have been truly lost. The matriarch had basically raised two generations of Carvers and had the respect of every man of Stone Ridge. Including him.

"Are you ready to go now, sugar?" Mrs. Carver huffed. "Beulah has left, so y'all don't have to carry on this way."

"We were *talking*," Daisy said.

"Can I drive you ladies home? It would be my pleasure." Never let it be said that his manners weren't impeccable.

*Are you watching me from heaven, Ma? How am I doing?*

"No, I drove," Daisy said. "Thank you, though."

"Yes, thank you, young man. Your mother would be proud," Lillian said.

It sounded a bit more sincere, at least. "Then I'll say good night."

He tipped his hat, then watched as they got in the truck and Daisy drove off. It was only then that he walked to his own truck alone. He managed to narrowly avoid Kari Lynn, who seemed to be angling toward him but couldn't walk fast enough to catch him.

He did *not* want to teach but it was tough to say no to a lady. The last thing he wanted was to watch others compete in the sport he'd loved his entire life. He couldn't go back, and he just wasn't ready to stand by on the sidelines. For now, he needed to be as far away from the rodeo as he could get. That part of his life was over.

The quiet surrounded him when he arrived at the ranch. He shut off the truck and sat in the cab alone, visualizing his home exactly as it used to be. Pens filled with heads of cattle, a stable full of horses. The red barn, not falling down on itself like now, but filled with equipment and a small tractor. A porch that didn't have peeling paint, his mother sitting on the steps. His father at the head of it all, rounding up the cattle, tagging the young ones. Him, racing his first horse, Trigger, across the plains, not a care in the world.

Now, he was alone. Not even any siblings, since, to hear his father tell it, he'd nearly killed his mother on his way into the world. He hadn't missed siblings much growing up because he'd had brothers everywhere in the form of lifelong friends. Lincoln, Jackson, Riggs, and his crew. Daisy, too, even if it had become harder to think of her as only a friend.

But now, well, now he found himself wishing he wasn't the last Cruz standing. A sister would have stayed behind and cared for their mother while he was off trying to make money the only way he'd ever known how. Instead, he'd left his mother to deal with her illness. He'd barely been home in time to say goodbye.

"I know you have to go," she'd say, palming his chin. "Just please, promise me you won't die before I do. Be careful, my love."

"Mom, you're not going to die."

"Yes, I am. It's just a matter of when."

She'd been right, of course. And though that could be said of anyone, they'd both known she'd already had a timer set. After her funeral, Wade wasted no time leaving again. He didn't want all the sympathy and casseroles. He couldn't stand the pitiful looks from everyone in town.

*"Poor lamb. He lost his father (good riddance, if you ask me) and now his precious mother. He's all alone in the world."*

But out on the rodeo circuit, he was still "Wild Wade" and no one had the slightest amount of pity for him. Just plenty of jealousy from his competition, and attention from the women. They'd line up outside his hotel room if they could find him. He was the cowboy du jour everywhere he went.

In Stone Ridge, he was just one of many eligible bachelors. Good thing he didn't care about settling down.

Figure he'd missed that train.

Sitting in the office with a cold beer, Wade twisted the cap off and took a pull. He opened his laptop and examined once more what he had left from his winnings. By his account, there was just enough to go into debt with several head of cattle and equipment. He'd have to watch, feed, and protect that cattle, hoping one day they'd feed him.

*Take your bets, everyone. Odds are two to one. Will "Wild Wade" save the family ranch or die of boredom in the pursuit?*

Hell, he wanted in on some of that action.

At this point, it was anyone's guess.

. . .

THREE MORNINGS LATER, the cattle he'd purchased at auction arrived and with them, a lot of tedious but back-breaking work. Wade was up at dawn every morning just like the good old days. He finished his coffee and lumbered outside in his work boots. Satan, who was getting old, seemed to observe the goings-on with mild interest and an occasional disgusted snort. Dante, always the friendly sort, was happy for the company.

And even though Wade hadn't asked for any help, later that morning Riggs and his brother Sean arrived and insisted Wade put them to work.

"I know a couple of ranch hands that work on the cheap," Sean said. "If you ever want to hire anyone just temporarily."

"Let me guess. Rodeo cowboys lookin' for the extra work?"

Not long ago, he'd been one of them, putting in the long hours for Hank Carver. Flirting with Daisy when she'd show up, pretending to help, but actually checking out all the cowboys' backsides. Including his own, he was always gratified to discover.

"It's going to be tough work," Riggs said. "But you can get this cattle ranch working again."

"Hell, for you, this should be easy," Sean said.

"When you're ready to breed, you can have some of my bull semen. Free of charge, of course," Riggs said.

"I've got a lot to do before I'm at that point," Wade said. "But thanks, buddy."

For the rest of the morning, they hauled hay and herded cattle. When a shiny clean truck drove up the lane, Riggs walked to meet his wife.

Winona leaned out the window. "Did you forget? It's time for the doctor's appointment."

Riggs cursed. "Is it noon already?"

*Noon. Oh hell.*

"This ultrasound should confirm that we're having a girl." Winona smiled, tossing her hair, batting her eyelashes. "And then I'll be the belle of the ball."

Riggs hopped in the truck on the passenger side. "See y'all later. Wade, come over anytime."

Wade turned to Sean. "I forgot I've got an appointment, too."

Sean chuckled. "Leave me to it, then. I'll clean up."

"I hate to have you do that, but I am very late."

Daisy was going to kill him. And he wanted to be there for her. Rushing inside, he took a spit shower, changed into better clothes, and covered his hair with his black Stetson. Breaking speed limits, he got to the Double C Ranch as Daisy was getting in her truck.

"I gave up on you," she said.

"Sorry, Peanut. I got caught up with all the new head of cattle that came in." He patted the door of his truck. "Hop in."

She climbed in and buckled up. "I guess I can't blame you for that. I sure know what it's like. Happens all the time around here."

"No doubt. It's new to me, all this cattle business." He took off down the dirt lane leading to the main road, kicking up dust.

"New to you? You grew *up* on a cattle ranch."

"You forget. I was introduced to rodeo early. My daddy had me in the corral practicing staying upright on a bull more often than not. Not that I complained. Anyway, it's been a while since our ranch was a working one, so it's like starting all over."

"I can help," Daisy said.

"No need, I've got it covered."

She grew silent for the rest of the drive to Kerrville and the clinic where they would meet Rusty's brother. Mark Jones, if Wade remembered correctly. He followed the directions Daisy gave him, and a while later they pulled into the parking lot of a plain-looking building. "Valley Health Clinic" the sign read.

"Okay, let's get this show on the road." Usually, Daisy beat him to the punch, always out the passenger door before he could open it for her.

Not this time. Now, she sat, still buckled up, staring off into space.

He opened the passenger side door. "Peanut? What's up?"

"I'm nervous. Maybe this is a mistake."

"You don't have to do this. We can go right now, turn this truck around and head back to town. Stop in at the Shady Grind for a cold beer."

Snapping out of it, she turned to him with narrowed eyes. "Are you trying to talk me out of this?"

"I'm trying to make you realize that *you're* the one calling the shots here. No one can make you do anything you don't want to do." He met her eyes, tipping his hat to get right in her face. "You hear me?"

"You're so right." She unbuckled. "And I'm doing this because *I* want to and for no other reason."

He held out his hand. "That's my girl."

Daisy hopped down and walked—no, strutted—her way to the clinic. It put a smile on his face just to watch those swinging hips.

DAISY WALKED INSIDE THE CLINIC, Wade holding the door open for her. Inside the otherwise plain office, there was a feeble attempt at holiday cheer with a tabletop tree on the counter and a clear glass jar filled with candy canes. Christmas music piped through speakers, sounding like the stuff they played in elevators.

An older gentleman was the only other one seated in the lobby and he stood.

"You must be Daisy Carver." Mark Jones held out his hand and offered it to Daisy and then Wade. "Thank you for coming. I hope you understand the situation."

"Sure. Of course I do," Daisy said, feeling far less confident than she thought she sounded. "Yes. That's fine."

"I turned over Rusty's DNA sample. Don't worry, it was done in the hospital by professionals."

"He's in the h-hospital?"

"Yes, Daisy." He lowered his gaze. "Unfortunately, he's dying."

"I'm sorry to hear that." That made sense, of course. He was taking care of things ahead of time like any organized and responsible person would do.

Rusty's brother also seemed very organized. He even had a small hanky in the pocket of his suit jacket.

She couldn't possibly be related to these people.

"Why is he dying?" It sounded like a dumb question even to her own ears. Old people died.

"Congestive heart failure."

Daisy filed that away in case she wound up being Rusty's daughter. She'd have to watch out for signs of early heart disease because it was hereditary. Right? On the other hand, her grandfather Carver dropped dead of a heart attack, too, so either way, she could be screwed. As was fifty percent of the nation, if she recalled the statistics. It was either heart disease or cancer that killed a person. Great. She was rambling. Her thoughts were like wild rabbits, hopping away in the fields, trying not to get slaughtered.

"They're waiting for you." His arm made a sweeping motion to the clerk behind the desk.

"Right this way, Miss Carver." The clerk stood and led the way.

Daisy turned back and found Wade right behind her. She felt her shoulders unkink in relief because she hadn't wanted to ask but it was good to have him follow her. Nice to have someone with her who didn't have a horse in the race, so to speak. Wade didn't care whether she was Hank's daughter or Rusty's. In fact, he didn't even seem to mind that she was Maggie's daughter. He'd said Maggie was nice. *Nice.*

"This is a lot quicker than you can imagine," the lab clerk said as she grabbed a box from the medical cabinet. "Just have a seat. It will be over in no time."

But this was the easy part. The tough part would be the wait. Daisy's heart raced and her palms were damp. In a few minutes, she'd have the start of discovering her heritage. Of understanding who she was. Or simply confirming who she'd always been.

"I just need to swab the inside of your mouth to get some cells and then we're done."

"S-sure." Daisy gripped the edge of the molded plastic chair with both hands until Wade pulled one of them off.

Holding her hand, he squatted in front of her. "You remember what I said?"

"I'm…okay." She nodded, tipped her chin, and opened her mouth for the swab.

It was over faster than Daisy would have imagined. One second to possibly change the course for the rest of her life.

Outside, Mr. Jones waited and stood when she walked out.

"You'll both be mailed the results," the lab clerk said. "It should be no more than a week, maybe sooner."

"I don't want mine sent home," Daisy said. "Maybe I'll just pick it up."

"Send it to my house," Wade said and then gave the clerk his address.

"This place is very reputable," Mr. Jones said. "Are there any questions I can answer for you?"

"About?" Daisy asked.

"Rusty, my brother, the man who might be your father. If you want to see him, we can arrange—"

"No." She could not deal with anything else today. Or possibly this year. Also, she did not want to see this man, who'd had an affair with a married woman. With a woman who had small children at home. "I'm sorry but we have plans."

"Okay, some other time maybe. Depending on how this works out, I imagine." He handed Daisy a business card. "Contact me at any time."

The card was that of an autobody shop. Daisy turned it over in her hands. "You're a mechanic?"

He nodded and tipped back on his heels. "Rusty and I both. He worked for me after he retired from the rodeo. That was his first love, but he's a natural-born mechanic. It's in his blood. Had an affinity for it all of his life. I hear you do as well."

A buzzing sound went through Daisy's ears and the room rocked and swayed.

*It doesn't mean I'm his daughter. So what? We're both good auto mechanics. And so are a lot of other people in the world. Coincidence, that was all. Chance.*

"I'm sorry to put you through this, Daisy, but Rusty doesn't always think things through. If it's true, and you're his daughter, you certainly deserve the gift he wants to leave you."

Still, her stomach pitched because she did *not* want to be Rusty's daughter. Although it made no sense, standing here, and talking even briefly about him, realizing they had something in common…it stretched the possibility in her mind. It took the breath from her body.

She tucked the card in her jeans and ran out of the waiting room without saying goodbye. Outside in the cool December air, she clutched her chest and tried to breathe. But she was breathing out, and not taking breaths in.

*Why, why, why did this have to happen now?*

This man had been out of her life for decades and he just showed up a year ago? What on earth made him decide that he suddenly wanted to be a father? Face it, he'd been running from the *possibility* of being her father for decades. If by chance Daisy was his, he'd been fine with another man raising his own child.

Which meant that if she was Rusty's daughter, she'd been abandoned twice.

*Twice.*

"Daisy, breathe. Just breathe."

She heard Wade's voice, sounding calm and clear and warm. And look at that, he'd called her Daisy. Not Peanut or some other childish nickname. He pulled her into his arms, her back to his front, his arms wrapped around her, hands around the fists she held clutched against her chest.

"I'm s-sorry. Sorry." She forced herself to slow her breaths.

"Don't be sorry, sweetheart." He lowered his head to her shoulder, nuzzling her neck. "You don't need to be sorry."

He smelled delicious. Like leather and fresh-mown grass. She leaned against him, using him as a post to hold her up.

This had all been a mistake. She'd lied to her family. A horrible sense of fear took root in her, raw and pulsating. Fear pulled at her shaky soul. Chest tight, she heard blood rushing loudly through her veins.

She turned in Wade's arms, facing him, burying her face in his warm neck as he bent his head.

And they stood there for several minutes, Wade's arm moving up and down her spine in slow and soothing strokes.

# CHAPTER 10

"*H*ope you don't mind a stop first. I left Sean to clean up, since I was running late." Wade drove down the highway back to Stone Ridge. "I want to check in before I take you home."

And as it so happened, Daisy didn't want to go home right now. Mima, who had a sixth sense about all of her grandchildren, would know something was wrong. Daisy would just walk right in the door and Mima would figure it out. Then, she'd worry right along with Daisy until they received the results. And she did not want her grandmother worrying about the possibly stupid decision Daisy had just made.

"That's fine." Daisy rolled the window down and propped her head on her stretched out arm. "I need to get my act together before I go home. I'm sorry I fell apart on you like that."

"Hey, any excuse to hold you tight." He winked.

*Incorrigible flirt.* At least now he was also flirting with *her.*

The thought cheered her a little. She wasn't off-limits to him anymore. And there was that hot and amazing kiss behind the tree. No, she hadn't forgotten. That was the night *everything* changed.

"I guess I haven't been much fun lately."

"Fun is overrated."

"Liar."

He chuckled. "Okay, so I've always liked my fun. But I'm all about the ranching now."

"Which is not always a whole lot of fun."

"Tell me it's rewarding, at least."

"Sure. From what I've seen, it can be. Lincoln sure loves it. Eve, too. Jackson not nearly as much but he does his part."

"And you?" He turned briefly to her, a smile tugging at his lips. "I noticed you seemed to have dodged a bullet there."

"Doesn't mean I don't know my way around a ranch, mister." She crossed her arms and turned toward him, pressing her back against the passenger door. "Mima taught me."

"And what did she teach you?"

"Mostly how to make sandwiches and beef burritos, load them up, and deliver them to the cowboys." She smiled, knowing that Mima knew a hell of a lot more than that about running a ranch.

"Food always has its place on a ranch. Especially burritos."

"Tell me about it. But *some* people think burritos are boring. During the summers, when Sadie is home all day, she scours recipes from *The Pioneer Woman* and that's what she feeds Lincoln. Every single day. It's a wonder he doesn't weigh three hundred pounds."

"She works it off him, I'm sure." Passing the Henderson ranch on the right, he then turned down the long lane leading to his ranch. "Every night."

Daisy wished she understood what all the fuss was about. Sex sounded wonderful. But according to Eve and Sadie, who seemed to believe it their civic duty to keep Daisy pure, it was only good with the *right* person. But of course, they happened to know this because they'd been with the *wrong* man at least once. How else would a woman know? Divining rods?

The Cruz ranch sure looked different from the last time she'd been here, asking Wade to give her some experience. She slunk in her seat, not quite believing she'd even suggested that. At this point she didn't want to bring it up again even if being around Wade tended to inspire all manner of randy thoughts. Maybe it was safer to stay wholesome, as far from her mother as she could get. And last she checked, she couldn't have a baby without sex, so she'd be safe from reproducing, too. At least until she could be certain she had some good genes in there. The Carver DNA.

"Impressive," she muttered, getting out of the car when Wade pulled to the side of the barn.

The pens were now filled with cattle and the place looked like a real honest-to-goodness cattle ranch again. Not like a ghost of its former self.

"I'll be right with you, Daisy." Wade hopped out of the driver's side and headed to the cattle pen.

"Take your time."

Daisy wandered over to the red barn looking for an old truck or farm equipment she could help fix. Every holiday season she was out of sorts and usually wandered around the Double C looking for something mechanical to fix. But recently the ranch had enjoyed a nice infusion of cash from Jackson's songwriting royalties. Every piece of old farm equipment had been upgraded which was nice for the cowboys. Not so great for her.

She pulled a blue tarp off, finding an old classic Model T under it. This beauty was probably worth some money. Sliding her hand down the hood of the classic design, she wondered if this was Wade's, or one of his father's vintage cars. She'd never seen one of his father's cars, but heard he collected them for a time but sold them off. Apparently, he'd kept one.

There wasn't anything else of interest until in a dark corner she saw an antique plastic reindeer. Using a broom for protection against evil spiders, she advanced, wielding it like a sword. She brushed the reindeer off and pulled it into the light shining through several slats in the barn's roof.

A memory tugged of a time long ago when she'd run into this very barn at a family picnic. Wade and Lincoln were teenagers at the time, Daisy probably around ten. She'd climbed up the ladder, looking for her brother, and found a couple rolling around in the hay. But the guy wasn't Lincoln. It was Wade and his girlfriend, making out. Daisy had a clear and mostly unobstructed view of Judy Marie's right boob. It was big and pink and…wet.

Daisy gasped and her hand flew over her mouth.

"Hey, you little rat!" Judy Marie squealed and covered herself. "Get on out of here. And you better not tell on me."

"I'm sorry!" Daisy cried.

"She's just a kid. What the hell is wrong with you? Go on, Squirt." Wade winked. "Go find Lincoln."

She'd nearly fallen off the ladder trying to fly back down. A few months later, Judy Marie broke Wade's heart by cheating on him. Maybe with someone who didn't have a best friend's little sister interrupting their make-out sessions in the hayloft. In the intervening years, she hadn't seen Wade suffer much in the girlfriend department even if there had never been anyone serious. Daisy would have known if there had been.

After brushing off the reindeer, Daisy found a treasure trove of other Christmas lawn ornaments. There was a plastic Santa with an extension cord, a plastic snowman, and under another tarp, a full-sized sleigh. It was like a gift. She'd found a winter project. Something to keep her mind off those DNA results for the next few days. This could be scrubbed, polished, and oiled.

One after the other, she brushed the holiday loot with the broom and dragged them outside the barn into the bright sunlight.

"What's all this?" came Wade's voice.

"Look!" She made a wide sweep of her hand over the treasures.

"I am. It's a heap of junk. I've been meaning to go through that barn."

"It's not *junk*!" She went hands on hips. "I can fix this. Look. This one probably used to light up. And this sleigh! It should probably go in a holiday parade."

"That's just...sad." He slowly shook his head.

"The kids will love it."

"I'm afraid the *kids* will think Santa has fallen on hard times."

"If nothing else, we can set these outside and give your ranch some nice Christmas charm."

"Christmas charm, huh?" He tipped his hat.

"What? Aren't you going to get a Christmas tree?"

"Well, I hadn't thought of that. I'm a little busy here." He made a sweeping motion.

She turned to see that he'd separated the cattle into two different pens while she'd been busy in his barn. She'd obviously lost track of time.

"That's fine. I'll get the tree for you. And decorate, too."

"Somethin' tells me you're looking to stay busy for a while. Maybe a few days or so?"

"Sure, yeah. You got me. I'm out of work until after Christmas and there's nothing left to fix at the Double C."

"Such a problem." He grinned. "As you can see, I have no such issue here at Casa La Cruz."

"I told you I can help."

"Yeah, everyone keeps offering. I forgot what that was like."

"This is home. And we help our neighbor."

"In this case, we especially help our neighbor if we're lookin' to avoid thinking other, more complicated thoughts."

"Okay, smart aleck. Where's your toolbox?"


THE SENSE of relief that pulsed through Wade was almost palpable. He appreciated the smile and enthusiasm from Daisy, even if misplaced. This was all junk that his parents had never gotten around to throwing out. But hey, if it gave Daisy a project that made her smile, he was on board. Because seeing the way she'd fallen apart after taking that test was more than this cowboy could take.

"Is that your father's old Ford Model T?" Daisy pointed to the tarp she'd removed. "It's a vintage 1926 coupe hardtop. *Very* cool."

The girl knew her cars. He was not at all surprised. "It's my inheritance from the old man."

The car, and this ranch that he'd nearly driven into the ground with his gambling debts. And the *car*, a gift, came with conditions. He walked over to it, pulled the tarp back on to cover it.

Daisy followed him. "It's a classic. And worth something."

"I'm sure it is. And it would be great if my father hadn't insisted that I keep it and never sell it."

The old man's last joke on Wade. What good would a Model T do on a cattle ranch? He needed a new tractor, that's what he needed.

"Well, sometimes things are worth something more than money to the people who give them."

"That's a nice sentiment, though not to someone who needs the money." He tapped the hood of the car. "What am I going to do with this, even *after* I get it running?"

"It doesn't run?"

He could see the wheels spinning in her head. She'd lit up, a fire in her eyes, an anticipation.

"No, it doesn't. Let me guess. You want to *fix* this."

"Oh, I would love to! Thank you, Wade." She practically jumped into his arms. "Thank you."

He tightened his arms around her and lowered them to her waist. He was enjoying this hug a little too much.

*It's probably not wise to spend this much time around Daisy. You might be tempted.*

They were in a fake romantic relationship, and though the idea had become more enticing to him than he could have ever imagined, it still wasn't *smart*. He put himself in Lincoln's place, an easy thing to do with a friend who was far more like a brother. Would he want *his* little sister dating someone like him? Someone who didn't know the meaning of commitment? She was too good for him. He had nothing to offer her but his friendship and she already had that. Always would. Best not to mess with that and wind up ruining both of them.

He cleared his throat and gently moved her away from him. "Sure, Peanut. You go ahead and fix away to your heart's delight. Now, let me find you that toolbox."

A few hours later, the sun setting, Wade was ready for a shower and dinner. He found Daisy working on the lawn ornaments. The reindeer were flanking Santa who, though he looked worn and faded, now glowed. Same with the snowman.

"It was just a short circuit." Daisy had found a power cord

and extension cord and plugged them into the nearest outside power outlet. "Working fine again."

"Good job." He removed his hat and shoved a hand through his sweat-dampened hair. "Well, I'm hitting the shower. Then I'll drop you home. I'm probably headed to the Shady Grind for a cold beer and some dinner."

"Okay, but I should probably go with you." She rubbed her hands together and brushed off her jeans.

"You don't have to," he said carefully.

"How will it look if you're off at the Shady Grind without your girlfriend?"

"Maybe like we have separate lives and aren't joined at the hip?"

"I guess I can understand why you might think that. But believe me, I know what real couples do."

"I'm not sure that Lincoln and Sadie are the best example." Wade was happy that his best friend had fallen in love, but Jiminy Cricket, the two of them spent *way* too much time together.

"What about Jackson and Eve?"

"Hmm. Also, probably not the best example."

"And Riggs and Winona?"

"Okay!" He went palms up in an "I give up" gesture. "Are you hungry?"

She shrugged. "I could eat."

"Then it's a date."

Though he didn't feel like company tonight, Wade showered, shaved, and dressed to be a proper companion. But the stupid Model T, like his sore and throbbing arm, refused to relent. Daisy had taken off the tarp and exposed a raw nerve ending.

The car was his father's final slap in the face. Something he didn't need, want, or would be able to use, but given to him anyway. It would have been nice had the old man left them anything else, like a life insurance policy for his mother. But no, the old man hadn't prepared for anything. An antique he couldn't sell was Wade's inheritance.

*I should sell it, old man. What would you know, or care, wherever you are now?*

But Wade would know, and he'd made a promise.

He was his mother's son, after all. Honorable to a fault. She'd taught him that anything worth doing was worth doing well, worth doing honorably, and that went far beyond the rodeo.

"Ready?"

Wade turned to find that Daisy had also spruced up. Somehow. She'd ditched the high ponytail from earlier and her long hair was loose around her shoulders. She never wore much makeup and didn't need any.

"You look...good," he said, like a teenage boy with zero game.

"So do you. I wish I could have taken a shower, too."

"Next time you want to join me, just say the word." He winked. "Or just walk right in."

*"Really?"*

Right. Well, *that* happened. He'd slipped that little gem out.

"I'm practicing being your boyfriend, Peanut."

"Oh. Well, I never took a shower with a man before."

Frankly, it was amazing that Daisy had remained untouched this long. Either she was right, and there were a bunch of cowards in Stone Ridge, or she'd been the one to keep them all away. But why? Had she really been waiting for someone special? If so, he wanted that for her. He didn't want her to give up what she'd protected so long to just anyone.

"You don't know what you're missing." With that, he tried

his best to lead her out the door and into the safety of his truck.

*There will be no more talk of showers with the little sister of your best friend. Little sister. Little. Sister.*

Hand low on her back, he gently pushed her forward. This worked, until she stopped inches from the safety of the great outdoors. This time, her backside bumped into him, and he swallowed a groan.

"Oh, sorry." She turned to face him, and he'd swear that a tiny electrical shock passed between them. "I was just going to tell you that I'll intercept any talk of the rodeo if you'd like."

"Thanks."

Normally, he would have thought to ask her to come along and do exactly that. But after that "lesson" under the tree at the Riverwalk, he'd remembered that Daisy was not someone he could fool around with. Even if she'd asked for lessons, it was up to him to restrain himself.

The tension between them was thick with something he couldn't even name. An emotion, cloudy, thick and heavy.

"Let's go," he ordered, ignoring the raw pulse of desire that spiked.

The question was how long he *could* ignore this.

INSIDE THE SHADY GRIND, Wade found stools at the bar, where they served the full menu. The Dallas Cowboys were on the flat screen, Lenny yelling and shaking his fist.

"Learn how to pass!"

A grand total of about five women in the joint. All were surrounded by about three men or more apiece. There was Jolette Marie in the mix, her admirers holding court. No Lincoln, Jackson, or Riggs in sight. Even Sean and Levi appeared to be MIA. Behind the bar was Lucy, one of the regular waiters/bartenders.

"Man, I missed this place." Wade chuckled, glancing up at the mistletoe hanging from the ceiling every few feet.

"Hey, Daisy, Wade," Lucy said, giving the bar a wipe. "Welcome back, champ."

"Thanks, darlin'." Wade winked and got an elbow in his gut from Daisy.

Her gaze slid to the mistletoe, then him, then back to the mistletoe. Ah. Yeah, he caught the hint. Later, he would explain that elbows were not the best way to get a lover's attention.

"C'mere." Hand on the nape of her neck, he tugged her close.

The kiss, a performance, should have been beautiful, chaste, tender. But...there seemed to be no way to kiss Daisy that way. Not anymore. She clung to him, threading her fingers in his hair, drawing him even closer. Drinking him in.

Suddenly her tongue was in his mouth, she was nearly in his lap, and they were engaging in *precisely* the kind of PDA he'd declared off-limits. When and where and how had she learned to kiss like this? She kissed like her whole body was involved and not just her lips. Her whole heart.

"Oh my Lord, you two, get a room," Lucy said with disgust, setting down two cold beers.

Wade broke the kiss, lowering his hand from her neck to settle on her shoulders. He felt the unnerving sensation that he was way out of his league.

"How was that?" she said.

"Um, yeah. Good."

"I'm a quick study."

"Well, well, well. What have we here?" came Lenny's voice.

Wade cleared his throat and grabbed his beer. "What's up, Lenny?"

"I should ask you what's up." Lenny pulled up a stool and sat next to him. "Now that the game is all but a painful memory, we should chat."

"We're about to order some dinner," Daisy protested.

"I'll deal with you later, young lady," Lenny said, shaking a finger. "What are you, twelve?"

"*Excuse* me," Lucy said, polishing a glass. "We don't serve minors."

"She's older than you realize, Lenny." Wade clapped the older man's shoulder.

*Older than I realized.*

Yep. Not a young kid anymore. Not *Peanut*.

"I'm beginning to realize that. The little whippersnapper that always wanted me to make a balloon in the shape of a car."

"That was almost twenty *years* ago," Daisy deadpanned.

"Seems like yesterday." Lenny shook his head. "Where does the time go."

*Where does the time go, indeed.*

"I'll have a Shady Burger with special sauce," Wade said. "Shoestring fries, and whatever my date's havin'."

Lenny cleared his throat as Daisy placed her order.

"My, my, my," Lenny said. "Date, is it?"

"Surely you've heard about us," Wade said. "You have your fingers on the pulse of this town."

"Must have missed somethin'. What a riot. Your mother was right, after all." Lenny slapped his knee. "Son of a biscuit eater."

Wade froze. He'd forgotten that people in this town knew far too much about his private family lore. Including too much knowledge about his well-meaning, at times a little too romantic, eccentric, and don't forget melodramatic, sainted mother.

Daisy took a pull of her beer. "What was Mrs. Cruz right about?"

"How about a game of pool while we wait?" Wade interrupted, climbing off the stool and offering his hand to her. "I'm sure I could beat you with my hands tied behind my back, but I'll use them anyway. I don't want to insult you."

Daisy blinked. He did know how to push her buttons. Maybe she shouldn't be fake dating someone who knew her as well as he did.

"Just try it, buddy."

They waited their turn at the table. Next to them, Jolette Marie talked about barrel racing and horse training. The men hung on her every word. Wade had to admit, she knew her stuff.

"What did Lenny mean?" Daisy asked.

"Who knows? He's upset about the game and probably not thinking straight."

No way would he tell Daisy that his own mother swore that he would someday marry Daisy Mae Carver. She'd seen it in a dream, and no amount of rational talk seemed to dissuade her from this crazy belief.

Not when he'd told her that he only thought of Daisy as a younger sister.

Not when he reminded her that he was seven years older than his best friend's little sister.

She insisted, until her dying day. He wondered if she was watching him now as he struggled between his attraction to Daisy and his duty to behave himself around Lincoln's little sister.

"Hey, champ," Jolette Marie said, walking up to them.

How he wished people would stop calling him that. "Hey, there, Jo."

"Hi, Jo," Daisy said. "You were right about those boots, by the way."

"Oh, good. And hey, I had no idea that you two"—she gestured between them—"were a thing."

"Yes, we are," Daisy spoke up. "We're dating now. It's new."

"Remember when we dated for about two minutes, Wade?" Jolette Marie said.

He'd done his best to wipe away that memory. Two minutes was about right.

"I think all those concussions have done their job. Those high school memories are long gone."

Jolette Marie took no offense, laughing and tossing her hair. "Concussions are good for something, at least. But you stood me up."

"Did not."

"You sure did, but you didn't break my heart."

"I'm sure that's tough to do."

"Hey, Jo!" one of the men she'd been talking to, called out. "Come on back, sweetheart. You owe me a kiss."

"No, she owes me a kiss," the other one said.

The third guy shoved another, and Wade's senses went on high alert. Bar fights over women were not common, but also not unheard of. And he'd expect Jolette Marie to be at the center of most of them.

"Now, no fighting, boys. Excuse me, guys." She smiled and went back to her adoring public.

He'd always found her exhausting to be around. They'd gone to school together and she'd been engaged to one of Wade's friends. The poor man had been one of three she'd left at the altar. In a town known for runaway brides, Jolette Marie held the record.

"Finally," Wade said, both at her leaving and the table being free.

He moved forward, and Daisy wrapped her hand around his bicep. "You'll never forget me."

"That's a given, Peanut."

"Or anything about me."

"I'm sure I won't. If I ever dare to forget a thing, I'm sure you'll elbow me in the gut again." He racked them up, then picked his pool cue, and used the chalk.

Daisy did the same. "Point taken. Elbows in the gut are not attractive."

"They're not a problem, but don't exactly inspire a man."

"You were flirting with Lucy."

"Not flirting. Just being nice."

"Maybe you should take 'keep a girlfriend' lessons from me. That looked like flirting, which is *why* I elbowed you in the gut."

"Keep my attention next time."

"And how am I supposed to do that, Wade?"

"You figure it out." He chuckled. "I can't teach you everything."

Lining up, he winked, and neatly made his shot. Then the next, and the next. "I spent plenty of time in a pool hall blowing off steam."

Daisy stewed, crossed her arms, tapped her foot. "I'm pretty good, too, if you'll give me a shot."

He chuckled and prepared to make his next shot when she gasped. "Oh, no!"

"That won't work on me. I have the focus of a—"

When Wade looked up, he lost all concentration and probably several brain cells.

Daisy's top was undone low enough for him to see the red satin of her push-up bra. He swallowed hard.

"I broke a button."

She'd busted more than one, and he didn't appreciate the

wolfish smiles on some of the men as they took notice. He sent them all a glare.

"You want to cover up?" he growled.

Shot ruined, concentration pulverized, he shrugged his jacket off and handed it to her.

"Thanks." She put it on, picked up the pool cue, then proceeded to mop the floor with him.

Score:

Peanut: one.

Wild Wade: zero. Zilch. Nada.

Lord help him, he just might be a little bit in love.

# CHAPTER 11

*D*ear Albert,
*Well, I'm in a pickle again. Things have calmed down some in recent days. It seems Daisy will not take the DNA test and simply leave the matter to rest. That's probably for the best as I'm certain she's Hank's daughter. She certainly doesn't need the money the old man wants to leave her, and it should all be left to his brother. I sincerely hope that's the end of the mess.*

*But lately, I haven't seen hide nor hair of Daisy. She was with me at the tree lighting, and I later found her and Wade outside "talking." Albert, as I live and breathe, it was the kind of "talking" young lovers do. Sitting close. Sultry looks and glances. Knowing secret smiles. This is a lot more than a pretend romance! Now, as you know, I have someone quite different in mind for our Daisy. Not that Wade. He's too wild and I refuse to allow Rose Cruz to be right. Her, and all her whimsy and far-fetched ideas, which had no place on a cattle ranch.*

Albert appeared, arms crossed, chuckling, shaking his head. "You just hate that she was right about them two."

Lillian dropped her pen and turned to him. "She wasn't *right*. Mistakes happen when you walk around with stars in your eyes. You bump into things and hurt yourself. That was Rose for you."

Rose also didn't schedule regular doctor visits and by the time she found out she had cancer it was already too late. Lillian was upset with Rose for a few reasons, but the biggest was her having the nerve to die on them. It wasn't fair. She was a good person, albeit a little too eccentric. Too given to far-fetched notions and dreams. But far too young to die, and here was Lillian, pushing eighty. She sometimes wished the good Lord had taken her in the place of Rose.

"She swore that she saw it in a dream. In the future, Wade and Daisy were in love and married. Don't get me wrong, I didn't believe her, either. Bunch of cockamamie stuff. But I've learned things over here, and well, sometimes things are not always as they seem."

"I know better than most that's true. You're not even really here right now. You're just my imagination. And Rose's imagination worked overtime. She always wanted the best for Wade, as any mother would, and of course she wanted Daisy for him."

"Of course." Albert nodded. "She's a Carver. Can't do any better than that."

"And our girl deserves the best. She's been through enough pain in her short life. What I want for her is a loyal and devoted man who will never leave her. Who will choose her every time over *anyone* and *anything* else."

Albert squinted. "And why can't that be Wade, exactly?"

"You want to play dumb with me? Okay, I'll tell you plain as day. Jorge Cruz ruined that boy. And Rose, well, God rest her soul..." She crossed herself. "She wasn't strong enough to stop it happenin'."

"Uh-huh. So, a rodeo champ who made a name for himself, and paid for his mother's medical bills when his father left her practically penniless? *That's* not a loyal and devoted man?"

"Oh, I see what's happening here. You're trying to confuse me." Lillian waved her hands dismissively.

"I thought I wasn't even really here," Albert chuckled.

"*Of course*, Wade was loyal and devoted to Rose. How could he not be? He's a man of Stone Ridge, after all, born and bred. But when it comes to a lifelong partner, I don't see it in him. He's far too good-looking for his own good. Terrible flirt. He loves women! All the *women* are after him, even in a town without many of them! No. Daisy deserves better."

"You want her to marry an ugly man that doesn't like women? Am I hearing you right?" Albert canted his head.

Lillian's eyes nearly rolled hard enough to fall out of their sockets. "I didn't *say* that."

"As usual, my advice is to stay out of it. But you'll do whatever you want anyway. You've done well so far with the DNA thing, so why not let this go? Daisy will make her own decisions, and there's nothin' you can do about it."

"You're wrong there, old man. There's something I *can* still do, and it might even help *Wade* in the long run."

And with that, Lillian launched Plan A: get Wade hired as the bachelor for the *Mr. Cowboy* dating show.

Fake should never stand in the way of real.

She picked up the landline and dialed. "Beulah? We need to talk."

DAISY HEARD Mima on the phone the next morning, so she gulped down a cup of coffee, skipped breakfast, and decided it was time to see Hank.

She hadn't ridden for a few weeks, and now she walked to the stables to get her paint horse, Oreo. If Daisy loved anything more than cars, it was horses. She might not be in love with ranch life and all the back-breaking chores, but she loved a horse as much as the next girl. Always had.

She led Oreo out of the stable, brushed her, cleaned her shoes, and saddled her. Oreo was a calm and docile horse and Daisy had loved her from the moment Daddy brought her home.

"Bought you a horse, Pumpkin!" Daddy had announced. "This one is yours."

"Oh, Daddy!" Daisy had easily launched herself into the arms of the best father on earth.

"Missed me, girl?" She now mounted Oreo and stroked her soft forelock. "I missed you."

Daisy didn't get to ride often enough. Too many little distractions here and there took time away from riding, though she never neglected to check in on Oreo. As a teenager, she'd barrel raced for a while mostly to please Daddy. But though she loved horses, she didn't like racing them for competition. And when she didn't have a passion for it like some girls did, she let the sport go. But contrary to what some believed, she hadn't always had a passion for cars.

But in high school, she'd taken a class simply so she wouldn't have to rely on her brothers or her father to change her oil. There, she'd discovered she had a knack for mechanics.

What must it be like to have known one's passion from the time you were a child? It had been like that for Wade, who'd been on a bucking horse since he was a kid. Wade's father sure loved the rodeo and had been proud of his son, said by everyone to be fearless. But no one was completely without fear despite what risk-takers and adrenaline seekers believed. Everyone had at least one person or thing they were terrified of losing.

For Daisy, that had always been her family.

Funny, she didn't see Wade the way everyone else saw him.

He wasn't cocky, no matter what anyone else said. Everyone else saw a flirty, charming, confident rodeo cowboy with a wild hair. The first time she'd seen Wade afraid, he hadn't even known she was watching. As usual, she and Jackson had both managed to tag along with Lincoln to the Cruz ranch.

Wade would have been fourteen at the time and already in training. He'd been pulled away by his father from whatever game they'd been playing outside.

"Son, if you don't practice every day, you'll never be a pro," Mr. Cruz had said.

By then, Wade was training with miniature bulls. She'd watched from the sidelines as Wade had gone up onto that bull and stayed on for several interminable seconds. Daisy's heart had plunged to her stomach as she watched, terrified Wade would fall and be injured. His father had him wearing a helmet and other protection, but that might not be enough.

"That was five seconds less than the last time," Mr. Cruz yelled. "You gotta beat eight. Do it again."

Wade had removed the helmet, and she'd seen the expression in his eyes and been struck dumb. In a moment she'd never forget, Daisy had seen the truth clear as a bell. Wade wasn't afraid of the bull.

He was afraid of his *father*. The one thing Wade feared was disappointing him.

Now, both of his parents were gone, and she wondered what else he could be afraid of losing. He'd lost his career, too, when he'd identified for so long as a rodeo rider.

Was it possible that Wade had nothing left to *lose*?

Her chest tightened. The thought was a punch to the gut.

"I'm not going to think about that now," Daisy told Oreo.

She rode on and waved to Lincoln and Jackson, with a

few other ranch hands in the distance, steering cattle. She didn't see Daddy and thought he might be working inside. He was doing less field work these days.

Hopping off Oreo, Daisy tied her to the fence post and walked up the porch steps to the front door. Normally, she would walk right in, but it was still early. Lord knew what she'd find if she walked right in the door like she'd been able to what seemed like not so long ago. Brenda could be inside, half-naked. Though she really couldn't picture that. Brenda Iglesias was so conservative that Daisy bet she didn't even take her clothes off to have sex.

She face-palmed. Okay, yuck. She did *not* want her mind going there.

Daisy knocked on the door, and Brenda opened it. Fully clothed, thank you, wearing jeans and flannel. Her long, dark hair was peppered with gray and pulled back in a ponytail.

"Daisy!" Brenda grabbed Daisy in a hug. "Come in, querida. Do you want some coffee?"

"Yes, please."

"Almost no one comes to visit us." Brenda walked into the modest kitchen.

The small ranch house was cozy these days, Daisy had to admit. When Daddy had lived here by himself, half the time everything was as dark as his mood. Now the curtains were pulled back to let in sunbeams of light. There were bright splashes of color everywhere. Turquoise blue, orange, jade. Everything neat, clean, and tidy. The house looked like a home where a happy couple lived.

It occurred to Daisy that her father had been miserable for years, and she'd been too stupid to see it.

Brenda handed Daisy a cup of coffee. "Hank is in his office looking over the ledgers."

"Oh, okay. I'll go back there in a minute. I need to talk to him." Daisy looked at the floor, wanting to make casual conversation but not really knowing where to begin. "Um, so how have you been?"

"Wonderful! It's all very exciting. Eve is going in for an ultrasound next week and she might find out if she's having a boy or a girl."

"If she's having a girl, she'll probably be given some kind of an award."

"Well, I was lucky to have a girl, so I hope it's hereditary."

Wouldn't it be nice if everyone could only inherit the good parts from their parents and leave the bad parts out? But more often than that, it didn't happen that way. You got the good right along with the bad. If you were lucky, there was a nice balance.

Brenda went on for several more minutes, talking baby showers, due dates, and how likely they were to be accurate. Then labor, and delivery, until Daisy started to tune her out.

"Pumpkin." Daddy ambled in the kitchen. "I thought I heard your voice."

Daisy set her now empty cup down.

"Daddy." She went into her father's arms, always so warm and open.

Brenda briefly touched Hank's arm as she brushed by him. "I'll be outside."

"You never come up here to see me anymore," her daddy said, pulling back from the hug.

It was true, but that was because she always saw him down at the bigger house where Mima cooked Sunday dinners. Lately he'd been bringing Brenda, too, but Daisy had never been up here to see them living together. Getting ready to be married soon. They weren't planning a big wedding because Brenda didn't like all the attention.

"Lincoln told you?"

"Yes, he did." Daddy lowered his head. "I'm sorry you're havin' to go through this. It's not fair to you."

"Not fair to *me*? Daddy, it's not fair to you, either! I think we know whose fault this is, and it isn't yours."

"Well, I used to think that." He closed his eyes and rubbed his forehead. "But I think there's always enough blame to go around when a marriage doesn't work out."

"That's generous, but she's the one who left us."

"And I'm sorry that we never sat down and talked about this." He walked to the kitchen table and took a seat. "If there's one good thing about this mess, it's a chance to talk about your mother."

"I don't know that there's anything to say. She *cheated* on you, Daddy."

"Well, I never broke my wedding vows, but sometimes I think I cheated on her, too."

"No, you didn't." If she'd had any doubts that her father was an honorable man, and Daisy didn't, *Brenda* would have never broken up a marriage.

"But there are different kinds of affairs. I'm learning that mine was an emotional one. Brenda and I remained close even after we were both married to other people. I tried to tell myself it wasn't true, because I did love your mother, but I think I never really stopped loving Brenda."

Oh my, her father sounded so enlightened. It was as if someone had switched Sam Elliott for Dr. Phil. What in the world.

"I worried that my mother had broken the two of you up, but Mima said that's not what happened."

"No, what happened is I let my feelings get hurt because Brenda's parents didn't think I was good enough for their daughter. And I didn't fight for us the way I should have."

"I can't *believe* they didn't think you were good enough."

Daddy chuckled and patted her hand. "I wasn't always all that good. Mima can tell you if she ever gets a hankerin' to be honest about her children's many faults. I drank too much, had a hair-trigger temper, and possibly had my head turned by a beautiful woman or two."

A beautiful woman like her mother.

"I'm sorry my mother broke your heart."

"Don't you worry about me now. I got my second chance whether I deserved it or not. While I was angry for many years at your mother, it was mostly on behalf of you kids. She didn't do right by you, even if she believed y'all were better off with me."

"She was right about that, at least. Daddy, you should know that I've decided not to take the DNA test."

While Daisy felt guilty lying about this, even now, this was a gift she could give her father. He wouldn't have to worry or wonder while he was supposed to be enjoying his second chance.

"You do what you want to do and don't worry about me or anyone else. This is your life, and I won't be upset if you have to be sure." He reached out, tucked a lock of her hair behind her ear. "But I'm sure. Besides, no matter what biology has to say about it, you're my daughter. You always will be."

Daisy rarely cried. She figured she'd done enough crying after her mother left to get her through the rest of her life. But when there were tears in her hard-edged father's eyes, it was inevitable.

She hugged him, and blubbered through a wall of tears, assuring him that she was *his* daughter.

And she always would be, no matter what those results had to say.

# CHAPTER 12

*W*ade had a rough night. Between his aching arm and intrusive thoughts of Daisy, this time with her top *completely* off, he'd rolled around in bed like an alligator. Good thing he didn't have to share his bed with anyone. No one pulling on the covers, complaining he didn't know how to share, and no one kicking him to get more room. Lord knew that would be Daisy, were she in his bed. She'd probably clock him should he dare snore and wake her up.

*Okay, that's enough thinking about Daisy in your bed.*

Nope. Not going there. Moving on.

She hadn't brought up giving her any more lessons since the night of the Riverwalk, and he was just fine and dandy with that. He wasn't going to be forced to take on that responsibility. Okay, not forced. Wrong word. Um…privileged? Yeah, much better word for that deal. So, he wasn't going to be *privileged* to introduce her into the world of sex. That was good. Yeah. Because with that privilege came a huge responsibility. And he didn't need that piled on top of everything else. So, yeah, great news.

Even if he was certain he could make it good for her. More than good. How about fantastic? Her first time should be memorable. Spectacular. It should be a high benchmark for any other fools to try and beat. Not that they could if they even tried. Oh, he'd make sure of it.

His mother must be having a field day in heaven, looking in on him now and then, watching him tied up in knots over Daisy. Having a good laugh at what she claimed he'd never be able to fight. Destiny. He'd been against the notion of this supposed "destiny" of his for years because Daisy was young and *sweet*. Too innocent for the likes of him. He'd never be good enough for her, and she'd never be "bad" enough for him.

But his mother firmly believed and insisted to her dying day: he and Daisy were meant for each other. She'd seen it in a dream.

He glanced at his mother's framed photo on the mantel. "You think this is funny, don't you?"

He forced himself to do the physical therapy exercises he loved to avoid. This time before sunrise, so he couldn't talk himself out of them. Afterward, the pain was intense enough for him to count the pills he had left and allow himself two.

Then he had his coffee, showered, dressed, and went out before dawn to start his day.

Since he'd need to move the cattle to another pasture for grazing, he drove the ATV out to a good patch of land and pounded posts into dirt to create the start of a cattle drive lane. That took him several hours after which he realized he was hungry. He hadn't thought ahead to bring a lunch pail with him like his father used to, but then again all he had in the kitchen were casseroles. Time for a run to the General Store at some point and load up on cold cuts. He'd been spending too much time eating out at the Shady Grind and it wouldn't hurt to curb expenses.

He parked the ATV at the bottom of the hill and hiked the short distance to the house. It was then that he heard a rustling in the barn and wondered if he now had the mice taking over, too. Super. Time to get a cat. Also, time to get a new barn for that matter, but that would have to hold for a bit.

As he drew closer, he saw a blonde spitfire under the hood of that classic vintage piece of crap.

After the other night's busted button/lacy-red-bra torture, watching her bend over that engine, her heart-shaped butt sticking out, was *not* helping. Why had he always been attracted to bright and shiny buckle bunnies with tassels on their jeans when *this* kind of a woman existed? She was real, earthy, and dirty in the best kind of way. She had his mind doing cartwheels.

And she's *Lincoln's little sister*. Whoa, cowboy! Whoa. That's one ride you'll never recover from.

He groaned. "Peanut! What are you doin' there?"

"Hey, Wade." She straightened, used a rag to wipe motor oil off her hands. "I didn't see you when I came by earlier, so I got busy."

"This is a waste of your time."

"It will never be a waste of my time to restore something old to new again."

"You can't do that. It's an antique. It won't ever be new again. Give up."

"It will still be just as good, and classier, too. They don't make them like this anymore."

"Suit yourself."

"Also, I got you a little surprise inside. It's an artificial tree and a few ornaments. You really *need* a tree. It will cheer you up, believe me."

"What makes you think I need cheering up?"

"You said you *have* to be a rancher, Wade. I hear you loud and clear. You don't have a choice. You're stuck here with us."

"I'm not *stuck*."

"Really?"

"Trust me. I'm good with my choices. I'm here, or haven't you noticed?"

"Where else would you be?"

He hadn't been much of a gentleman if he'd let Daisy believe that her fake boyfriend would rather be anywhere else. "Hey. I don't want to be anywhere else. Stone Ridge is my home."

While she didn't appear convinced, at least that shut her up for a moment. She gnawed on her lower lip and wouldn't look at him.

"Um, did the mail come?"

*The mail.* He mentally face-palmed. Of course she would be here, probably every single day, waiting for the results. He hadn't checked the blue wood mailbox at the end of the lane.

"I haven't checked. But he's always late, so he probably hasn't come by yet."

"You'll let me know the minute my envelope comes, right?"

He pulled off his hat and ran a hand through his hair. "I'll go down there and check after lunch. First, I gotta eat."

"You go ahead, I'll just be out here." She went back to her wrenching.

He should have realized she would use the car as a distraction. She could have been using *him* as a distraction, but that wouldn't be a good idea. He'd already established that.

*Just keep telling yourself that, champ.*

"Not hungry? You don't want some casserole?"

"Ew, no."

He chuckled and shook his head. "Can't blame you."

Inside, he washed up, mainly because of Daisy. He hadn't even shaved this morning but figured he'd let that go for now. He chose the leftover enchiladas casserole, fuming a little bit. Daisy acted like they'd never even kissed, and really...did she kiss *everyone* the way she'd kissed him?

He'd just pulled the plate out of the microwave when someone knocked on the front door. Frustrated, he stomped over, swung the door open, and found Beulah with someone he didn't recognize. A tall brunette in a black pantsuit gave him an eager smile.

"Wade, let me introduce Savannah Ackerman. And this here is Wild Wade, our rodeo champ, in the flesh!"

He offered the woman his hand, then turned to Beulah. "What's this about?"

Beulah waggled a finger. "This is about discussing you as Mr. Cowboy for our new reality show."

"We already talked about this. I'm—"

"No need to play this game with me. I have it on good authority from Lillian Carver that y'all are just pretending. And she would know better than anyone else. At least hear Miss Ackerman out. She came all this way."

"May we come in, Wade?" Savannah asked in a smooth voice. "I'd just like to talk to you for a few minutes."

"Yeah, sure."

He waved them inside and led them to his great room. Propped in the corner stood the tree with a box of ornaments nearby.

"I'm glad to see you're finally gettin' into the spirit of the holiday," Beulah said, nodding toward the tree.

Miss Ackerman took a seat on the leather couch and pulled a folder out of her briefcase. "As you know, we're in developmental talks about this reality dating show here in Stone Ridge."

"It would be good for the economy," Beulah added.

"Yes," Miss Ackerman continued. "But more importantly, it could be good for you. Do you know how many of our former contestants go on to be TV personalities with successful broadcasting careers?"

Wade crossed his arms and sat on the edge of the couch. "Nah, I don't want to be on TV."

"He's already been on TV." Beulah nudged Miss Ackerman's elbow.

"I don't want to be on TV *again*," Wade added.

"That's fine. There are also plenty of other opportunities behind the scenes. Once you're on our show, opportunities open up everywhere." She splayed a series of eight-by-ten photos of women who looked like fashion models.

"These are just some of the ladies who are interested in becoming Mrs. Cruz."

"Wait. What?" He stood. "What do you mean, *Mrs. Cruz?*"

Miss Ackerman help up a palm as if to silence him. "Not right away. Some *day*. And, of course, it may not work out. We understand, things happen. But we do ask for our single men to walk into this situation with the expectation that they are trying to find true love. Their one and only soul mate."

"Miss Beulah? Are you serious right now?" Wade glared at her and hooked a finger to his chest. "*Me?* Married?"

"What's wrong with that, *Wade?* Surely you don't want to be single the rest of your life. You don't have that many choices, seeing that most women your age are already married. You may have missed the boat, son. I'm trying to help you. Our town needs more women. Look at these gorgeous women, and they'd all move to Stone Ridge." Beulah swept her hand over the glossy photos.

"For six weeks," Miss Ackerman said.

"Well, except for the woman he marries."

Wade crossed his arms, ready to dig in his spurs. No one would talk him into this mess. No way. No how.

"I'm not getting married to someone I've dated for six weeks."

"But that's the premise of the show. Sometimes, you have to take a leap of faith."

"Lady, I'm not leapin' anywhere." He touched his arm. "Maybe you heard. I had a career-ending injury and I'm sure that's not too attractive to these gorgeous women. I'm sort of a broke-down cowboy."

"That's actually *very* attractive. We do love our wounded heroes, don't we?" Savannah smiled.

"I'm sorry I can't help you. It's just not going to happen."

"Would an offer of money help?" Savannah said.

"What's going on here?"

They all turned to the sound of Daisy's voice. Great. She was about to find out their little game was over.

"Daisy Mae Carver! I have a bone to pick with you." Beulah shook her finger. "Pretending to date Wade. What a fine mess you've made. Well, I hope you're proud."

"Your grandmother told Beulah we're a fake couple," Wade explained.

"But—"

Beulah cut her off. "It's time for you to do your duty and help us convince Wade to finally settle down and have himself a wife. I know you hate that gigantic billboard, and the sooner we find our Mr. Cowboy, the sooner it's coming down."

"What about my other suggestion? Jolette Marie's brother? Sean Henderson? Beau Stephens? *Levi?*" Daisy said, with Levi's name sounding like a squeak.

Savannah piped in. "Hello. Daisy, is it? I'm Savannah Ackerman. I've just offered Mr. Cruz the possibility of some money since he's not interested in a broadcasting or enter-tainment career after the contest ends."

"M-money?" Daisy turned to him, her voice going from squeaky to shaky.

"I can see the ranch needs work and we could help with all that. Now, I can't make any offers without first consulting with one of my executive producers. But though it's frowned on, there might be a way we can do this," Savannah said. "We really want a rodeo cowboy. Obviously, it would be perfect for our *Mr. Cowboy* show. It's all branding."

"Wait a cotton-pickin' minute. Money? Isn't the offer of marital *bliss* enough?" Beulah held a hand to her neck. "I'm absolutely shocked that this would come down to money. Why isn't love enough?"

Savannah chuckled as if she too understood the unlikeli-ness of one of these women being Wade's true love.

"That's often not enough for young people. Times are different, Mrs. Hayes."

"Butter my biscuit!" Beulah said. "This proves money is the root of all evil."

"Money is also the way I could get my ranch back in busi-ness a hell of a lot sooner." Wade couldn't help but point out.

Not that he would consider it, of course. That is, unless he could get it in writing that he didn't have to marry the woman. That would be important. He'd also have to figure out how much his soul was worth.

Savannah stood. "And on that happy note, I will leave you to consider the idea. And I'll be in touch when I hear back from the studio executives."

Beulah followed her out, clucking her disapproval the entire way to the door. "I do declare. Never heard of such a thing."

Wade closed the door, chuckling. "That was fun."

Daisy stood in the middle of the room, looking as vulnerable and lost as on the day he took her for the test. "You're thinking about this, aren't you?"

"Not in a serious way." He couldn't lie to Daisy.

"Are you *ready* to get married?"

"No, but hell, Beulah is right. I'm thirty-three, and if I'm going to settle down, I guess I should do it fairly soon. Or at least try."

"With a *stranger?*"

He scratched his temple. "Probably not. I'm definitely not one of those who believe in love at first sight. You may not have heard that part, but Savannah said that they understand sometimes these things don't work out. They want me to at least try, but they understand they can't *force* me to marry one of their women."

"You *are* thinking about it!"

"Just *thinking* about it, Peanut. You can't blame me for that." He stalked back to his forgotten lunch. "And I still haven't eaten lunch."

"How can you eat at a time like this? You're about to sell your soul for a little money."

Damn if that didn't hit him square in the solar plexus and he felt it clean as a punch. "Don't judge me. I'm trying to start over. And I don't have any other way to earn money. A little influx of extra cash wouldn't hurt."

"I know!" She brightened. "You could sell the car. It won't take me much longer to get it running."

"No, I *can't* sell the car."

"I swear, I'll work my magic and—"

"Told you. My old man made me promise never to sell it. The car is my 'inheritance.'" He made air quotes. "A gift I'm supposed to hand down from Cruz to Cruz."

"But he's not going to know."

"*I* would know." With a spoon, he served himself a heap of enchiladas.

"Don't let him keep controlling you when he's already long gone. You didn't even like your father!"

"That's not the issue."

"No, the issue is you're being bullheaded and stubborn, and *such* a man!"

"A man?"

"You saw photos of beautiful women. And you're thinking, my, wouldn't it be nice to be surrounded by women and be the only man in the mix. But that kind of thing can be highly overrated."

"As spoken by a *woman*." He snorted.

"Okay, fine. If you're doing this, I'm not going to fix your car." She crossed her arms. "I refuse."

"I didn't ask you to fix it anyway!" Okay, now he seemed to be yelling.

*Calm down, idiot. She means well.*

"Fine, you jerk! I'm leaving." She turned and stomped out his front door.

"Good. Great!" He stared at the door after she banged it closed, appetite completely gone.

How in the hell had he gotten himself into this holy mess?

Oh yeah, he remembered. He'd come back to Stone Ridge to see if he could resuscitate the ranch he'd inherited with what little money he had left of his savings. Now he was dealing with Beulah, who wanted him to get married, and Daisy who didn't want him to get married. She wanted to fix his car. And kill him slowly. She'd asked him to teach her how to attract a man, then forgotten the whole thing. Well, he was going to forget about it, too!

Someday.

At times like these, he was almost glad there weren't many women in Stone Ridge.

. . .

Daisy was so furious she slammed the door behind her. It was bad enough that Beulah knew the truth but now Wade was actually considering the contest. Just the idea had created a wall of anger so big she almost couldn't breathe. Her breaths were coming short and brief. She didn't want to believe that Wade was the kind of rodeo cowboy Mima had warned her about. An opportunist and a womanizer.

Like Rusty.

No, not Wade. He was the boy she'd loved for half her life, if she were finally being honest. She didn't have a *crush* on Wade. Crushes didn't last for over a decade. The feelings he inspired in her went far beyond physical attraction. Her heart and soul craved him in a way she did not fully understand.

He was hers. He'd always been hers, but just didn't know it.

*Tell him. Stop making stupid excuses to be with him. You swore you were going to take risks. Change your life from boring to adventurous.*

She'd just reached her truck when Wade came out the front door. "Daisy! We're not done here."

"Oh yes, we are. We're done when *I* say we're done."

"Look, let's talk about this like adults."

"Is that another crack about my age?" Her hands formed into fists and she gave him her back. "I might be younger than you, Wade, but at least *I* have common sense."

"And I don't?"

"Not when you can't see what's right in front of you."

"Let's not fight. We don't do this. We've been friends for a long time. And I don't want to lose…us."

She turned to face him, some of the hot air fizzling out of her at the sound of his soft tone. Because he was right. They were friends, tied together by community and family. And years of memories. She wanted so much more than that, but she couldn't force him to be ready for her.

"Okay."

"Come back tomorrow. Work on the car, or don't. But I know you need to keep busy until the test results come."

"Yeah. I'll be back." She turned to reach for the handle of the truck.

"Okay, good. See you tomorrow."

In the next moment she and Wade had reached for each other at the same time. She was in his arms, and they were both holding tightly to each other. His arms were around her waist, pulling her closer.

"I'm sorry," he whispered those sweet words into her neck and sent a tingle of pure desire slicing through her. "I shouldn't have yelled at you."

"No, it's my fault. I'm sure I'm not making any sense to you. I can barely understand myself."

"You're waiting for news on something potentially life changing. That's not a small thing. I'm an idiot not to realize you're going to be more sensitive than normal."

She pulled back to face him and placed her hands on his shoulders. "No, but it's...it's a lot more than that."

"Are you sure? What is it, then?" He tugged on a lock of her hair.

"I don't want you to be Mr. Cowboy."

"That much is clear. I don't want to do it, either."

"I do want you to have the money and that's what you want, too."

"It would be nice, sure."

"But there's a bigger problem. At least for me. Maybe not for you, though."

*What if he said, you're too young for me? I'm too old for you. You're Lincoln's little sister. We're better off as friends, aren't we?*

*I'm sorry but I think of you as a sister or good friend, not as a lover. Not as a potential wife. But don't take this personally.*

He could say some, or all of this. Many of the same things she'd been saying to "men who were not Wade" for a very long time. Now maybe she would get the rejection back tenfold.

But she'd made her decision, no matter how scary. She was tired of playing it safe. She'd suggested to Wade that he pretend to date *her* to rescue him from the contest. To "save" him from dating all these women and possibly marrying one of them. Because if this happened, it would be too late to tell him how she felt. He'd be engaged and Daisy would have to find a way to live with that.

"I-I don't want you to date all these women because I want you for myself."

Wade gazed at her from under hooded eyelids she couldn't read. Then she did what he'd advised and lowered her gaze to study his lips.

He kissed her, a soul-reaping kiss that made both her skin and nipples tighten. Her thoughts were a jumble, if they could even be called thoughts. They were more or less snippets of anticipation. Hope, bright and clear. Single words.

*This. Now. Mine. Him.*

*Finally, finally, finally.*

Something good had happened to Daisy. Something precious and special and wanted. The one man she'd always yearned for. Prayed for.

"About time you got honest with me. I've been waiting. I don't even know how long."

"Oh, Wade. I'm a hot mess right now and I know it. But it won't always be like this."

"You're *not* a mess. You're brave and strong. And you turn me on without even trying."

"How do you know I'm not trying?" She smiled up at him, trying to bat her eyelashes.

"Because if you were really trying, I think you would have killed me by now." He tugged on a lock of her hair. "Are you wearing the red bra tonight?"

"No, this one is black." She started to unbutton her top to demonstrate, but Wade stayed her hand.

"Don't tease me."

"I'm not."

"You don't mean to, but it doesn't take much for me when it comes to you. I got hot and bothered watching you wrench on the car."

"And I always thought being good with cars made me less attractive to men."

Wade cocked his head and smirked. "I admit that I prefer you dressed in your Wranglers than in your auto-shop jumpsuit."

"See? I was right."

"That's just because the uniform hides what I know is underneath." His hand lowered and lingered on her behind.

"You don't *know* what's underneath."

"Oh, but I have a *great* imagination."

She kissed him to shut him up. Pulling back, she pressed a finger to his sensual mouth. "There."

"What was that?" One corner of his mouth tipped in a smile.

"You're talking too much. Less talking, more kissing. And more...*you* know."

"More what, Daisy?" He tugged on her bottom lip. "If you can't talk about it, we can't do it."

"Sex."

"Oh, we are going to have sex, but we're going to take it slow."

"Why?"

"Because you deserve someone who will take his time with you, someone who will—"

"Wade, I can make my own decisions. I'm *ready*. I've been waiting a long, long, *long* time for this."

He chuckled. "And I appreciate the enthusiasm."

"It's the right time. You're the right man." A man she'd never regret loving, no matter what else happened between them.

"We're still taking it slow. I'm afraid you're going to have to trust me." He reached behind her to open the driver's side door. "I'll see you tomorrow."

With that, he helped her into the truck and shut the door.

Daisy drove home, and for the first time in several days, she took a deep breath and let the air fill her lungs.

And she didn't once think about Maggie *or* Rusty.

## CHAPTER 13

*L*illian found Daisy humming to herself in the kitchen, happy as a bluebird.

"Well now, good morning," Lillian said, walking as if she might step onto a landmine at any moment.

She figured she'd have hell to pay for letting Beulah know the truth. And up in heaven, Rose would be *quite* unamused, but she didn't know what Lillian was going through down here. Only Albert did. Her Daisy needed a man who would never abandon her, for the rodeo, cattle, or anything else. She needed to be first. She required certainty and security. Safety.

"Hi!" Daisy turned, then gave Lillian a huge hug. "I've been up since dawn, so I started breakfast. The bacon is frying, and the grits are in the pan."

Oh good heavens, the girl was terrible in the kitchen. Lillian would be lucky if the grits were edible.

"Thank you, sugar." Lillian helped herself to a cup of coffee. "I have to admit, I expected you to be a little upset with me."

"Why? For telling Beulah I was fake dating Wade?"

"Let me explain—"

Daisy waved her hand dismissively. "It doesn't matter. I'm fine. I know whatever you did, you did it for my own good. And I appreciate it."

Lillian cupped her ear. "Um, what, now? Speak into my right ear. I think I'm going a tad hard of hearing in the left."

"Ha, ha. You're funny."

"You're not upset that Wade is being courted to be Mr. Cowboy? I heard that they're offering him money and Lord knows the boy needs it. I would like to see him bring that ranch back."

"Whatever Wade decides to do, that decision will be entirely up to him."

"Yes, it certainly will be. And I guess it wouldn't be such a terrible thing to see him settle down, find the right woman. Have a couple of kids."

"And will you feel sorry for this woman? Winding up with Wild Wade?"

Lillian worried this was a trick question. "Well, of course not. Rose raised that boy the right way. He's a true man of Stone Ridge. I think I'll be pleased as punch to see him finally settle down. Rose always wanted the best for him."

*Even if she'd mistakenly believed that had been Daisy.*

"I'm glad to hear you say that." Daisy turned the bacon over in the skillet. "Because he's a friend of the family and I for one want nothing more than his happiness. Whoever that woman works out to be."

"That's very mature of you. I'm quite proud." Lillian patted her back. "I'm sure the right man will come along for you any day now. There are so many available."

"I'm not going to think about any of that for now."

"Of course. You've had a lot on your mind lately. Let's get through the holidays and Eve's baby shower. Then we'll find someone just right for you."

"Eve and Sadie invited me Christmas shopping with them, so I'll be taking off for a while today. We're going to dinner. Don't expect me back until late. You might as well go to bed."

"Oh, child. Did you leave all your shopping to the last minute again?"

"I'm afraid so."

"Well, don't spend your hard-earned money on me. I already have everything I could possibly want." Lillian took a sip of her coffee, then sent up a little prayer of thanks and mouthed, "Thank you, Albert."

Things were going according to plan, and best of all, Wade would soon enough be happy and settled down with a lovely woman.

Like Rose used to say, "You just can't fight destiny."


"Please Sadie, not another toy store," Daisy begged. "I still have to find a few grown-up gifts."

She'd been wracking her brain for a present for Wade, but nothing seemed good enough.

"What did you get for Sammy?" Sadie said.

"I thought I was giving him that little push toy that makes all that popping noise?"

"No, that's what Eve is giving him." Sadie turned her gaze in the direction of Eve, now taking a load off, sitting at a table enjoying a Cinnabon roll.

"Then what am I giving him?"

"*That's* why we're here," Sadie said, walking into yet another toy store. "Follow me. I know just the thing."

Daisy followed dutifully, avoiding parents hauling their kids around as they pointed to what they wanted from Santa. As with every store they'd been inside today, holiday music pumped loudly through speakers and every toy ever created had a Christmas version. A Santa doll with a jiggly belly in the front of the store danced to the tune of "Feliz Navidad." But as much as she was enjoying spending the day with her sisters-in-law, listening to talk of sciatica pain in the last trimester, latching-on problems for nursing babies, and when to start solid foods, she really wanted to get out of this shopping hell.

She'd planned to see Wade later and hadn't intended on spending this much of the day shopping. But the minute they'd arrived, it had been one blessed thing after another. They couldn't find a parking space and they'd circled the lot until someone finally left. Then Eve had to find a restroom every few minutes. Sadie kept texting Lincoln to make sure that Sammy was able to survive for a few hours without her.

News flash: he was.

Finally, thank you Jesus, Sadie handed Daisy a plastic fire truck that could double later as a ride-on toy. Braving the lines, Daisy paid, and they both went to find Eve.

"I still need to find Jackson the perfect present," Eve said.

"What? It wasn't that shirt and the boots you got him *five* stores ago?" Daisy said.

"No, that's an okay present but I know exactly what he wants from me." Eve waddled over to the Victoria's Secret store.

Oh, well. This was more like it. Daisy's eyes didn't know what to take in first. She loved all the silky lingerie. Mostly she bought her lacy undergarments online wondering when she'd be able to finally share them with someone. Well, the time had finally arrived. Wade had loved her red bra. She chose push-up bras and matching thongs until Sadie elbowed her.

"These are for you?"

"No, they're for *you*, Sadie," Daisy snapped. "Why? Why can't they be for me? I like lingerie, too, you know."

"Of course you do. These are just so…sexy."

Daisy not so subtly elbowed Sadie out of her way. "Why don't you go bug Eve? She seems to be buying a dominatrix outfit. Maybe you should stop her."

Sadie burst out laughing. "That's called a teddy. But I don't see how Eve can wear those much longer with her growing belly."

"Let her dream."

"I guess this means there's someone special?" Sadie asked, looking through the push-up bras right along with Daisy.

"Maybe. But there doesn't have to be, you know. This is for *me*."

"Yeah, that's what I used to think. Now, whenever Linc buys me lingerie, I know who it's really for," she chuckled. "Why do you think Eve's buying a teddy? It's so Jackson can enjoy his present."

"Nice to know y'all keep the magic alive." Daisy flipped through the bras, looking for her size in a strapless.

"Well, with your brother, it's easy. He—"

Daisy held up her palm. "You're about to cross the line."

"Got it. Hey, I like this new little system we have."

"And thank *you* for no longer going all the way to 'red alert' before I stop you."

They paid for their purchases, and on the way back to Stone Ridge, they again passed the billboard of the man with blinding white teeth. This time Daisy smiled back at him. From now on, she would view this giant man as a win.

As long as his photo was up, Wade was out.

"We haven't talked about *Mr. Cowboy*," Sadie said. "What do y'all think about this reality show Beulah dreamed up?"

"It's silly," Eve said. "I don't see how anyone can find true and lasting love in six weeks."

"Do you know that they're insisting the man be prepared to propose at the end of the show?" Daisy piped in.

"How do you know that?" Eve asked.

"That's how *all* these shows are, Eve," Sadie said.

"I was there when Beulah came over and the woman from the show offered Wade money to do this. They want him to lie and pretend he'd propose to a woman at the end of the show."

"The women probably wouldn't come out to stay in Stone Ridge if there wasn't an engagement at the end of it," Sadie said.

"Beulah thinks some of these women will stick around, just like Winona did when she found out about all the men," Eve said.

"I disagree," Daisy said, and hoped. "There is only one Winona James-Henderson."

"You can say that again." Sadie snorted.

Even if none of them had liked Winona when she'd first arrived in Stone Ridge, a Nashville star with her hair extensions and false eyelashes, they'd all grown to adore her. Riggs had married her, and she'd been a big part of the only medical clinic in town getting up and running as soon as it had. Now Eve wouldn't have to go to Kerrville to have her baby. The baby could be born right in Stone Ridge.

When they passed the clinic on their right, a large pink bow was strung from one end of the clinic to the other with a sign:

*It's a girl!*

Both Eve and Sadie squealed. "Winona is having a *girl!*"

"See? This problem will be solved in no time. When do you find out what you're having, Eve?" Daisy asked.

She and Winona were having babies within a couple of months of each other.

"I find out next week." She held up crossed fingers.

"I preferred being surprised," Sadie said.

"I like surprises now," Daisy said quietly, not sure if they could hear her.

She'd had her share of them lately. The fact that Rusty thought he could be her father was not a great one. But there were other surprises, too. To learn that her daddy was truly happy now, reunited with the love of his life in a late-in-life romance.

But possibly the best surprise of her life was to learn that Wild Wade Cruz had been waiting for *her*.

WADE CHECKED the mailbox in the afternoon, half anticipating that Daisy's results would have arrived. But still no envelope for Daisy. A few more bills for him even though he'd switched everything to online banking. And today, a letter from the Rodeo Cowboys Association. Ripping it open, he read that they were trying to start an association of retired rodeo cowboys and would love his support. Imagine that. They planned to elect a board and use their former influence to help ranching communities. Sounded honorable, charitable, and also boring. A chance to be a sad old man recreating some of his younger and more active years. That wasn't ever going to be him. He was still young, though this letter made him feel sixty-five. Did they not realize he'd *retired* young, or was this simply a form letter they sent to every cowboy on their massive list?

Depressing. He considered ripping the letter into shreds, then realized the immature response wasn't him. Instead, he'd bury it somewhere in the office with all the other paperwork he still had to go through.

By the time Daisy rolled up late in the afternoon, he was done with his chores for the day. And ready to collapse.

"Hey, there. I got caught up Christmas shopping with Eve and Sadie. It was *torture*."

He nodded. "No letter today. Sorry, I already looked."

"That's okay. I don't want to think about any of that."

"No?"

"Just happy thoughts are allowed inside this brain." She gestured to her temple.

"I could use some of those happy thoughts." Wade pulled her into his arms, holding tight.

The rush from being with Daisy had become addictive. She'd essentially taken the place of his former adrenaline kicks. She was everything wrapped up in one package for him. Excitement, thrills, danger, and...oddly enough, the comfort of home. Not a normal combination for him.

The other difference was that he'd become eager to please. Maybe far too eager. It felt strange, like walking around in someone else's too-tight jeans. He'd always been a gentleman, but he'd never actually courted a woman since he'd been a teenager. But today, he'd planned to take Daisy to the farthest point of his property that faced west. So they could watch the sunset.

He told himself this was because she wanted to give him something and he wanted her to know that he didn't take that lightly. This was setting the stage for the rest of her life. She didn't deserve less than everything even if he wasn't certain *he* could give it to her. Not his heart and soul, anyway, both of which felt a little battered these days. And okay, sure, she was taking his mind off his own problems so he didn't have to consider whether or not he could truly be happy for the rest of his life simply being a cattle rancher. Point being, he had to try.

It was enough for some, like Lincoln, and it *should* be enough for him.

He was no stranger to hard work, so that wasn't the problem. And he told himself that the issue wasn't having no one cheering him on as he mucked stalls and hauled hay bales.

No one timing him even though, truth be told, he often timed himself.

But fame and adulation were fleeting, he understood, and so what if he was no longer the flavor of the month. Every time Daisy looked at him with all her eagerness, every time she kissed him and sent heat spiraling through, he didn't need anything else.

"We should really decorate your tree." She pointed to it.

"Whatever possessed you to get me a tree, anyway?"

"Your mama would be upset that you didn't have one up. *She* always did."

He ignored the ache that memory sent through him. Maybe it was precisely why he'd avoided getting a tree.

"Haven't you had enough Christmas for today?"

"I guess you're right. The stores were full of it."

"Are you hungry?"

"I managed to get out of dinner with Eve and Sadie."

"Great, I packed something to eat."

She deadpanned. "Not a casserole?"

"Do I look crazy? You've made it clear how you feel about those." He took her hand and led her. "Beef tacos."

"You remembered."

"We're going to go watch the sunset."

"Really?"

He grabbed the cooler and strapped it on the new ATV. Tapping the seat, he indicated for her to hop on. Many ranchers used ATVs to get around a large property. He would always prefer a horse, but frankly, they were far more expensive to own and maintain. Until he started to break even, Wade would not be able to take on any more horses. They were a luxury he couldn't afford.

With Daisy a passenger behind him, he didn't even attempt pushing the ATV to the high speeds he craved. He took it easy, a leisurely drive along the outside perimeter of his property, hoping she'd notice much of the work he'd done. His cattle drive a few days ago had his cows now grazing along the north pasture where they had plenty to eat. One advantage of his situation had been plenty of grass after he'd cleared out all the dead brush. This would save him a lot of money on feed for now.

He pulled over at the fence line of the west pasture, and Daisy spread out the blanket. Together, they laid all the food out.

"This is nice," she said, biting into a taco. "I'm surprised you remember how much I love these."

"I remember everything about you, Peanut." For once, this wasn't a line.

He imagined this happened when you grew up with someone. Always noticing every small thing. Remembering. She liked rocky road ice cream and picked out the marshmallows. She told everyone she enjoyed romantic comedies, but he knew her favorite movie was actually *Tombstone*.

"They're from the taco truck, right?"

"Yup."

It made its way down to Nothing every other week. The actual location was top secret because it always varied, but Wade knew a guy who knew a guy.

"Nothing's claim to fame. The *El Abuelo* taco truck." She faced the skyline and the descending sun. "I wish they'd take the stupid *Mr. Cowboy* show over to Nothing."

"They could use the attention, but don't think that's going to happen. Beulah is on this like white on rice."

She put her taco down. "Wade, if you want to do the show, if you really need the money…maybe you—"

"After all this trouble, you're not goin' to tell me I should do the show?"

"No, I don't want you to. You know why."

"We already established that."

"I just figured you'd do whatever you wanted to anyway."

"And you'd be right about that. That's why I'm here right now. This is where I want to be."

"Yeah?" She smiled at him shyly, and he felt a strange pulling and tightening in his chest.

Heartburn, maybe. Damn. Maybe he *was* getting old. But in the next moment he completely rejected that idea outright, reached for Daisy, and rolled with her on the blanket. She wound up on top, straddling him, and wasn't *this* a beautiful sight? Better than the sunset. Her blond hair fell over her face as she bent her head, then tucked her hair behind her ears and smiled down at him. Her eyes were the most mesmerizing shade of green. They were the color of the warm and lush leaves of an apple tree.

A surreal memory punched through him, one of lying on his back looking up at the bright blue California sky. Thinking that life as he knew it was over.

But this didn't feel like the end. It felt like a beginning.

She threaded the fingers of their hands together. "Tell me something and be honest with me."

*Here we go.* She was going to ruin this moment by asking him about other women. By asking how many women he'd been with. *Too many.* He wanted to forget about that part of his past and leave behind the reputation he'd earned over the years. Lincoln had been no saint, either, by the way, but he'd been far more discreet. Wade had to give him that.

"I'll be honest. Just don't ask me about something you don't want to hear."

"Okay," she said, cocking her head. "How's your arm?"

"Fine. Great." This was, of course, a lie.

But he didn't feel comfortable telling Daisy that some mornings his arm hurt so much he wanted to scream. Cry. Put a hole in the wall, with his *good* arm. He wouldn't do it, of course. What would be the point?

"You *said* you'd tell me the truth. I could feel it the night you carried me on your back. Your arm was working so hard it was trembling."

"That's nothing for you to worry about."

"But I *do* worry because I care about you."

Whenever he'd told a woman that he *cared* about her, it was the ultimate kiss-off. And they knew it. But Daisy wasn't jaded about love. She was still hopeful and eager, like someone he once remembered…oh yeah, him. Before he'd had his first heartbreak.

And Daisy… well, it occurred to him that Daisy might have never had a broken heart.

"Alright, it hurts. Now you tell me something true. Has anyone ever broken your heart?"

"Why do you ask, so you can go beat him up?"

"No, because I want to know."

"Never mind." She rolled off him. "I can't tell you the truth."

The way she pulled away sent daggers of fear slicing through him. Someone *had* hurt her. How bad? He forced himself to take it down a notch, let the fear go.

"Tell me."

"No."

"Whisper it in my ear."

"No," she snorted.

"Spell it."

"No!"

"Charades?"

She laughed and smacked his shoulder. "Cut it out."

He pulled her back into his arms. "Look."

Together they watched as the sun lowered beyond the horizon, the last rays of the sun darkening against the skyline. The night was clear and cool.

"There's going to be a lot of bright stars tonight," he said.

They were quiet for several moments, just listening to the sounds of sparrows twittering in the tree branches and settling in for the night.

"It was you, okay?" Daisy whispered into the darkness. "*You* broke my heart."

She might as well have shoved a knife in his heart.

"When?" He turned her to face him, palming her chin.

"That time you kissed me and ran away. I felt like I'd done something wrong because I enjoyed it when you kissed me like that."

"Sweetheart, I was the one who'd done something wrong. And I shouldn't have run out on you. When I kissed you, I knew I'd crossed a line, and it scared the crap out of me. Not crossing the line, but the way you made me feel when I did."

"It *was* good, wasn't it?" She took his palm and kissed the inside of it.

"You were young. And yes, it was way *too* good for my comfort."

"I don't think it's a coincidence that it's still good between us. There must be a reason."

"I can't argue."

"For once."

And then she smiled against his mouth and kissed him, a kiss so warm and tender that he knew without a shadow of a doubt he was in deep, deep trouble.

# CHAPTER 14

*D*aisy had just told Wade a difficult truth, and yet he still wasn't being fully honest with her. She understood why, and it was easy not to hold it against him. But his arm was a problem for him. He kept pushing through, working through the pain, but he had no one to talk to. No one but her. Both parents gone, his mother with whom he'd always been so close.

His father, a man Wade seemed to have both loved and mostly feared. Even Lincoln didn't have as much time for his best friend these days, though she would bet that Wade wouldn't tell him the real truth, either. It was easier to be tough. And it was expected from the men of Stone Ridge. Certainly, from a former rodeo cowboy.

And she understood better than he realized. She behaved far stronger than she felt most days because she didn't want anyone's pity. But he hurt, too, and didn't want her to feel sorry for him. Understandable, but it wouldn't stop her from helping him.

In the middle of their heavy make-out session under the moonlight and stars, she casually massaged his arm.

"What are you doin'?" he said through hooded lids.

"I'm trying to ease some tension."

"Baby, you're already doin' that."

"I just don't want you hurting." She sank her fingers in his thick cocoa hair.

"And I don't want you to hurt, either."

While that could be taken many ways, Daisy fixated on one of them. She didn't know what would happen after they entered into this brand-new territory together. It wouldn't just be Mima having a difficult time accepting them. Lincoln would probably not be thrilled, either, but he'd get over it. Eventually. Sadie would help.

The real problem being, of course, what to do if she and Wade *didn't* work out. They *should* be able to seamlessly go back to being friends again because she'd done that many times in the past. She'd dated everyone from Jeremy to Troy. And when it hadn't lasted, they were still friends even to this day. No hard feelings.

This was different, of course, and her heart knew it. She'd already memorized everything about Wade. It helped that she'd been doing that most of her life. She only wanted to be with one man her whole life, and Wade could be her one and only. Forever. She didn't care if he was her first and last. Maybe that's the way it should be, old-fashioned though it sounded. She was okay with that, given her mother's example. Best to be as far away and different from Maggie as possible.

This night couldn't have gone better if she'd planned it herself. Now that the sun had set, only ambient moonlight remained and a spread of sparkling stars. It gave her a courage she might not have had otherwise to take the lead from a man who probably always led.

Straddling Wade, she slowly unbuttoned her shirt, ready to reveal her new plunging demi bra. Judging by his reaction, which she could feel beneath her more so than see, he approved. Wholeheartedly.

"Wait. I want to see this."

Before she realized, he'd reached for a small pen light and shined it on her boobs.

"Wade!" She rolled off him.

"What?" He laughed, rolling to tuck her under him. "Don't you want me to see?"

"I wanted you to see with the benefit of *mood* lighting. You know, the moon! You're cheating. I don't think anyone looks good with a bright light on them."

"You do. But I want you to feel safe."

He dropped the light, then quite skillfully unsnapped her bra. He slowly kissed and licked from the column of her neck, to her shoulders, lowering the strap of her bra. When his warm mouth covered her breast, Daisy's entire body tightened in response.

Wade stopped. "Am I going too fast? Is this too much?"

"No," she whispered. "It's good. I like it."

The tightening of her skin wasn't out of nerves or anxiety. An intense pleasure she'd never experienced before made her want to buck against him. She did, and he groaned in a way that sent waves of satisfaction rolling through her.

Then Wade went after her jeans and panties, lowering them past her hips.

And Daisy got to experience some of what she'd been missing.

"I'M STILL A VIRGIN," Daisy said once they were back at the ranch.

"Only technically." Wade pulled her into his arms. "You didn't want your first time to be a few feet away from my grazing cattle, did you? In the dark?"

"I'm not complaining."

Far from complaining, she'd been incredibly responsive. It was a crime to think she'd been denied this experience for so long. She was also eager, to the point of wanting to return the favor, as she'd pulled on his jeans. But he'd denied himself that pleasure because tonight had been all about her. He'd simply stayed her hand and told her that was the advanced course.

She batted her eyelashes. "When are you going to let me into that silly advanced course?"

"You have to be patient. Maybe next time."

"Maybe *next* time?"

"Here's something no other man would ever tell you, so I'm glad you picked me." He tipped her chin to meet his gaze. "The first time might hurt."

"I'm not an idiot. I know that."

"And you already know how I feel about hurting you."

"Yes, and I trust you. I feel safe."

"I will make it good for you, as good as it can be the first time. But baby, it really doesn't get much better than what happened tonight."

"That *was* amazing."

"And the rest will be amazing, too, because I'll make sure of it. It won't hurt as much with me, but it will hurt the first time."

"So why is every woman going on and on about sex like it's better than chocolate?"

"Because it is, after a couple finds their groove." He sent her a wicked smile. "And I know we will."

She believed that, too. "I can't wait."

He kissed her again, holding her close, inhaling her sweet scent. He still tasted her on his tongue, and just that thought sent him into a tailspin. Holding himself back from what he had wanted to take tonight was an excruciating exercise in self-control.

"I'm not going to lie. I can't wait, either."

Lately, it was all he could think about. As if he were a teenager going at it for the first time. Excited and eager. And a little nervous, too, but it happened to be his favorite kind of tension. The anticipation before the chute opened, the thrill in the air all around him.

That was Daisy.

Wade walked her to her truck, opened the door, and waited as she strapped in. She gave him one last kiss, deep and promising, and then drove off.

He would be lucky if he slept at all tonight.

PREDICTABLY, Wade tossed and turned all night long. Memories of what he'd done to Daisy the previous night mixed with the anticipation of what he planned to do to her. As soon as possible.

The next morning, he knew exactly what he had to do.

He hadn't been out to Lincoln and Sadie's cabin since they'd moved into the large home Lincoln had built for them on several acres of Carver land. When he'd been home for his mother's funeral, he'd come to see the frame. Then he and Lincoln sat together, for hours, drinking beer, exchanging memories. Lincoln letting Wade be quiet and stew in his grief. Like best friends do.

And it didn't sit well with Wade that his relationship with Daisy had recently changed, and Lincoln had no clue. Most of this was none of his business, but Wade couldn't get past the fact that he had to say something. After all, in the beginning the whole thing had been a lie. He had to tell Lincoln that he was dating Daisy, and he had to frame it in such a way as to let him know that this relationship wasn't business as usual for him. Because it was true, and also the only way he and Daisy could work.

Daisy was a grown-up now and no one needed to protect her, but least of all from him. He would rather be impaled by an angry bull than hurt her. Even if she wasn't in love with him, for the first time in many years, he was the one open to a serious relationship. But if Lincoln didn't get a clue, if Wade didn't share how his feelings had changed, he might feel betrayed. Wade couldn't have that. He wasn't going to hide a thing.

That's how he found himself knocking on the door of the cabin of his oldest friend.

Lincoln opened the door, holding Sammy. "Oh, hey, bud. Come on in. About time you came by to see the place. The only other time you've been here since it was finished was with Daisy. We had other things on our minds that night."

"Yeah, I'm sorry I've been scarce." He shut the door and stepped inside the marbled foyer. "I actually need to talk to you about something, and I probably should have come sooner."

"Don't tell me you're thinking' about doing that stupid reality show. I heard that both Beulah and Mima are after you. You want my advice? Don't let them pressure you. You're just like me. And you're going to have to know a woman a lot longer than six weeks before you propose." Lincoln snorted. "Probably, like, years."

*Years. With someone that I've known for most of my life. Someone who in many ways I've always loved.*

Someone who his mother believed was right for him even before Wade did. The strangeness of that never failed to amaze him. How had she known? Was it just a coincidence because she liked the Carver family and had been friendly with Maggie? It had to be.

"That's actually what I need to talk to you about."

"Yeah?" Lincoln set Sammy down on the floor and the kid started to crawl around.

"He can do that already?" Wade pointed. "Isn't that early?"

"Hell if I know. But it's sure made our lives a lot more complicated." Lincoln turned Sammy around when he was headed straight for the fireplace. "Forgot I have to stop cursing around him."

"Well, I—"

"Go ahead, I'm paying attention." Lincoln turned Sammy around again. The kid was quick, he'd give him that.

In the corner, there was a playpen. "Can't you put him in that contraption?"

"I would, but he screams his head off. I'm only thinking of you. The screaming is loud. Boy has a good pair of lungs on him. No, Sammy, you can't have that." Lincoln took a pen that had been on the floor.

Sammy screamed, apparently offended that he couldn't start scribbling at eight months, or however old he was.

"Damn, only Sadie can calm him down when he works himself up like this."

And Sammy's face had gone tomato-sauce red.

"Where is she? Taking a shower?" Wade prayed. This confession time wasn't going too well. He would need Lincoln's undivided attention.

"No, she went to meet with Mima, Beulah, and the ladies of SORROW about some knitting-thing fundraiser. She won't be long," Lincoln yelled over the sounds of Sammy's wails.

"Okay, well, listen. You have to know I didn't see this coming. I swear I didn't."

"What?" Lincoln said, swaying the baby back and forth. "Say that again."

"I should come back another time. You're busy."

"No, seriously, just give me a minute to calm him down. I

wanted to talk to you about a fishing trip. It's been a while," Lincoln yelled.

"Your bachelor party weekend," Wade yelled back. "Too long ago. We definitely need to do that again."

This was ridiculous. Two grown men couldn't carry on a conversation with a screaming baby in their midst. Lincoln continued to sway Sammy, hand him various toys, and nothing worked. Nothing. Feeling completely useless, Wade made silly faces. They only made Sammy cry louder.

Then came a squawking sound from the walkie-talkie nearby. Lincoln, like so many, used them as a means of communication on a large ranch.

"Lincoln, we need your help pulling a cow out of the mud," came a man's voice and sounded like Jackson. "Got herself stuck pretty good. I got some help already, but it's going to take a few more men. West pasture, same place she did before. Figured you'd want to get this done now. Is Sadie back?"

"No, damn it. Aw, shit fire. Sorry, Sammy." Lincoln spoke into the handset, then turned to Wade. "Watch Sammy? It will only be a few minutes. I swear."

Wade took a step back and threw his hands up as if he'd been asked to sit on a stick of dynamite. "What? That's *not* a good idea. I don't know much about kids. Let me go help pull the cow out."

"Thanks, buddy, but not with your sore arm. I wouldn't be much of a friend. Besides, I know the location better than you do." Lincoln handed a screaming Sammy to Wade, who took him with the ease he did holding a woman's purse.

"Just hold him and rock him like I was doing. It does nothing but you feel better trying. Be right back."

But the minute the door shut behind him, Sammy was shocked into silence. He simply stared at Wade with a stiff bottom lip as if he couldn't believe his father had handed him off. Backing up carefully, not wanting to risk dropping the kid, Wade took a seat on the couch.

"My name's Wade." Wade cleared his throat. "Um, do you like horses?"

AN INTERMINABLE TWENTY MINUTES LATER, during which Wade told Sammy his entire life's story, Sadie waltzed in the front door.

"Wade," she said, smiling. "What are you doing here?"

Sammy had fallen asleep during Wade's recounting of the National Rodeo the first year he won the grand prize. He'd been holding him for the past few minutes, and the boy was going to be big like his daddy. Wade's arm ached but he was afraid to move the kid.

"Came by to see Linc, and he had an emergency in the field, so he left Sammy with me."

She drew closer and ran a hand through her boy's soft curls. "Did he cry much?"

"Oh, you know, a little. But I bored him to sleep. He pretty much calmed down when I recounted the first time I was on a bucking horse." He shrugged because it was one of his best stories.

"You two look good there together," she said.

"Well, he's asleep. This part is easy."

"He doesn't usually nap for long. I'll put him down in his crib," Sadie said, easily taking him from Wade. She pressed a kiss to the boy's forehead. "Doesn't he look just like his daddy?"

"He does."

A few minutes later, Sadie was back. "How about some iced tea?"

Wade followed her into the kitchen he hadn't seen since it was little more than a framed room. It was spacious, and this he did remember. Granite countertops were offset by gleaming cherrywood cabinets. In the center, a large kitchen island. The colors were blue and yellow, bright and cheerful.

"We haven't seen much of you lately." Sadie set a pitcher on the bench table set against the kitchen's nook. "How's the arm?"

Why was that all anyone ever asked about? Why not ask him about the ranch and his new cattle and equipment?

"It's fine. I've recovered well."

"Doing your physical therapy exercises?"

"Yes, ma'am." He took a gulp of the sweet tea. "I would drop by more often but there's a lot of work to be done on my ranch."

"Of course, you're busy. So is Lincoln. And you know what we've all been through lately. Poor Daisy. And poor Linc, he's been miserable wondering how she'd take it."

"She's handling it pretty well, I'd say. Linc should have trusted that she would."

"You know how he is, trying to protect everyone he loves from any kind of pain."

"Yeah. I sure know."

"The two of you aren't any different that way."

"He's a lot better at it than I am. I seem to wind up hurting the people that I love one way or another," Wade said, wishing he hadn't said that out loud.

He was thinking of his mother, whom he hadn't seen much in her last months. And really, what had been the point of keeping her alive when he didn't have any time to spend with her? He'd paid her bills and kept her treatments going longer, which had stretched her days, for her friends and family. For him, the times he got home. Maybe that had also been selfish of him. Some days the guilt ate him alive, though he knew she'd understood. At one time, in the exuberance of his youth, he'd actually thought he could save her somehow.

That money meant good medical treatment and that would equate life. Didn't quite work out that way.

And time was the one thing he would never get back.

"I'm sure that's not true." Sadie studied him, then pushed a plate of cookies in his direction.

He took one, of course. It would be rude not to. They were holiday sugar cookies in the shape of green trees and yellow stars.

"You're not actually doing that reality show, are you? I heard that Beulah figured out you and Daisy were fake dating."

"No, ma'am. They did offer me money, but at this point, I couldn't in all good conscience participate in that kind of show."

"Oh," Sadie said, her eyes wide. It was as if he'd told her everything.

*Everything*, in one simple sentence.

This is why he loved women.

"Yeah."

"You and Daisy." Sadie folded the edge of a paper napkin. "When…when did this happen?"

"Recently. I didn't plan it. We really were faking in the beginning."

"Well, *you* were, anyway."

"Yeah, but it took me a while to figure that out. I'm an idiot."

"Another way you're like Lincoln. I don't understand how you missed it. She adores you. Always has."

"I know she did at one time, but I thought she got over that. She was always so much younger than me, that it was unthinkable. And awkward. She had a crush on me, that was all. I never acted on it."

Unless one wanted to count that kiss long ago, but he didn't. He'd done the right thing and rushed out of there

177

before he regretted doing more. The idea that he'd been Daisy's first heartbreak had crushed him, just ripped into a piece of his soul.

But he would make it up to her now.

"I know you didn't. And frankly, Wade, she's old enough to make her own decisions."

"That's what she tells me." He managed to crack a smile.

"Are you worried about how Lincoln will take this?"

"Even my oldest friend can't tell me who to date. But it's out of respect for him that I'm here."

"You haven't told Lincoln yet?"

"I tried, but…there were a few distractions, and then a cow got stuck in the mud."

"Oh, not again?"

Wade chuckled. Some cows got stuck in bad patterns.

"I told him I'd come by some other time and we can talk then." Wade stood, not wanting to impose any longer. "Thanks for the tea and cookies."

Sadie followed him to the door. "Wade? I wonder if you'd let me prepare the way first? I'd like to help. I won't tell him anything, since I know you want to do that. But I could…you know, ease him into the idea."

"Whatever you think is best." He reached for the door handle. "I have no intention of hurting her."

Sadie waved her hand dismissively. "I know that."

Wade drove home, a little unnerved by the fact that Lincoln's wife wanted to "prepare" the way for him. Why? To "soften the blow"?

He'd like to think Lincoln wanted to see his sister happy, especially with everything she'd been through recently, but maybe Wade's reputation had preceded him.

And this time he actually cared what someone thought of him.

# CHAPTER 15

*N*ot surprisingly, Sammy didn't nap for long and was up five minutes after Wade had left. Sadie's little boy was always anxious to get moving the moment he woke up. She put the baby gate up and set him on the kitchen floor with a couple of plastic bowls while she made dinner. Meatloaf, Lincoln's favorite.

In a way she was still celebrating the moment when all the worry had been taken off her cowboy's strong shoulders. When Daisy told her big brother that she wished he would have told her sooner, Sadie had wanted to cry with relief. Late that night, they'd stayed in each other's arms long after making love, talking about everything they'd been through from the moment Hank started receiving emails from Rusty Jones.

"Are you glad she's decided not to take the test?"

"Yes, because that means this is really over. We can put it behind us." His warm and calloused hand skimmed down her naked back. "Why? Do you think she should take it?"

"I don't know. I'm glad for you that she decided not to do it. I like having my husband back."

"You like having all my attention, don't lie. I keep wondering when you'll get sick of having me around."

"I'm never going to get tired of you. Just wait and see."

Sadie wanted this kind of happiness for everyone she loved. And certainly, a former playboy could be reformed when he fell in love. She'd seen it firsthand.

Good thing, because Sadie now knew whom all that sexy underwear Daisy purchased was for. Sadie understood what it was like to pine after a brother's best friend. Her brother, Beau, had accepted that she and Lincoln were together, in fact trusted that no one else could love and protect her better than he could. She had faith that Lincoln would eventually do the same for Daisy.

Lincoln showed up just as she was setting the table, looking like he'd been dragged three miles through mud and grass. Mud caked his jeans, shirt, and face. Still, he had a grin on his face because her man was definitely a rough-and-tumble cowboy.

"Oh, phew, baby!" Sadie fanned a hand in front of her.

"What? You don't want a kiss?" He stood in the doorframe of the kitchen, just on the other side of the baby gate, arms splayed wide.

"No. Kiss me *after* you take a shower."

"What about you, Sammy? Want to give your daddy a big hug?"

Sammy squealed and went back to gumming the Tupperware bowl's lid. It was an expensive toy, and Sadie already washed enough dishes for a five-person household these days. She wished Sammy found his actual toys this intriguing.

"I'll be back," Lincoln said and sprinted upstairs.

"Okay, Sammy. No tantrums tonight. I need Daddy in a good mood."

This latest development was not a big surprise to Sadie.

She'd seen Wade and Daisy together and you couldn't fake that kind of thing. While she'd fully expected that from Daisy, the surprise had been watching Wade, a bit gobsmacked with love. She'd never seen him so taken with any woman.

But Wade had always been a full-blown flirt, yes, even with *Sadie* before she and Lincoln got together. Pretty much with every woman in town from birth to death, giving Wade the appearance of always being available to *everyone*.

Twenty minutes later, the table was set, Sammy in his highchair, and Lincoln back down from his shower. Dressed in clean jeans and a pearl-button shirt, his hair still damp, he still made her knees liquid. Her heart sped up simply because he'd entered the room, never mind that she worried what she might find when she put her pulse on his feelings about a Wade-and-Daisy relationship. After what she'd been through lately, Lincoln's dial was set to optimize protective mode with Daisy.

"What's the occasion? Are we still celebrating?" He pressed his hand low on her back before he drew her chair back for her. "You don't even like meatloaf."

"I should eat more of it. Meatloaf is good for me."

*Careful, Sadie. Don't lay it on too thick.*

He smirked. "Yeah?"

"I got to chat with Wade today."

"I'm sorry I had to leave before we were done talking," Lincoln said, serving her and then himself. "I want to get together and go fishing soon, if you don't mind."

"I think that would be a great idea!"

"Wow, *you're* excited. You hate it when I even have to go away for a cattle auction and that's business."

"Well, I miss you. But you deserve some fun with your oldest friend."

"Thanks, baby. I think I will make plans. I have to check

the weather reports. I'll be sure not go until after the holidays."

"You know, I was just thinking. Wade really was *so* great with Daisy at the Riverwalk when that man showed up, don't you think?"

"Yeah, he was. I appreciated him handling things until I got there." Sammy squealed and Lincoln tousled his hair. "Everything worked out and that's all that matters."

"Um, do you know if Wade is actually seeing anyone?"

"Besides Daisy, you mean?" He winked. "You know Wade. He'll never settle down."

"Never say never. Isn't that what people used to say about you?"

"That's true. Then you came along."

"I was always right in front of you."

"What can I say? I'm a slowpoke cowboy." He chuckled and squeezed her hand.

"So, since Wade is sticking around and not in the rodeo anymore, I bet he's going to consider settling down with someone special."

"You think?" Lincoln cocked his head as if the very idea puzzled him. He shook his head. "I can't imagine that."

"Then you need to expand your imagination. He's thirty-three."

"I don't see what age has to do with it. He'll get married when he meets the right woman. *If* he meets the right woman. I expected him to come back home with some buckle bunny and hope to make things work with her on his ranch. He had his choice of women on the circuit, now not so much."

"But he *didn't* come home with a woman. I think Wade is more discriminating than you realize." Sadie handed Sammy a piece of bread to gum on. "It was nice seeing you handle him and Daisy dating, even if it was fake."

"It's not like I'm going to find it weird when Daisy winds up in a relationship. It's bound to happen sooner or later. I wonder what's taking so long. She's old enough."

"This is what I'm thinking, too!"

Lincoln grinned. "What is it? Do you have someone to introduce her to? Want to know if I think she'll like him?"

Sadie playfully pointed her fork. "*You* don't have any *idea* of whom she'd like. But no, I think she can find a guy all by herself."

"You're right about that. Daisy does what she wants and always has."

Really, it was uncanny how little insight her man had into other people's love lives. Probably for the best.

"Have you ever thought about the fact that it might be hard on Daisy, finding and keeping a boyfriend? You and Jackson put together can be pretty intimidating. And that's even before they get to *Hank*."

Lincoln grunted. "The *right* man won't be afraid of us."

*You can say that again, cowboy.*

"You just remember that, baby. You remember that's what you wanted."

"If I forget, I'm sure you'll remind me."


WADE DROPPED by the General Store on his way back to the ranch. He was determined to have food on hand for the next time Daisy came over.

Unfortunately, he wasn't quick enough to avoid Kari Lynn in the dairy aisle.

"Hiya, Wade."

"Hey there, darlin'. You sure look fine today."

*Why had he said that?*

Force of habit. It was like he got diarrhea of the mouth

around women. Reality check. He didn't *have* to be liked by every woman, did he? No. He didn't.

"You're so sweet." She batted her eyelashes. "I thought maybe I'd come by your ranch sometime. I'd love to see what you've done with it."

"Better not. I wouldn't want your pretty boot to step on a nail or a rut. I've got a lot of work still ahead of me."

"Alright, well, when you're done."

"Sure thing, I'll let you know."

"Well, hello there, *Wade*," came Mrs. Carver's voice out of nowhere. She'd appeared at his elbow like a ninja.

"Mrs. Carver, don't you look lovely today."

Kari Lynn took that moment to strut away in a bit of a huff, he noticed, but rather convenient for him.

"Kari Lynn is so lovely and you're *such* a charmer. Do you ever get tired of laying it on so thick?"

*Yes. Try exhausted.*

Unfortunately, he'd never learned how to turn off the charm. "I never exaggerate. I do think you look lovely."

"What about me is *lovely*, young man?"

He didn't hesitate because he noticed things about women. All women, young or old. "That's a new coat, isn't it?"

Mrs. Carver blinked. "Why, yes. How did you know?"

"I haven't seen you wearing it before."

"How do you know it hasn't been in the back of my closet?"

"It hasn't."

"You're right." She tugged on the buttons of her coat. "Thank you for noticing."

"Welcome."

He would win Mrs. Carver over yet. She was one of the few women in Stone Ridge who didn't fall under his spell.

Wade wasn't sure why other than the fact that Maggie had been friendly with his mother. But Lillian didn't think him good enough for Daisy, no shock there. He didn't have a whole lot to offer her but a broke-down cattle ranch, a falling-in-on-itself barn, a house in need of repairs, and a man with an injured arm.

She could do much better than him. Whether or not she should was the real question. He wasn't the most impartial judge at the moment. Clearly, he had an agenda. He didn't want her to find anyone else.

When he got back to the ranch, he found Daisy in the barn wrenching on the car again.

"You don't give up, do you?"

She wiped her brow, her blond hair held back in a high ponytail. "This is a classic. Trust me on this."

"You sure do ask a lot of me." He headed into the kitchen with his bags. "I'll be right with you."

He quickly put away the milk, bread, eggs, bacon, cereal, soup, and other food he'd bought. An utter feeling of domestication settled on him but this time with an ease he didn't expect. How about that, he seemed to be growing up. Just as his mother said he would someday. Maybe he'd make dinner for Daisy tonight. She couldn't cook, and he wasn't exactly a four-star chef, but he could manage. He'd eaten on the road for years, in diners and bars, but for a while there when he'd been trying to save every penny, he'd learned how to cook an exceptional batch of ramen noodles.

From outside came a sound so loud and jarring that Wade instinctively went for his shotgun. But even as he rushed outside, he should have recognized the sound was unique. Different. Not the sound of an animal threat. Not the sound of cattle hooves. Not the sound of a bull loose and creating havoc.

*This* was the sound of a building coming down.

Terror was a real and tangible vice that clawed at his throat, cutting off his breath.

Part of the barn had fallen in right where Daisy had been working on the car.

# CHAPTER 16

"*D*aisy!"

Fear uncoiled in Wade like a poisonous snake. The adrenaline rush hit him with the force of a bull coming straight at him. His pulse raced. The sound of his heartbeat thudded in his ears. He couldn't take in a full breath.

He didn't understand why he thought he'd missed this feeling.

"I'm okay." A piece of the barn's old rotted ceiling lay on her legs, but she was surrounded by dust and wood. She kicked the plank off with her feet. "I think."

He cursed. "You're not *okay*. The ceiling fell on you. I told you not to work on this car. Damn it, Daisy!"

"Hey, be nice! The roof just fell on me!"

"Let's get you out of here before the rest of it falls down."

Without another word, he dusted debris off her shoulders, arms, and legs. He picked Daisy up and kicked the door open, carrying her into the house. Setting her down on the couch, he went for his first-aid kit. It was a required staple when he was growing up and he'd used it just last week when he'd cut his finger mending fences. He found it under the kitchen sink where he'd left it, then grabbed some ice and a dish towel.

"Okay, let's see." Plopping himself next to Daisy, he tried to push up the leg of her pants, but the jeans were too tight. "Pull this up so I can take a look at your legs."

Daisy didn't bother tugging, but simply raised her hips, unzipped, and slid her pants completely off. She wore tiny frilly pink panties with only a small swatch covering her. He made a valiant—he was sure—award-winning effort to ignore this, and inspected her legs. *Her curvy, creamy legs and thighs.* And holy cow, even her *ankles* looked delicious.

Okay, so he wasn't doing such a great job of ignoring.

She had a few bloody wounds and scratches on her shins. He used ointment to clean and bandage her. She could have a concussion. He'd had plenty in his life and knew exactly what to look for.

"Did anything hit your head?"

She gave him an odd look through narrowed eyes. "I don't think so."

"I don't *think* so won't work for me. You have to be sure."

"Okay, maybe a small piece hit my head, but it was so small I barely felt it. My body took most of the punishment. I'll probably just be sore tomorrow."

He handed her the towel with ice. "Put this on your head, just to be safe."

"Ahem. Are you just going to ignore the fact that I'm lying here nearly naked?"

"Daisy, cut me a break. My barn just fell on you. You're injured, and I'm worried and trying not to think about how much I would like to pick you up like a caveman and throw you in my bed right this second."

He rose and went to the medicine cabinet to get some anti-inflammatory meds for her.

This he knew exactly where to find and was gratified to

see that he had plenty left. In the beginning, after the injury, he'd counted the pills in the bottle and told his arm he'd get through the day with one pill. One. Some days that worked, others it didn't. He kept careful count, however, and tried to beat his own score.

He grabbed a glass of cold water but when he walked back in the room, he almost had to dunk it over his head.

Daisy had removed her shirt, too, and lay there on his couch, up on her elbows, a slow smile crossing her Cupid's bow lips. She had the sexiest lips he'd ever seen in his life and now that he'd tasted them, he couldn't get them off his mind.

"Can you ignore this?" The pink matching bra pushed up her breasts like an offering.

He swallowed hard and his words were more of a croak. "I'm not *ignoring* anything. This is willpower, girl. Are you trying to kill me?"

"Why are you resisting me?"

"I'm trying to do the right thing here, Daisy. You don't need me to throw you over my shoulder and haul you into my bedroom."

"Hm, maybe I do." She chuckled, took the pill and swallowed it, then licked her lips. "Wade, the thing is, when the ceiling fell on me…it hurt my mouth, too. Right here."

Oh man, she was good. Fine, he would play along.

He gently pulled her up by the waist and pointed to the corner of her lips. "Where? Here?"

"Yes, and you better not even *think* about a Band-Aid."

"No, baby. No more Band-Aids for you. I can see that you're dandy. You may have hit your head but you're obviously firing on all cylinders."

He tugged on her full lower lip, then kissed her. *Not* sweetly.

Not tender. The kiss was long and deep and promised everything he meant to deliver. He was done waiting and done being the honorable good guy. *Done, done, done.* She was getting what she wanted tonight.

But he'd have to slow his roll and not just go for sex the way he wanted. The way his body reacted and the way he craved. Hot, sweaty, raw. No frills. Down to basics. That would come later, were he lucky enough to have more than once with Daisy. Tonight, he'd take his time, even if it killed him.

Wade picked Daisy up in his arms and carried her to the bedroom where, for the second time today, he kicked a door open.

This time, his heart raced for a different reason.

His favorite reason in the world.

Daisy stood on her bare feet inside Wade's bedroom, facing him, wearing only her new lingerie.

At last.

Minutes ago, when she'd heard the sounds of the crash before part of the ceiling came down, she swore that her life flashed before her eyes.

She nearly wept it was so boring.

Always the good girl. She'd never taken any chances, never laid her heart on the line. *Or* her body. Finally, it was time to create some memories.

Wade took her in, all of her, as if seeing her for the very first time. His hand slid from her waist to her hips. "You're so beautiful, Daisy."

"I'm glad I have your attention." She stepped forward and went on tiptoes, her arms reaching for his shoulders. "But *you* have too many clothes on."

She slid his jean jacket off his shoulders with his help, then slowly unbuttoned his shirt. Beautiful tanned, sinewy muscles were revealed, a light smattering of dark chest hair, a taut and flat stomach, and…wait. A tattoo? She traced the edges of the design, a long lasso rope that circled his bicep and lowered, ending at his forearm.

The words read, *Do or Die*.

"We were all drunk one night in Oklahoma," he said.

She kissed the tattoo right where the rope met his bicep. "I like it."

Then she ran her hand down the large red scar on his arm and kissed that, too.

"Had I known, I would have had the tattoo done on the other arm. It could have covered up the scar."

"Maybe then you'd have a broken rope, too. But I happen to love this scar. It says that you have a history and a dangerous past that you *survived*."

He met her eyes, his own hooded and dark with heat. "You're a survivor, too, Daisy."

She'd never considered that, but yes, she *was* a survivor.

She'd survived Maggie Mae leaving and now she'd survive everything else, too. She could have been a different girl than the one she'd turned out to be. She could have gone after the attention of men in an unhealthy way. There had certainly been plenty of them always surrounding her. Instead of asking for attention, she'd been too cautious, but there was some good in that, too. She didn't want to make the same mistakes someone else had made before her.

She would have to make her own.

He toed off his boots, then shucked his Wranglers off. Daisy always thought he had a great body, judging by the way he filled out his clothes, but reality went far beyond anything she'd expected. His body was male perfection. A fine work of art, the hard body of a man who had a life filled with tough physical labor. Mending fences, mucking stalls, corralling cattle, pulling newborn calves out, hauling hay.

"What do you want? Tell me." His fingers traced the curve of her face.

"Everything. I want a memory I won't ever forget. Something real. You."

Gently, he pushed her back on the bed and covered her body with his own. He braced himself above her. "I want to give you all you want."

"Finally."

He slid her panties off, then teased her mercilessly with long, deep kisses, his tongue tasting every inch of her flesh as if he could eat her alive. As if he were a hungry man offered a five-course meal. When he pushed her bra aside with his mouth and suckled at her breasts, she went on fire with heat.

Reaching for him, she tried to pull him to her, tugging on the waistband of his boxer briefs. But it occurred to her that she'd forgotten something important. Protection. If there was one thing she'd learned from women like Jolette Marie, who loved to talk about sex, it was *never* to rely on the man bringing the goods. She'd planned to buy condoms, but she'd never gotten around to it.

"Wade, wait. I meant to…but I don't have any…any—"

"Protection? I've got you. It's my job to protect you in every way."

Oh, whew! She hadn't wanted to rely on him, but how nice to know that she could.

Once, she thought she'd be afraid of this moment. Worried to be so completely bare and vulnerable. Exposed. But she felt nothing of the sort. Instead, she felt cherished, safe, even…loved.

*Okay, let's not go there. Don't get ahead of yourself.*

*This doesn't have to mean love. It doesn't have to mean forever, just because you want it to.*

This was a risk, and she was taking it, right along with him. They were in this together, drawn to each other and giving in to this connection between them. An awareness that had always been there. Something deep and unguarded in her assured her that Wade would never be a mistake. She didn't know where the thought had come from or if it simply sprang from her own wish, but it felt real. Powerful. Like fate.

When she orgasmed once more under Wade's skillful ministrations, it was as if she'd left her own body. It was delicious.

"Oh my, that's so much better than chocolate *or* coffee." She threw back her head and moaned.

Wade snorted. "I would hope so."

"But you don't know how much I love coffee. I can't live without it." She reached for him, pulling him to her. "Please. I'm ready."

"Yes, you are. As ready as you'll ever be."

Within seconds he'd protected them both and then slowly entered her. Daisy gasped which made him stop.

"Too much?" Braced above her, he met her eyes, his own so dark and hooded, she hardly recognized him. "Want me to stop?"

"No, don't stop. It feels good. Really."

She didn't want to say it out loud because it sounded a little silly, but she felt a brand-new realization about herself. It seemed as if she now had an empty space inside her waiting to be filled. And she would stretch to make room for him. In her mind she pictured opening up for him, and when Wade went deeper it stopped hurting. She only felt a delightful friction that grew in intensity as he began to move.

A tide rose inside her that, for the life of her, she couldn't hold back. The sensation was one of losing control while gaining it back. She orgasmed again in a flood of waves of pleasure, releasing a tension she didn't know she'd been holding back. Wade followed, giving her the sweetest knowledge that she could bring him this kind of pleasure.

Her body was more powerful than she'd ever imagined.

Afterwards, he rolled and tucked her under his arm. Pressing a kiss against her temple, he said, "I swear it will be better for you next time."

*Better?* Better than this? No way. "I'm already addicted. How long before we can do it again?"

"Not long." He chuckled. "Give me a minute."

She caught her breath and kissed the scar on his arm. "Wade, do you ever miss the rodeo?"

"Sometimes I do, but I thought I missed the adrenaline rush. I found out that isn't what I miss at all."

"What is it?"

"It's the community. The way we would come together, and everyone knew their part. Even the animals. We competed against each other, but there's also a grudging respect. It's a sport not just anyone can do and we're proud of that. But the main person I've always competed against is myself."

"What does that mean?"

"I wanted to do better each time than I did the last time. It goes back to those early years, sitting on the miniature bull that was my first ride. Trying to beat my own score." He hesitated a beat. "Guess it's the way I was taught."

"I remember. Your father pushed you hard."

"You saw some of that."

"And how badly you wanted to please him."

"When I was a boy. But then the rodeo became all mine. The one thing I had that he could no longer control."

They were both quiet for several seconds, just caressing each other. She pressed her cheek against his chest and listened to the thudding sound of his heartbeat.

"Daisy, do you ever worry what will happen if you *aren't* Hank's biological daughter?"

"No, I don't think about that. It won't happen."

"I just wondered. I've been thinking that biology is only one part of what makes a family. Jorge was my father, but I never understood him. I doubt he ever understood me."

"I feel the same about Maggie, but I always had my father. I know him, or at least I thought I did."

She hadn't realized how truly unhappy he'd been for years. Foolishly, she'd imagined that she and her brothers were all he should need. The thoughts of a self-centered child.

"Maybe we don't ever get to know everything about our parents."

"Sure, I know that. It's just…I can't think of what it would do to my daddy." A sob she hadn't expected caught in her throat. "He's already been through so much. And I don't want to add to his pain."

He squeezed her tightly and kissed her temple. "Are you ever going to tell him you took the test?"

"I'm not sure. If I tell him, it will only be because I want to reassure him. But will that make it seem that I had my doubts I was really his daughter?"

"You know him better than I do, but I doubt that. He will understand that you had to be sure. Just please tell me you didn't do this because it's what I would have done."

"No, of course not." She put a finger to his lips. "This is all me. I made the choice."

"To be honest, I use to wonder if I could actually be my father's son. We were so different."

"But you loved him. I know you did."

"Yeah. I would have done anything to please him when I was young. To make him proud. But we had a difficult relationship. It's made me wonder if I should ever have children. I wouldn't want to ruin them the way my dad ruined me."

"You really feel that way? That he *ruined* you?"

"No, guess not. But for him, the rodeo was a status symbol. He'd brag about his son, the rodeo champ. That's not the way of the circuit. We try to keep it real. One day you're on top, the next you might be in traction. And skill isn't *always* a part of this. Sometimes it's luck which, by God, you never take for granted. But nobody liked my father much, and I had to defend him whenever he came around. Make excuses for him. Ultimately, he thought he created me. Turned me into the cowboy I became. You would think he considered the dangers of the profession. I don't think I'd want my son on a bucking bull. There are a lot of risks, and one of them is death."

She shivered at the thought of Wade dying. "You're talking to someone who rarely took any risks in life so maybe I'll never understand."

"It's not necessarily something to admire."

"For me, it is. The biggest risk I've ever taken is taking that DNA test."

"I'm glad to hear you admit it."

"Okay, you're right. It may not come out the way I want it to, and then I don't know what I'll do."

Wade brought her hand to his lips and kissed it. "You'll be okay because it won't change anything unless you let it. Hank is the father who raised you, who loved you, and never left you. That's a family."

But it would also mean she'd been abandoned twice, both by Rusty and Maggie.

"I didn't mean for this conversation to get so serious," Wade said, rolling her on top of him with a slow smile. "I'm ready to play again."

"Oh, yes, I can tell." She straddled him, threading her

fingers through his. "Am I ready for the advanced course yet?"

"Let's say *I'm* not ready to show you the advanced course yet. But let me show you something else. And I think you'll like this."

Two hours later, she could say that she did. Oh, very much.

IT TOOK MUCH LONGER than Wade thought it would to disentangle from Daisy.

First, he didn't want to go anywhere else. Second, he didn't want to do anything else.

Third, whenever he thought to go back outside and see about the barn, she'd change his mind. She'd move a certain way or give him a wicked smile and he was gone. Just toast. For someone who had no experience, she was gifted and talented. Incredibly responsive to him.

Normally, he'd have never let anything he owned sit in complete ruin, but he had Daisy in his bed. Eager and willing and sweet. Addictive. He wasn't going anywhere for a while.

And face it, the barn wasn't something that could be repaired overnight. It would take time, effort, and was he stalling? You bet.

"What was it like, when you got injured?" Her head was resting on his abs, silky hair fanned out.

She wasn't asking him how much it had hurt, but the question might have normally extinguished any flame. Or he'd have thought it would. He didn't speak for a moment, simply collecting his thoughts. Beyond those memories of the moment just after the injury, he hadn't allowed himself to think much about that day.

"If you don't want to talk about it, it's okay." Her hand slid up and down his arm, in soothing strokes.

"I was tired, but otherwise I was having a normal day."

Out in California, the day had been warm and dry. His favorite kind of weather. Not as dusty as Texas, but hot and dusty all the same. A typical rodeo. A disastrous outcome for him.

"What happened?"

"I just… I lost my focus."

He wouldn't mention the woman who'd been vying for his affection at that moment, because he'd determined long ago that hadn't been the problem. No woman had ever distracted him from his job and purpose: winning. He still hadn't put his finger on what had gone wrong. Hadn't zeroed in on why and how one normal day went south in an instant.

Were he still riding, he'd have worked this problem out. Analyzed back and forth until he had the answer, just so he'd never repeat that particular misstep again. But as it worked out, he hadn't been pressed to do that. His career was over. Now, he wasn't sure this would be worth exploring. To what end?

"Do you think you lost your focus because of her?"

He didn't have to ask who she meant. Daisy was talking about his mother. "No."

"We'd lost her so recently, and after the funeral you went right back out."

"I had to."

"I know, but…maybe that's why. It was too much, too soon. You were out there again like nothing had happened."

"No, that's not it. I'm sure. I was doing fine."

That's what she'd wanted. She'd wanted him to move on, live, love, and move forward with no regrets, knowing she was in a better place. And that's exactly what he'd done.

"Because I know I wasn't doing fine. I loved her, too, Wade."

"I know. And she sure loved you."

*You have no idea.* He threaded his fingers through her soft strands of hair, wanting badly to redirect this conversation.

He hadn't allowed himself to wallow in grief because that was not productive. So, he'd moved on, even if that had become exponentially tougher when coming back to his family home. Her home. Try as he might talk himself into the thought that this hunk of junk, this land, was his, too, this still felt like his mother's place. Eventually, he'd put away all her knickknacks and finally clear out her desk.

For now, he would live the rest of his life to the fullest, ignoring the pain in his arm.

And if he ever wanted to forget, he currently had himself a nice distraction. "Daisy?"

"Hm?" She lifted her head and turned to him with a lazy smile.

He beckoned. "C'mere."

She did, straddling him with a smile, and for the next few hours he did his best to distract them both.

WADE WOKE before dawn the next morning and slid a hand down Daisy's naked back. "Peanut, we have to go see about the barn. I can't believe I let this go all night."

She rubbed her eyes, her sleep-mussed hair falling every which way. "I had you otherwise occupied."

"I enjoyed that a lot more, true, but I think it's time for me to stop being selfish." He rolled out of bed and walked toward the shower. "Care to join me?"

"Yes." She sat up, sheets falling to reveal her beautiful breasts. "Wade?"

"Yeah?"

"I think you definitely need to stop calling me Peanut now." She winked.

"If you say so, sweetheart. But I do like Peanut."

"You should call me 'honey.' Peanuts are salty."

He quirked a brow. "And your point is…?"

She threw a pillow at him, which he caught midair.

After a pillow fight, and a shower together, they'd had a quick breakfast. Quick, because Daisy burned the grits. And the bacon. Fortunately, he had cereal.

"Don't come in the barn until I'm sure the structure is safe enough out here," he instructed.

Wade *had* secretly hoped the Model T would be toast and he could justify junking it and getting it off his ranch. If he couldn't sell it, he could donate it. He didn't need it around but he'd kept it till this point because it made Daisy happy and distracted her from her problems for a while. But no such luck. Not a dent or scratch to be found on the auto. Shit fire!

Daisy, of course, ignored his request to stay away and followed him into the barn.

"This is amazing. Look at how well it held up." Daisy ran her hand down the hood of the car.

"Careful or you'll get a splinter." He handed her a pair of gloves and she slipped them on.

"I wish you didn't hate this car so much."

"I don't *hate* it. Hating it would take too much energy." He bent to pick up pieces of wood, throwing them outside in a pile.

At least a beam hadn't fallen. A shiver went through him. He didn't want to think about the kind of damage that could have done to Daisy.

Daisy picked up a shingle and threw it in the pile. "If you don't hate it, then what would you call it?"

"A bad reminder."

"Of…?"

"Pride. Excess. Ego. Greed." He stopped to think. "I think that's it."

"Wow, no wonder you hate it!"

"The car reminds me of my father's worst traits. You might not remember, but he collected these. Bought one from my tournament winnings every time he could. Said it was an *investment*. For a rancher, that makes very little sense. We invest in farm equipment, ATVs, feed, cattle, horses. Of course, he wound up using these cars to further feed his gambling habit. When he lost, he sold a car, and went back to the tables."

"But he kept this one for you. There's probably a reason for that."

He thought the reason might be that his father simply ran out of time. One more loss and this one would have been gone, too. There was no real way to know. It was only after his death that Wade learned the enormity of his father's gambling addiction. And it had been a punch to the gut. Had Wade known he was funding his habit, instead of simply supporting the ranch, he would have stopped the rodeo a while ago. Or at the very least, he'd have stopped the bleeding. No pun intended.

Daisy stared up at the ceiling, and at the beam of sunlight, no longer held back by the impediment of a roof. "It's time for a good old-fashioned barn raising."

But he'd have to dig deep into the small amount of cash he had left for the materials even if he got the help from his neighbors with manpower. The plan had been to get this ranch profitable and *then* fix the barn.

"I'll start the phone tree," Daisy said.

CHAPTER 17

*The phone tree.*

Wade had almost forgotten about that anti-quated benefit of living in Stone Ridge. Any time someone needed help, the phone tree was alerted, and all the available men would head to the destination. Because he traveled so much, he hadn't been around for many of them, though he had participated whenever he was home.

The most recent of those times had been when little Jimmy Ray had wandered off after a town barbecue. A whole squad of men organized a search, and it had been Lincoln who found him. Shortly before that, he'd helped on repairs of the town's first school.

Being on the giving end of their system was one thing, but Wade never expected to be on the receiving end of the phone tree.

"Hang on." Wade followed Daisy into the kitchen where she picked up the landline. "I don't need to bother them. I can probably take care of this on my own. I'll just add it to the list."

*The growing list.*

"Wade, are you too *proud* to accept help?"

*Yes.*

He scoffed. "Absolutely not. But the phone tree is for people who are desperate. I can take care of this myself."

"Riggs asked for help when someone put a hole in the fence between your properties and let Satan through it. He had to repair it quickly, so he used the phone tree."

"That's different. There's no danger here, as long as *you* stay out of the barn."

Daisy ignored him, picking up the phone. When he reached to take the handset from her, she put a finger to his lips.

"Hello, Mima? Wade needs some men over here. The barn fell down. Yes, you heard me right. It's an old-fashioned barn raising. Tell Lincoln and Jackson, and then the next man on the list. I'm going to stick around and help the men."

She hung up, and when he held out his arms wide, she folded right into them. "There. It's done."

"And how are you going to help us, exactly?" He kissed her temple, taking in the sweet coconut scent of her hair.

"I'm going to take care of the car."

"Of course."

She wrapped her arms around his waist. "I would decorate the tree, but we need to do that *together*. Later."

"Right. We'll decorate the tree and then we'll decorate each other."

"I can't wait to see a big, red bow on you."

"I'm going to put a lot of tinsel all over you." He slid her a slow smile.

*"Tinsel?"*

"The silver stuff that takes forever to pull off, you find it in the house year-round, and probably still on the tree next

Christmas. I'm going to have a lot of fun taking it off you slowly and all year long."

"Aw."

For once, he'd said the right thing, judging by the sparkle in her eyes.

*Yes, Daisy. I want to be with you for a long time, should I be that lucky.*

He and Daisy pushed the Model T out of the barn and off to the side. They cleared the area of debris and wood. Then Wade went for his hammer, saw, and tools. Not long after, the men began to arrive in trucks. The Henderson brothers, Sean and Riggs, both upset that Wade hadn't run right over there yesterday after it all happened. He almost told them he'd been otherwise occupied and quite distracted but instead told them he'd been sulking.

"That's what we're here for," Riggs said, grabbing his tools from the truck bed. "Neighbors helping each other."

"But I haven't been around enough to help much."

"Well, that will change." Sean clapped Wade on the back.

It was good to know no one resented him for being gone so much, coming back only occasionally to see his mother or work for Hank between tournaments. Wade didn't think he'd been a good enough neighbor, not for years, but he would do better now.

Lincoln, Jackson, and even Hank arrived shortly thereafter, carrying tools and plenty of wood.

"I'll pay you back for all this wood," Wade protested to Lincoln.

"Yeah, you will. You can pay me back next time any of us is in trouble or in need. I'm sure you'll come through." Lincoln turned to Daisy. "Hiya. You got here quick."

"Yeah, well, I was already—" Daisy began, then stopped. Clearly, she'd lost her nerve. "Um, I was here to work on the car and saw all the damage."

"Did you *already* find a project while you're on furlough?" Jackson asked.

"She's fascinated by my old man's Model T."

"It withstood the roof falling in on it. Solid steel," Daisy said, flexing a muscle.

The way she loved that car was rather annoying. And also, a little inspiring. She didn't give up on old and broken things. Good to know.

"Did you hear it fall, Wade?" Lincoln said.

"Oh, I heard it. Ran for my shotgun until I realized the building had fallen down."

"Lucky thing that no one got hurt," Jackson said.

"Yeah, lucky." Wade met Daisy's eyes. She smiled at their private joke.

Within the hour, a whole crew of men had arrived. Jeremy, Levi, even old Lenny, who brought cold cuts and beer and set it all up on his tailgate. It was incredible to see the outpouring of support. Wade couldn't remember a time when his father had called for help. There had been plenty of times when he needed it, too, but to Jorge Cruz, asking for help meant admitting failure. He'd drilled that into Wade, too, and that's why he'd never asked for help from anyone in digging his way out of the hole that his father created for him.

This would be one more way he'd take a different path from his father. He would take the help same as he would always willingly give it. It was about community, and he'd fallen out of the rodeo just to find one that had always been here.

Around dinnertime, Winona and Delores drove over in a truck loaded with food. They served up fried chicken, mashed potatoes, onion rings, corn, fried okra, peach and apple pies.

"We've been cookin' all day between wrangling twins,"

Delores said, one baby on her hip.

Winona carried the other one on her hip as she dished out apple pie. If she'd ever been a stuck-up Nashville celebrity, as the rumor went, it sure didn't show. And Wade hadn't tasted food this delicious since his mother's home cooking. The memory brought about a fresh new wave of pain and he pushed it back down. She'd be proud of what they'd all done here today. And happy that Wade had accepted the assistance.

By the end of the day, the new frame was up, and part of the new roof, surprising even Wade as to how much could be done quickly with serious manpower. But the sun was setting and the temperatures dropping. A cold wind rapidly descended, the air moist and…

"It had better not snow," Wade muttered seconds before the first snow flurry fell.

They fell one after another like little pieces of cotton straight into the new barn. Wonderful. It almost never snowed in this part of Texas.

"Look, Joey!" Winona cried out, bouncing the baby in her arms. "It's snowing! Cal! Check it out!"

"Don't get too excited." Lincoln chuckled. "I'll be lucky to gather up the size of a snow cone to show Sammy."

"Everyone who can, meet back up here tomorrow and let's finish up the roof," Riggs ordered. "For now, let's all get somewhere dry and warm."

He took one of his sons and led his wife back to the truck. Delores followed them, holding the other twin. Knowing his time was limited, Wade ran from one man to the next, thanking him personally. Shaking each hand.

"No problem, son. This is what we do," said Hank.

"I'm happy to help." Derek clapped Wade's shoulder.

Wade thanked twenty men or more. The last men he had to thank were his best friends in the world. Lincoln, Jackson, and Beau Stephens. They accepted his thanks, adding their own disappointment that Wade hadn't called them all sooner.

"I still need to talk to you, Linc," Wade said. "But I've taken enough of your time today. Your wife and son are no doubt waiting for you."

"We'll talk soon. I'll be back tomorrow after morning chores." Lincoln headed to his truck, then called after Daisy, "Need a ride home? The roads will be icy."

"No, I'm fine," Daisy said from behind Wade. "Thank you, though."

"If it gets too icy, I'll drive her home," Wade said. "Don't worry."

"Oh, sure. Yeah." Lincoln climbed in his truck and adjusted his long legs. "Thanks."

He exchanged a quick look with Wade, and in that moment, he was sure that Lincoln understood something had changed. In the old days, they could almost read each other's minds. Then Lincoln shook his head as if he were talking himself out of the thought and drove off with a wave.

Wade pulled Daisy close. "He knows."

"Well, so what?" She burrowed her face in his jacket. "He'll be fine."

"I noticed *you* didn't tell him you were here all night."

"I started to, but…best to ease him into this, don't you think? And not start off by letting him know we're already sleeping together."

"Yeah." He pulled her into his arms, knowing she had to be cold. She wasn't wearing much of a jacket. "Get your sexy butt inside right now before you freeze."

As if last night and today wasn't enough, Daisy would also have a white Christmas.

207

She didn't think she'd ever been happier in her life. Just watching Wade's eyes light up when he saw how much help had come his way. Almost the entire town, save some men who were probably too old or too young to be of any assistance. Even Lenny showed up just to help with food and beverages.

Her heart expanded with joy for Wade. He was finally understanding that he didn't have to do this all alone. He'd mentioned missing the community of the rodeo circuit, and hopefully he'd see that he already had that here in spades.

He belonged. He was finally home for good.

"I'll make a fire," Wade said. "Then I'll drive you home."

She watched him work, squatting in front of the fire, the muscles on his forearms and back bunching. Lust swept through her like a tidal wave. She'd seen good-looking men before, but Wade was different. You couldn't label him handsome or a pretty boy. He was strong and...rugged. His dark hair and olive skin made him stand out in a crowd.

When the flames licked out of the fire, Wade came to sit beside Daisy on the leather couch. He put his arm around her, and she curled into his body.

"If you're trying to get rid of me, this isn't the way to do it."

"I don't want you to go. But you don't live here, Pea— I mean, I need to take you home."

That slip to call her Peanut again was classic, trying to throw up his walls again. Creating a safe distance between them. Because this cowboy had taken risks all his life but clearly never many with his heart.

This time, Daisy wouldn't have it. She was a risk-taker, too, damn it, and she'd proved that.

"What are you doing, Wade? Are you trying to put some distance between us again?"

"No!" he protested just a little *too* quickly.

"It's Lincoln, isn't it? It's bothering you that he suspects."

"I tried to tell him. It didn't work out. Today didn't seem like the right time, either." He studied the fire, his fingers playing almost absentmindedly with her hair.

"Please don't pull away from me. Lincoln is going to be just fine. It's none of his business."

"It's just…more than that. I'm in uncharted territory and while normally the thrill of that would be calling to me this… is different."

"How so?"

"When I saw you lying there, part of the barn on top of you…" He squeezed tighter. "It's different when someone you love is in danger. I don't mind it for me, but I don't ever want to see you like that again."

All Daisy heard out of that sentence was the word *love*. "You love me?"

"You know I do. I've known you all your life. Loved you for at least half of it."

"That's not what I meant."

He chuckled. "I know what you meant. You don't let me get away with much, and I like that. Now I realize it's exactly what I need."

"Because I love you, but I'm also *in love* with you. I'm not sure exactly when this happened, but before you say it, this doesn't have anything to do with last night. It's not that I think I have to wind up with the first man I ever slept with, even if it is you. It's just that…it's *always* been you. You know?"

He slid her a slow smile. "What do you mean last night had nothing to do with it? That wasn't love-inducing sex?"

"You know it was."

He kissed her, a long and deep kiss full of promise.

"You're not in this alone. I doubt that I'll ever be good

enough for you, but if you'll have this broke-down cowboy, then…I'm in. Sweetheart, I'm all in."

She smiled against his lips and kissed him back with all the love and emotion in her heart.

Because for the first time in her life, Daisy Carver felt truly and wonderfully…chosen.

# CHAPTER 18

*Dear Albert,*

*Well, I am just beside myself with worry. Daisy spends less and less time at home and more at that Wade's ranch. Claims it's something about a car project. Sometimes, I fear she's far more like her mother than any of us want to believe. She's always favored Maggie, looks-wise, but that's where their similarities ended. Because while Maggie thought of herself as the queen of England, little Daisy has always been a tomboy. Chasing after her big brothers, bringing home frogs and sticks.*

*Boys were her best friends. She rarely played with girls and dolls but preferred cars. But after she became a young lady, I'd be lying to say that I didn't notice little changes here and there. She wore only a certain type of Wranglers, and a size too small. She occasionally had her hair cut and styled by some fancy schmancy salon in Kerrville, and please let's not talk about the shoes.*

*Now, she's after a rodeo cowboy just like Maggie Mae. What is this mess? Albert, if she winds up pregnant, what am I to do? Help! I need help from beyond!*

"Get ahold of yourself, woman! You're hysterical. If I

wasn't a figment of your imagination, I'd have to slap you."
Albert appeared, sitting on the edge of their bed.

Still wearing the same Stetson he'd worn on the day he
dropped dead halfway to the barn.

"I've always loved you in that hat."

"Want to know what I think? You worry she's more like
*you*. After all, you were the one who raised her. The only
mother she's ever known."

"You're talking about Ray, aren't you?"

"The rodeo cowboy that broke your heart. Yeah, that's
who I'm talkin' about. Luckiest day of your life when you
met me. I was the best thing to ever happen to a heartbroken
teenager." He tapped his chest proudly.

Truer words were rarely spoken.

"He turned my head around, Albert. So bright and shiny
he blinded me with his devastating good looks and attention.
I thought he loved me."

"And where was this man from, again?" Albert cocked his
head and narrowed his eyes.

"Stop that! You know very well that he wasn't from Stone
Ridge. What does that have to do with it?"

"I think you know."

"You make it sound as if there's something in our water."

He shook his head. "Not the water. There's something
about the women."

Albert always did know the right thing to say. She'd give
him that.

"The biddies of SORROW always talk on and on about
how special the men are. But let's talk about you women
now. You *know* you're special, so you don't accept scraps
from your men. You want to be first, and so you are. Demand
what you deserve, and you'll get it. And our women *are*
special."

If this were true, and Albert was right, then maybe Daisy

also would demand to be first with Wade. This didn't have to be another "rodeo cowboy breaks young lady's heart romance."

This wasn't Lillian's story, after all.

It was Daisy's.

"Wade was raised by Rose, and he will love and treat our Daisy the way she should be."

"Oh, Rose." And just like that, tears flooded her eyes. "She should be here to see this. If only..."

"Those are the two saddest words in the world, you used to say. *If only*. Why not switch it up to 'but instead'? But instead of getting to see her son be with Daisy while she's alive, she'll have to see it from wherever she is right now."

"Albert, surely she's in heaven."

He winked. "Of course, darlin'. Don't you doubt it."

Lillian heard rattling around in the kitchen.

"She's home."

Lillian threw on a housecoat over her nightgown and rushed to the kitchen. Lately, she hadn't been getting up early enough to cook breakfast. She didn't see the point anymore. Now that Brenda took care of the ranch hands and cowboys, Lillian only had herself and Daisy. More often than not, Daisy ate a light breakfast on her way to work. All she seemed to care about was a steady diet of caffeine.

"Good morning, sugar."

Daisy spun around, a big smile splitting her face. "Morning."

*Oh, my girl, it is good to see you this happy.*

Every once in a while, the memory of those tear-streaked cheeks on three-year-old Daisy stole Lillian's peace. The rest of her life had been spent happily wiping away that pain. Daisy deserved true and lasting love. Happiness and security. A man who adored her. Everything.

"I haven't seen much of you around here lately."

"I'm sorry. I've been getting in so late every night, but I'll start having breakfast with you every morning." Daisy set a mug of coffee down in front of Lillian.

"There's no need. I just wonder who is taking up so much of your time."

Daisy froze in the middle of pouring her coffee and Lillian had her answer. "I've been meaning to talk to you about this."

"What is it, baby girl?" Lillian patted the seat next to hers, indicating Daisy should sit.

She did, but Lillian sensed a thread of reluctance. Fear struck her heart and for the millionth time she wished Albert were here if only to simply hold her hand.

"I have something to tell you and I...hope you're not angry with me."

Lillian steeled herself for the news. It couldn't be horrible news because Daisy seemed happy. Could she already be *pregnant*? But no, Wade hadn't even been home long enough. Maybe they'd run off somewhere to get married? No. She discounted that immediately. That wasn't Daisy's way. She'd want her family there. Perhaps...

"I took the DNA test."

Lillian set her mug down with a thud, and coffee sloshed around inside.

"Please don't be mad."

"I'm not mad, child. Just...surprised. I assume the results show you're Hank's child?" For what other reason could Daisy be so happy?

"I don't know yet. The results will come any day now." Daisy took a swallow of her coffee. "You're the first person I've told."

"You've been keeping this to yourself all this time? You must be in knots."

What a burden for her poor Daisy.

"No, I told Wade. He was the only one who knew what I was doing. And he's been there for me every step. He went with me to get the test when I asked him to take me. He held my hand. He…he…" Daisy's voice grew thick with emotion and her breath hitched. "We've grown so close because of all this. I just don't think I would have made it through this without him."

"You're scared, aren't you?"

"There are no guarantees. No matter what, I'll always be a Carver. I'll just find out if I'm one by blood, too. But there are all kinds of families and you'll always be mine. The only mother I ever had."

Lillian pushed back the emotion clogging her throat, because if she didn't, she wouldn't be able to talk. She wouldn't be able to reason with Daisy. "It isn't like you to take a risk like this."

"I know. I've played it safe all my life. I dropped my middle name. And I've tried my best not to look like her." Daisy took a breath. "But, Mima, if I'm not Daddy's daughter, we don't *have* to tell him. It might break his heart and I don't want that. I just had to know."

"Why did *you* have to know?"

"Because I don't like not knowing. All my life, this was supposed to be an ugly rumor. What if it's true? I can't be afraid of the truth. No more secrets, not for me."

Lillian nodded slowly. "You will tell *me* the results, won't you?"

"If you'd like."

"Now, of course, I *have* to know."

But Lillian didn't think this was a wise thing to have done since the outcome mattered so much to all of them. Even Daisy, whether or not she wanted to admit it.

"Did Wade talk you into this?"

"No! Why would you say that?"

"The boy has taken a lot of risks in his life. This would be just one more to him. But maybe some things should be better left alone."

"I disagree or I wouldn't have done this. And it was entirely up to me. He had nothing to do with my decision. I think secrets that are kept buried can only hurt people more in the long run."

"What will you do with the money if you're Rusty's daughter? Will you take it?"

"I don't want any of his inheritance, so I'll just let his brother take it all."

"And if he *is* your father, you don't want to know him?"

"I don't see why. He abandoned me just as much as my mother did. It took him years to be curious whether or not he actually had a daughter. Years spent as a rodeo cowboy, having a good ol' time. I don't want to know him now, even if he is my flesh and blood."

Dear Lord, Lillian hadn't *considered* that. If this were true, and this Mr. Rusty was her father, her girl had been abandoned twice. And the one man who had never left her side might not even be her real father. No. *No*, it wasn't possible. Hank was Daisy's father. There could be no other way.

"I'm sorry, I shouldn't have told you any of this. I hadn't meant to, but…you could tell there was something on my mind."

"Thank you for telling me. I'll take this with me to my grave."

"*What?*" Daisy blinked and reached for Lillian's hand. "Why? Is something wrong? Are you sick?"

"Don't worry none, sugar. But I'm old and won't be around forever." Especially the way this heart of hers ached at the moment. *That* couldn't be good.

"Whew, you had me worried." Daisy went back to her coffee.

"You and Wade seem to be spending a lot of time together," Lillian said carefully.

"At first, he was the only one I could talk to about all this. It wouldn't affect him one way or another and so it was easier to talk to him. Then, there was my car project over there. The Model T was taking my mind off my troubles."

"And...that's it?"

She hesitated. "I know you don't like Wade for me."

"Well, I may have overreacted."

"You think? Having a fainting spell when you heard we were dating?"

"*Fake* dating, you mean, or so you said."

"I wasn't lying!"

"But it turned into something real, didn't it?"

Daisy lowered her eyes and nodded.

"And does he feel the same way?"

"Yes."

Lillian could have warned the girl not to play with fire, but then again, she didn't know that Wade's own mother had predicted their love years ago. And if she was right, and it appeared that she had been, a long and happy marriage with many children had been assured.

At least, Lillian hoped, if Rose was right about the two of them then she was right about all of it.

"You know, Rose loved you very much," Lillian said, patting Daisy's hand. "She was quite friendly with your mother. You used to spend a lot of time over there, you and Maggie Mae. Wade used to entertain you, according to Rose. Only he could get you to stop whining."

"I don't remember that."

"No, you were far too young. I probably should have allowed you to spend more time over there after Maggie left us, but you wanted to stay close to home."

Facts were, Lillian did resent Rose for a time after Maggie

Mae left. Surely Rose knew *something* about where she'd gone, and why? They'd been close, after all. But Rose claimed not to know.

"I asked Wade about Maggie Mae. He said she was always nice to him."

"Your mother *was* nice, sugar. She made a terrible mistake but until that day, she'd been a good mother to all of you and always done the best she could."

Daisy nodded. "I suppose she had her own issues, whatever they were. Now that I'm older, I can almost forgive her. Maybe she felt second best to Brenda. Maybe she didn't feel loved by Daddy."

"Hank could have done better."

"But maybe sometimes you just can't help who you love."

"Yes, Rose would have said it's written in the stars." Fanciful talk for a rancher's wife, but that was Rose. "Wade is shiny and bright, and he'll take any woman's breath away, but is he solid? Is he someone you can count on? Be sure that he will love you till the day he dies, just like my Albert did. Because I want nothing less than that for you, my sweet girl."

WADE WOKE the next morning before dawn, feeling well rested for the first time in weeks. His arm hurt, as usual, but even that was at an acceptable and bearable level of pain. No pill required. He couldn't give full credit to great sex, though that certainly hadn't hurt anything. But sex had never given him this kind of peace before. It had never given him this kind of…certainty and purpose. Clarity.

He wondered exactly when he'd fallen in love with Daisy Carver. Because, damn, he sure didn't see *that* coming.

Had he fallen for her the night she beat him at pool or the night she cautiously met him behind the tree at the River-walk? Maybe it was the day he'd taken her for the DNA test, and she'd shown him a kind of courage he hadn't seen in the toughest and craziest rodeo cowboy.

Realistically, it could have well been the day he kissed her for the first time when she was only eighteen. And something wild and untamed had unfurled inside of him. Something that scared the spit out of him and had him running from her ever since that moment.

But there was no doubt now. When she slid those green eyes in his direction, when she tossed that blond hair, or shook her finger at him, he was a goner. Certified, one hundred percent *lost*. Taken. She gave him back everything he thought he'd lost. All that adulation and approval from the masses was replaced by one little spitfire that gave as good as she got.

And if he lived to be one hundred, he now believed she was all he'd ever need.

Wade was drinking the last dregs of his coffee when Lincoln showed up. Earlier than everyone else, which was no surprise to Wade.

He walked outside to meet him, just as the first rays of the sun were rising. "Hey."

Lincoln shut the door to his truck. "I'm early, so we can talk."

"Walk with me."

The morning air still carried a chill, but as predicted, the patches of snow were nearly gone. Wade walked next to his oldest friend, who might someday be family. He hoped.

"I like what you've done here," Lincoln remarked, nudging his chin toward the pastures.

"There's more work to be done."

"Plenty and always. That will never change."

"Maybe, but someday I'll no longer be in the red and trying to catch up. The ranch will be self-sustaining."

They walked to the edge of the field where in the distance the cattle could be seen, some grazing, some lying down.

"This is about Daisy, isn't it?" Lincoln said. "That's why you wanted to talk to me."

Wade simply nodded.

"Uh-huh. My bride and I talked long into the night. She saw something that I didn't without you even telling her. But I didn't catch on." Lincoln shoved his hands in the pockets of his leather jacket. "How long has this been going on between you two?"

"Not long at all. It really was fake in the beginning. I wouldn't have lied to you. I never have."

"I know." Lincoln nodded. "I'm hardly in a position to judge you. I fell for Beau's little sister, after all. He was okay with it."

"Sadie has loved you half of her life. And Beau knew it."

Lincoln kicked a rock with his boot. "And if I'm being honest, I know Daisy has loved you for half her life, but I had hoped it was a crush. I just didn't see anything ever coming of it. You weren't ever going to settle down. You weren't going to leave the rodeo."

"I never thought I'd say this but I'm damn glad about the injury. Happy to be a broke-down cowboy. If I hadn't been stopped, I would have missed out on the best thing that ever happened to me."

"Daisy?"

"Don't sound so surprised." Wade chuckled. "Swear to God, Linc, I'm in love with her."

Lincoln grinned. "Hot damn. How about that?"

"Buddy, no one's more shocked than I am. Just didn't see this coming. Had I seen it, maybe I would have stepped aside."

"Why?"

"We both know that she can do better than me."

"Nah, I don't know a better man."

"I thought I couldn't fall in love. Thought it had been beaten right outta me. But she surprised me."

"Well, that's our Daisy. She never gave up on you." Lincoln clapped Wade's back.

"She doesn't give up on people. Anyone she loves."

"You're damn lucky to be one of them."

"And don't I know it."

They stood quietly for a few minutes, two old friends watching the sunrise.


By MIDDAY, Wade had himself a brand-new barn. And it was far better than the first.

After the crew had left, he was just about to rustle up some lunch when he remembered checking the mailbox for Daisy. And the envelope had finally arrived, a plain and white letter-sized envelope from the laboratory. Simple enough. Able to change many people's lives. This little piece of paper might destroy everything, or simply cement it into place. He walked back with the envelope, turning it over in his hands, wishing he had X-ray vision.

Because one thing had become clear to him since the moment he realized he'd fallen in love with Daisy. This suddenly felt like a huge risk to him as well, like one that had the power to upend his world. But only if it didn't contain the right answer. Surely it would. The odds were fifty-fifty anyway, and on some days, he'd call that good odds. He'd been a glass-half-full type of guy for most of his life.

If Daisy wasn't Hank's daughter, it would make no difference to Wade. That hadn't changed. But what had changed was that he understood, whether she wanted to admit it or not, the wrong outcome was going to destroy Daisy. And suddenly the risk felt a lot closer to home for him. He wished maybe he'd tried to talk her out of this, but if he had, maybe they wouldn't have become this close. He might not have fallen in love with her but still be ambling around this big ranch trying to deal with feeling so alone even with an entire town behind him.

He'd felt undeserving of anyone's help, but Daisy had changed all that for him. Because if she loved him, there must be something fundamentally good and worthy in him. And it was likely the same trait his mother saw. He was going to go out on a limb and call that good and worthy thing in him his heart. The one part of him that had never been battered, bruised, and broken on the circuit. He'd protected that organ fairly well, all things considered.

After lunch, someone was at his door again. He opened it to find the lady from the dating show, along with Beulah.

"Hello there, Wade," said Beulah.

"Come on in, ladies." Wade held the door open, making a sweeping motion with his arm. "Would anyone like some lunch? It's a casserole."

"How sweet of you to ask, but no. This should be quick." Beulah looked expectantly at the woman next to her.

*Was her name Georgia? Oh no, Savannah.*

"Great news, Mr. Cowboy!" Savannah said. "I was able to negotiate a cash offer for you to do the show. The producers are on board. All I need to do is have them watch some film of you in action, roping those cows and riding those bulls. You're exactly what we need. What size tux do you wear?"

"Now there's something you don't hear every day. I have no idea what size I wear, Miss Ackerman, seeing as I don't believe I've ever worn a penguin suit."

"No problem, we'll take your measurements."

Wade held up his palms. "Hold up. I *never* agreed to this."

"Why, Wade Cruz, are you saying no to this generous

offer?" Beulah nudged Savannah. "Show him the money. That's all these young people seem to care about."

"Of course." Savannah whipped out what appeared to be a several-inches-thick contract and flipped to a page. She handed it to Wade. "*This* is what we're talking about."

Wade was sure his eyes bugged out of his head. This figure was equivalent to winning a tournament, one of the biggest. This money could secure his future on the ranch. And realistically, when could he ever earn this kind of money again?

All for dating a bunch of women?

*And promising to marry one, Einstein.*

A lot of money, and he couldn't take a penny of it. No question. He handed the contract back.

"Very generous."

Beulah clapped her hands. "Wonderful!"

"And I can't take it." Wade removed his hat and ran a hand through his hair.

"Why can't you? Don't *tell* me it's not enough money for you." Beulah clutched her chest as if the very thought would bring on full cardiac arrest.

"It's plenty, and I would do it, but the thing is…I'm taken."

"Since when?" Beulah went hands on hips. "I want a *name*, and I want it now. Don't you care about your town, young man? This is your community. You're just lyin' to an old woman just like you did before."

"Not like before. It really is Daisy. At first, we *were* pretending. But I promise you that I'm not pretending anymore. I'm in love with her."

"Butter my biscuit! You mean Rose was right? You and *Daisy?*"

Wade nodded, smiling a little because he didn't seem able to help it.

"What's happening?" Savannah said. "Is he refusing the money? I don't understand."

"Yes, he is," Beulah said, holding up her index finger, pontificating. "Proving, as I firmly believed, that love has *nothing* to do with money."

"Well, of all the nerve," Savannah said. "Do you know how many heads I had to go over to get this money for you? How many hours of *rodeo* I had to watch? And now you refuse it?"

"Don't worry, we'll find someone else."

"Well, I don't know if we will," Savannah said, stalking off. "I don't understand you people."

"Our young ladies in town get first dibs on our men." Beulah followed her. "I thought you understood this. But we have plenty more where Wade came from. Why, I've already spoken to Sean…he's a rancher, and his brother is married to Winona…"

Her voice drifted as she followed Savannah out the front door.

Wade watched all that money walk away, wishing he could have taken it if nothing else for Daisy's sake. If only it wasn't a stupid dating show. He could promise her the future she deserved. Unfortunately, the strings attached to that mess would lose him what he really wanted. Kind of a catch-22.

Besides, he'd just determined the cost of his soul. Priceless.

Which didn't make this any easier.

## CHAPTER 19

*T*he night of the Nativity play arrived, and Daisy expected Wade to meet her at Trinity Church. She'd had to come with Mima, Jackson, Eve, Lincoln, and Sadie because Sammy was starring in the play. It was a family affair. Even Daddy and Brenda came, eager to see Sammy nail the part. The kid was so cute Daisy didn't see how anyone couldn't love him. Perfect casting. Ha!

The manger scene was set up outside the steps of the church, complete with a cow from the Henderson farm, and a couple of lambs from a farmer from Nothing. Some of the kids from Sadie's classroom were playing Mary, Joseph, and the Angel Gabriel. Pastor June was herding them all like tiny cattle.

"Do you think it's too cold outside?" Sadie said, clutching Sammy to her breast. "I don't want him to get sick."

"Now, sugar, don't worry," Mima said. "Our Sammy is made of tough stuff."

"Just like his daddy," Eve said.

"He is the savior to the world, Sadie," Jackson quipped. "You *have* to share him."

"Jackson!" Eve scolded, but she had a smile on her face.

"You're hilarious." Daisy elbowed Jackson.

"Thank you for noticing, Shortie."

"Has anyone seen Wade?" Daisy asked. "He should be here by now."

And then she saw him ambling toward them, wearing his black Stetson and a slow smile. Her heart tugged with an almost painful tenderness. She loved this man so much she almost couldn't breathe when he walked into a room. His gaze landed on her, as usual taking her in like he'd never seen her before, even though they'd practically grown up together. This had always made her feel...new.

"Go kiss your boyfriend like a proper girlfriend does," Lincoln said.

Daisy whipped her head around to see if her big brother was teasing. The expression on his face told her everything she needed to know.

"He told me just this morning."

"Told you what?" Jackson said. "What am I missing here?"

"Keep up, son," Mima said.

"I'll tell you later," Lincoln said, then turned to Daisy. "Or maybe Daisy will."

Taking her cue, Daisy walked straight toward Wade's open arms in front of the entire family. And she shouldn't have been surprised at the chorus of *Aws*. Mostly coming from the women, sure, but she would take it. She heard their voices carrying behind her.

"*What a shock,*" *Jackson chuckled.* "*Like I didn't see this coming.*"

"*It's so sweet and took way too long.*" *Eve sniffed.* "*I'm so happy I might cry.*"

"*Me too,*" *Brenda said.* "*Here, I brought some tissues.*"

"*Rose was right all along,*" *Mima said.*

*"I really don't understand how anyone could have missed this,"* Sadie said.

*"Baba, bibi,"* said Sammy.

*"That's right, Son,"* Hank said. *"About time."*

"Hey," Wade chuckled, folding her into his arms. "Guessing everyone knows about us now."

Daisy pressed her face into the warmth of his chest. "And they're okay with it."

"Even your grandmother?"

"As long as I'm happy."

As the play began, Pastor June reading from the Bible, everyone drew closer and assembled. Daisy stood, Wade behind her, his arms wrapped around her waist. The cow began to moo in the middle of the most important scene. One lamb wandered off, and Sammy had a fit when Sadie dared to put him in the makeshift crib and walk a few inches away from him. So, she carried baby Jesus, and the rest of the play had to go on like that.

It was funny, and cute, and just what one expected from a play starring a cow, lambs, children, and a baby.

Later, after the play had ended, and everyone got treated to Christmas cookies and hot cocoa, Wade drove Daisy home to his place.

And even though it was a little chilly outside, Daisy rolled the window down and stuck her head out. She let the Texas wind blow through her hair as she smelled the welcome scent of fresh-cut grass, the humidity in the air a gift at this time of the year.

It just didn't get any better than this. She had everything she'd ever wanted.

When Wade pulled in and parked, Daisy climbed out of the truck and ran into the moonlit field.

"Catch me if you can," she called out, spinning her arms like the lady in *The Sound of Music.*

Like some kind of a loon. That was her. She was a loon now.

Crazy in love and stupid happy.

"I can." Wade easily caught her from behind and pulled her to him. "How old do you think I am?"

"You're not old at all," she said, leaning her back into him.

"Older than you, but young enough to keep up." He spun her around to face him. "Hey. I need to tell you something."

"Tell me something." She curled her hands around his neck.

"Your results came today."

That took the steam right out of her. "Oh."

"You don't *have* to open that envelope." He lowered his arms around her waist, settling his hands at the small of her back. "Not if you don't want to. No one will ever know but you and I."

"But…I took the test. Why wouldn't I open it?"

"It scares you and I can see that now. You don't have to do this."

"You already told me that."

"Maybe I should have talked you out of it."

"Why would you?"

"Because I don't want you to get hurt, and it feels like a bigger chance to take now."

"I love you, too, Wade." She smiled. "Are you scared for me? Because I'm not."

"I love you, and I'm…yeah, a little bit scared."

To know her fearless rodeo cowboy was scared for her was the most tender thing she'd ever seen.

"And just like I was okay when the barn fell down, I'll be okay this time, too. No matter what."

"Swear that to me."

"I pinky swear." She held out her finger.

He took it, wrapped it around his own and brought both to his lips to brush a kiss. "Okay."

In that moment, with Wade's love and quiet, unrelenting support, Daisy considered that she might *not* open the envelope. Why bother when she had everything she'd ever need? She didn't need to know, when her heart was already so certain.

Later that night, she lay tangled in Wade's arms, her cheek resting on his chest. He had a powerful heart, thudding with steady, even beats. It reassured her more than she would have believed. He'd live a long life and she'd never have to lose him.

Not to the rodeo. Not to a reality dating show. Not to someone else.

Here was someone who loved and would never leave her.

"Do you know what we forgot to do again? We forgot the poor tree. It's two days before Christmas."

"We got it late. There's nothing sayin' that it can't go up on Christmas Eve."

"That's what we'll do. Make a night of it."

"Sounds good."

"Hey? Did you ever hear back from the show about the money?"

"Yeah. They came by earlier today. The offer was…generous."

Daisy sat up. "Are you kidding me? I didn't think they actually would. They never offer money. They must have really wanted you."

"It doesn't matter. I refused their kind offer because I'm taken."

Daisy's heart was a quivering mess of ribbons and curls. "I can't believe you did that for me."

"And I'd do it again."

"What did Beulah say?"

"She didn't believe me at first, and we sure didn't help the situation by lying. But in the end, I convinced her."

"Was she too upset?"

"Not at all. She explained to the lady that the women in Stone Ridge have first dibs." He tugged on a lock of her hair.

"Thank goodness I saw you first." She gave him a long, deep kiss. "But I hate that you didn't get that money."

"It's money I didn't have before so no big loss."

"I'll make it up to you. I'm going to be the best girlfriend you've ever had."

He cocked his head and smiled. "Sweetheart, that's a *very* low bar."

"We can't have that. But I do have an idea."

"What's that?"

She slid one finger slowly down his abs, and lower… watching his expression darken with heat. "I've been reading, and I think I'm ready for the advanced course."

"Oh, yeah." He grinned, splaying his hands behind his neck.

And then she proceeded to rock his world.

During the night, Daisy woke to rays of ambient moonlight spilling through the blinds. Wade was asleep next to her, soundly, one arm thrown over her waist. She shifted, not wanting to wake him, but desperately needing a drink of water. Those darn holiday cookies always made her parched.

Sammy was so cute tonight, his dimpled smile so reminiscent of her big brother. He was sort of Lincoln's mini-me. Just like that she pictured Wade's son, a little carbon copy of him. Running around climbing and jumping off everything. She would watch him like a hawk.

Finding a cold water bottle in the fridge, she uncapped it, then walked over to the framed photo of Rose smiling back at her. She picked up the photo and kissed Rose's sweet face.

"I miss you, Rose, and I promise to take care of him.

Forever."

The photo was one of those understated professional photos taken for Trinity's congregation directory a few years ago. Pastor June had hired a photographer and asked families to come and have their pictures taken. Daisy remembered the day well, feeling badly for Rose. She took her photo alone. Her husband had died, and Wade was away touring at the time.

She was such a sweetheart that, even though not technically or by blood, in every sense of the word she was a part of everyone's family. Daisy had loved her, too, like a mother or a special aunt.

No one ever thought Wade would be back to stay after Rose died, but somehow both Daisy and Rose knew that he would.

A sense of connection pulsed through her, a deeply rooted knowledge about the past and the future. If Daisy ever had a daughter with Wade, she'd be Rose's granddaughter by blood. And a finer bloodline could not be had. Her children would not just be *Maggie's* grandchildren, but Rose's grandchildren. And Daisy would make sure they'd always know about her.

On the way back to the bedroom, Daisy spied the envelope lying on the counter where Wade had apparently left it. How could something so thin contain such important information? Well, she was no longer afraid of this letter. Nothing here could hurt her when she had everything she needed.

Using a fingernail, she ripped open the envelope, took out the paper, and read. There was some verbiage about the testing process, their accuracy rating, their procedure. Three columns, the one for mother blank. There was a column for alleged father, one for child, and at the top of each "Alleles Called."

Skimming, Daisy went to the part she wanted and for the

second time, her life flashed before her eyes.

The lines on the paper were squiggly and hazy.

She had to read it twice. Three times.

*The alleged father cannot be excluded as the biological father of the tested child. This conclusion is based on the matching alleles...*

WADE WOKE with a start to the guttural cries of a wounded animal. He sprang out of bed. Daisy wasn't next to him but he wasn't processing all coherent thoughts at the moment. Just ones involving the urgency of that horrible sound. Pulling on pants, he ran for his shotgun, and found Daisy lying on the floor in the middle of the kitchen. *She* was the source of the caterwauling.

Curled in a fetal position, sobbing, the damn letter crumpled to her chest.

His heart must have certainly stopped. Just seized in his chest, stunned. Fatally wounded.

*No, no, no.*

"Daisy?" He squatted next to her, turning her face to him. "Sweetheart, look at me."

She handed him the letter though he didn't really need to read the results. He already knew, of course.

Daisy was not Hank Carver's biological daughter.

Because he didn't know what else to do, he lay on the floor, too, and curled her into his arms. He caressed her hair, her face, her arms, her back. He didn't bother talking but held her close until the guttural wails began to slow. Until her breathing was reduced to the painful sound of halting skips between uneven breaths.

"It's okay, baby. You're still you. Hank *is* your father. And no one else has to know about any of this. It's just between you and me."

"I d-don't care anymore wh-who knows. I'm a joke. The

biggest cliché in the world. I'm Daisy Mae, d-daughter of a buckle bunny and a rodeo cowboy who had a one-night stand."

"You know it's not that simple."

"How is it not simple? My mother was a terrible wife, a cheater, and my father was the man who *cheated* with married women! Does it get any worse than this?"

*Yes. It gets worse if I lose you. It gets worse if you blame me for taking you to get the test. For inadvertently encouraging you.*

*It gets worse if you can't bounce back from this.*

But she would. Had to. This was Daisy Carver, and she didn't take shit from anybody.

"No, *your* father is Hank Carver, and he does not cheat with married women. He never abandoned you and he never would. That man is your father."

"I wanted him to be more than anything. I was so sure. I wanted to be *his* flesh and blood. And I'm not. I'm just so *angry* with everyone."

"Yeah, I get it."

"These two *people* played with other people's lives and hearts for a few minutes of pleasure. For sex. No *wonder* I was a virgin for so long."

She gazed at him from under lowered lids, almost seeing straight through him, and in that moment, he wondered if she was seeing a piece of Rusty in Wade. If she was judging him, too, for every woman he'd ever casually slept with. Some of whom, Lord help him, might have been married for all he knew. He'd always asked, always wanted to be sure, but people were known to lie.

The fear that spiked through him was new and fresh and real. He thought for sure he was a dead man walking. This was judgment from someone he loved. Maybe it had all been too good to be true, this love and devotion from someone so pure and good.

He stood and reached for her. "Let's go back to bed. We'll think about this more in the morning. Things will look better, you'll see."

"I don't see how," she said, allowing him to pull her up to her feet. "Should I take the test again? Do you think the test could be wrong?"

He shrugged. Probably not, but why not leave that possibility open for now. But no, it *wasn't* wrong. He felt it. Knew it. And so did she.

"Either way, we both need some sleep. And I swear to you, I will find some way to make this better. To fix this for you." He brought her hand up to his lips and brushed a kiss across her knuckles.

Hand low on her back, he steered her to the bed and pulled back the covers. She crawled in, and in a moment that renewed his hope, she opened her arms.

She didn't have to ask him twice. He curled her into his body, holding her tightly against his chest. "You'll get through this."

She didn't reply, just buried her face in his neck and fell back asleep within minutes.

He dreamed of their children. Someday. One little blonde girl with green eyes like her mother's. She'd be interested in cars, too. And hopefully, with any luck, horses as well. He'd get a lamb and goat or two for the kids. A whole petting zoo.

Their children would grow up never having any doubt of who their parents were, or that they loved each other and were loved beyond measure. Wade would never abandon his family, and he'd never sacrifice Daisy for anything or anyone else. Not even rodeo, Lord help him, and he never thought *that* would ever happen.

He slept soundly all night long.

The next morning, he woke up, annoyed because Daisy wasn't in his arms. But she could be making the coffee or attempting for the second time to fix him an edible breakfast. He told her she didn't need to cook, that he would, but typically the girl wasn't giving up easily.

"Daisy?" he called out. "I'm going to hit the shower, but first, coffee. You've got me addicted, too."

He walked into the kitchen, finding no Daisy. And no *coffee.* Not even the rich, dark smell of it lingering in the air. More than anything, this hit him as ominous. Pulling the front curtains back, he peered outside to find his truck gone. *She'd taken his truck.*

"Damn it, Daisy. Where the hell did you go?"

It was early morning, the day before Christmas, and he knew for a fact not a blessed establishment would be open in Stone Ridge. Everything closed up tight as a drum, even the General Store. The church would be the only place open and he wondered if Daisy could have gone there to yell at God. It was possible, but his first order of business was to check closer to home. The crumpled letter sat on the counter, deceptively innocent. Taunting him. He quickly showered, dressed, and pocketed the letter. Then he went for his only option: the ATV.

He thought he'd calmed her down the night before. But either she'd faked it well, or she'd had her second wind of fury in the morning. While he wanted to believe there was some other, lighthearted reason she'd disappeared from his bed without saying goodbye, he had nothing. Zilch.

She clearly wanted to get away from him before he'd talk her out of whatever fool thing she was about to do. It would help if he could imagine what that fool thing *was* and get there fast enough to stop it. She already mentioned that she didn't care anymore who knew the truth, so maybe she was headed to the Double C.

On the way, he thought of everything he'd done wrong because the way she'd handled this *had* to be his fault. First, he could have more strongly discouraged Daisy from taking the test. He thought he'd been supportive, but at the time he hadn't fallen in love with her. A man protected those he loved from even the possibility of pain.

He should have stopped this test. Daisy wasn't like him, fearless, with possibly a bit of a death wish on his back. Well, that wish was gone now. He wanted to live a long and healthy life with Daisy even if the boredom of life on a ranch killed him. No matter. He'd die a slow death in her arms and would enjoy every single minute.

ATVs weren't meant for highways, even two-lane ones. Wade stuck to the dirt gutters as he pushed the sucker for all its horsepower. He slowed when a pickup came up next to him, and a window rolled down.

"Lose a cow?" Lenny called out.

Wade waved him away.

*Lost my woman.*

"I'll help you find the cow," Lenny said. "Not doing much else. Just got back from selling the last tree on my lot."

"You sell *trees*, too?"

"Idle hands, devil's work, and all that."

"I'm fine, Lenny! Move it along."

"Okay, champ! But you look a might ridiculous, you don't mind my sayin'." With that, he waved and finally drove off.

Wade could only *imagine* the picture he made driving down the main highway in an all-terrain vehicle. From the cheering stands of a rodeo exhibition to an ATV that was having trouble pushing sixty.

*You've come a long way, cowboy.*

He'd come home, defeated, to a ranch he almost didn't remember. A man with a bum arm. A beaten man he barely recognized. Now, he was head over heels in love with a woman whose entire life had just blown up.

Fortunately, he was familiar with that type of scenario.

And he wasn't going to just sit by and watch *this* destruction happen.

He had to fix this.

Finally, he got close enough to the Double C Ranch to turn down a dirt road that led to Lincoln and Sadie's cabin. Knowing ranchers' hours, they'd be awake. In fact, he'd probably find Lincoln in the fields. But Daisy wouldn't be out there with him. If anything, she'd be inside with Sadie. Crying. Commiserating. She'd have to tell someone in her family, and Sadie was possibly the person least likely to be invested in the outcome.

When he drove by the main house where Daisy lived with Lillian, he didn't see his truck. And he didn't spy it anywhere on their land. Still, he had to take a chance.

He knocked on the door and Sadie opened it, holding Sammy on her hip. "Hey, Wade."

"Is Daisy here?"

Her eyes widened. "No, why would she be *here*? Did you guys have a fight?"

"No, it's nothing like that. But…something happened."

"What?"

"She's upset, you're right about that. Took my truck and left early this morning."

"Did you check Lillian's yet?"

"I drove by and didn't see my truck. Thought maybe you'd seen her earlier."

"I'll call Lillian," Sadie said, and Wade followed her to the landline in the kitchen. "Hi, Mima. Is…um, Daisy awake yet?"

Wade winced. She hadn't spent the night at her home, but with him. What kind of a man didn't know where he'd put his girlfriend?

"No, I just couldn't remember if we were supposed to go to the church tonight at seven or at eight. Oh yes, you're right, I should have asked you first. Seven? Oh, okay. I'll talk

237

to you later." She hung up. "She hasn't seen her since last night."

He palmed his face, trying to think.

"Wade, what happened?"

"I need to find her. I'm worried she…" He pulled his hat off and ran a hand through his hair. "She…"

"Tell me."

Rather than tell her, Wade pulled the folded piece of paper from his pocket and handed it over.

He watched as Sadie's face crumpled.

"Oh, no. I…I suspected this. Did you know she was having the DNA test done?"

"I went with her. That night after she talked to everyone, she considered it. Then she just went for it."

*She asked me what I would do, and I told her I'd take the damn test. Should have kept my damn mouth shut.*

But he was a risk-taker at heart even if some risks, he'd now learned, shouldn't be taken.

"She asked me to not tell anyone and I didn't."

Sadie reached to pat his arm. "No, I totally understand."

Maybe sensing his mother's distress, Sammy started fussing.

"I…I need to tell Linc." She headed to the walkie-talkies they kept nearby.

Wade stopped her. "Maybe you don't need to do that yet. I'm going to find her, and then we'll come back and discuss this. It isn't the end of the world, and I told her that."

"It must feel like it to her." Sadie held Sammy close, kissed his forehead. "The day before Christmas. Poor Daisy."

"Some gift," Wade muttered, and then his brain woke up.

*Gift.*

Wade knew exactly where he might find Daisy, and he would need a vehicle.

## CHAPTER 20

*D*aisy strode through the pasty-white hallways of the hospital. This morning, she'd been awake before dawn and known exactly what she wanted to do. Still, she'd stayed in bed listening to the sound of Wade's quiet and even breaths. Trying to decide if she should tell him about her plan. But if she told him, he'd talk her out of this. Or he'd want to come with her.

This was one thing she had to do alone. Face the man who'd wrecked her family. The man who'd wrecked her life. Were Maggie anywhere to be found, Daisy would do the same with her.

Now, the sounds of her boot heels thudded against the linoleum floor.

She approached the nurse on the second floor of the cardiology wing. "I would like to see Rusty Jones, please."

"Visiting hours are after five o'clock," the snooty nurse said. "Come back then."

"No," Daisy said. "I'm his daughter, and I need to see him now."

"His daughter? Which one?" The nurse flipped through some forms on the desk.

*Aw, hell no.*

"He has more than one?"

"Two, I think? No one knows each other, apparently. But it's the first time I've seen *you* around." She studied Daisy with narrowed eyes.

"Yes, I've been out of town. Daisy *Mae* Carver. He'll recognize the name."

"Have a seat." The nurse indicated a row of empty chairs. "I'll check with his doctor and see if he's up for visitors today."

Well, if he wasn't up for visitors, Daisy supposed she would stick around until he was. She'd driven all this way, after all, not even taking the time to leave Wade a note. Regret pulsed through her because he'd likely wake up and be worried to find her gone. With *his* truck.

She'd seen the regret in his eyes last night. His girlfriend was the daughter of two horrible people who obviously didn't know the meaning of loyalty. Of faithfulness. Would Wade view her the same way? Had her stupid DNA determined that she'd wind up like her mother? No man would want a wife like Maggie.

Daisy had two strikes against her. She didn't have Hank's DNA, but that of a no-good, cheating, rodeo cowboy. With *three* daughters? Seriously? Were they all illegitimate, or was she the only one? Daisy burned with anger. If Rusty wasn't dead yet, maybe she'd help facilitate that.

A couple of long hours later, the nurse gestured to the room. "You can go in and see him. Make it a short visit."

"Oh, don't worry." Daisy stomped toward the room. "This won't take long."

But when she crossed the threshold of the doorway, all the hot air whooshed out of her. She barely recognized the man she'd supposedly met at her auto shop a year or so ago. That man had been lively and wily. Funny, with his South-west idioms. Now, his face was pale against his shock of white hair. His arms were attached to various leads, the skin purple and blotchy in places.

He didn't look like he'd ever been on a bucking horse.

"Daisy Mae," he said in a gravelly voice.

"I go by *Daisy*. Just Daisy."

"You look just like your mama. Man, she was beautiful." He beckoned her closer. "I heard the news. And I'm sorry."

*Sorry*. That's something she hadn't expected to hear out of the man.

"It's too late to be sorry."

"You're right about that, young lady. But I can't go back and change things, so all I have for you is the sorry."

It was hard to argue with that. "I don't want to be your daughter."

"I know."

"I… I'm just here to tell you that I already have a father. His name is Hank Carver and he never abandoned me. He was always by my side, practically my best friend when I was growing up. You and my mother both left me. So, whether or not my DNA matches yours, that doesn't matter to me." She took a breath. "I just wanted to tell you that I already have a family."

"Well said, darlin'. Well said. Hank is a much better man than I ever was. I guess what happened is an accident of biol-ogy. And I'm sorry you had to find out. I never wanted the stupid DNA test. I was going to leave you my money either way. It was my fool brother who insisted. Maybe we'd all have been better off not ever knowin' for sure."

"I thought so, too, but I'm glad I know. Secrets shouldn't be kept in a family. I plan on telling mine the truth and they'll accept me anyway. That's who they are. Good people, like me."

"I'm glad to hear it."

She cleared her throat. "Do I have *sisters*?"

"'Fraid so. They came out of nowhere when word got out I was dyin'. Funny how that is. I had a little money set aside from all my years in the rodeo. You're the only one I thought might actually be mine. The timing and all."

"Or because my mother was kind enough to tell you?"

"Now, I know you must hate her, and I can't blame ya. But ya know, darlin', your mother was a very sad woman. She told me that she'd fallen in love with a man who still loved someone else. After a while it didn't work anymore. She felt that she deserved better."

"You?" Daisy snorted.

"Heck no, not me. I think I was pretty much nothing to her but a diversion. Contrary to what you might think, hookin' up with rodeo cowboys was not something she did all the time. She wasn't what we like to call a buckle bunny. Got the feelin' this was a one-time deal for her. She said she was going back to try to work things out with her fella."

"Did you know that she was married?"

"No, I didn't. Can't recall if I asked."

"You *should* have asked."

"Maybe, darlin', but I wasn't the married one."

"Are all you rodeo cowboys like this?" She waved her hands. "Spreadin' your seed around, makin' the world a better place?"

Daisy had spent her life trying to be different than Maggie. How on earth had she wound up in the same place? Here she was, in love with another rodeo cowboy. Who knew how far and wide he'd spread his seed? The thought choked off her airway.

"We're not all 'seed spreaders,' as you like to say." He held up air quotes. "Some cowboys are family men who travel with their wives. Sometimes the children, too. Others are loners and dead serious about winning. No time for hanky-panky. Only some of us are like me, or how I used to be."

She didn't know that she believed this man, but it didn't matter.

"There's no point in talkin'. I just thought I'd come in person to tell you that I don't want your money."

"Take the money," a man said from behind her. Daisy whipped around to find the other Mr. Jones in the doorway, Rusty's brother. "Hello, Daisy."

"I'm only here for a minute."

He held up a palm. "I understand. Don't let me interrupt, but it's my opinion that Rusty owes you *this* at the very least."

"I owe her a hell of a lot more than that. But this is the best I can do."

"Think of the money as a gift. No strings attached. Rusty doesn't expect you to visit his grave or be a devoted daughter in death."

"Well, that's good. Because it isn't goin' to happen. What about the other women? My...my sisters?" The word felt foreign coming out of her lips.

To think she'd always wished for a sister. Not like this.

"Only one of them had similar test results. You'll share the inheritance with her."

*Sister.* She had a sister. Not a *real* sister, of course. Not someone who grew up with her, sharing a room, brushing her hair, reading to her, chasing frogs, and collecting rocks and sticks. Not someone who worried about her enough to invade her privacy and ask who the sexy panties were for. *Sadie.*

At the thought, Daisy was caught between a sound that was somewhere between a snort and a sob. Daisy already had two sisters who were more real to her than someone who had a biological link. The words should mean more. Sister. Father. Mother.

"I don't wish you any harm, Mr. Jones," Daisy said to Rusty. "Thank you, but I don't want your money."

With that she turned and left the room. She wasn't going to forgive him. The forgiveness was not hers to give. Hank should forgive, if he wanted to. He would be the only person owed an apology in this scenario. He'd raised another man's daughter all along believing she was his own. It wasn't fair to do that to a man.

Daisy was halfway to the nurse's desk when she heard the sound of Wade's deep voice.

"I don't care when visiting hours are, ma'am, I need to find Daisy Carver and I need to find her now."

The nurse turned her attention from Wade to Daisy when she stopped a few feet away from the desk. Wade's gaze followed and his eyes met hers. Gaze soft and warm, he slowly walked toward her.

It seemed like a lifetime ago since last night when he'd held her while she cried her heart out.

Her feelings had not changed for Wade, but now she had tiny seeds of doubts. Maybe she'd wanted Wade so much that she'd formed him into who she wanted him to be. Loyal and faithful. Trustworthy. Was he all of those things or were those just words, too?

"I'm sorry I took your truck," she said. "But I didn't want you to talk me out of this."

"Forget that." He pulled her into his arms, holding her tightly against him. "I was worried."

"I know."

"You should know that I went looking for you at the ranch, and I showed Sadie the letter."

"That's okay. There's no way I could keep this from my family. I was a dummy to think that I could."

"Sadie wouldn't tell anyone else. We can still keep this quiet, if you want."

"No, I need to do this. It's the right thing." She nudged her chin toward Rusty's room. "That's what I was doing in there with Mr. Jones. Facing him. Telling him exactly what I thought of him *and* Maggie."

"That's my girl."

She buried her face in his warm neck. "I've had a very long morning. And I just want to go home."

THE MOMENT WADE FOUND DAISY, every thought, every emotion he'd had for the past several hours just loaded, locked, and clicked into place. There was no longer even the slightest doubt in his mind that he loved this woman beyond what he'd believed humanly possible. If it hadn't been proven to him once, when he feared she'd been injured, waking up finding her gone solidified his feelings. He'd do anything for Daisy to give her the life she deserved.

He followed her back to the Double C Ranch, and he figured later, they'd both drive back to his house in his truck. First, she would tell her family, and he'd be there to support her. There was so much he wanted to tell her. His life had become clear the moment he stopped resisting his feelings for her. Without a doubt, nothing in this new life of his would ever again be boring with Daisy at his side. She challenged him in every way and made him a better man. She was simply…everything. And she had to marry him. She had to say yes to the rest of their lives together.

For the first time in his life, he wanted this security and safety with a woman. All the domesticity he'd previously rejected and found dull and complacent. It no longer felt that way. Not with her.

He parked the truck he'd borrowed from Sadie right behind his own.

Daisy hopped out of his truck and walked over to him. "I need to tell everyone. What a Christmas present, right?"

Right. It was Christmas Eve. Tonight, Daisy and her family would be going to the midnight service, most likely. He'd be there with them, too.

"You can wait, if you want."

"No, it's going to be all over my face that something is wrong. And Sadie knows. She can't keep a thing from Lincoln. I just…better get through this."

"If that's what you want. I'm there with you."

Then she fixed him with those deep-emerald eyes and what he saw in them killed him.

*Regret.*

"I think I need to do this alone, too. You should just go home and I'll…talk to you in a few days. When everything has calmed down some."

"You don't want to spend Christmas together."

"I think it's best…I…I know we made plans, but everything has changed."

"Nothing has changed for me. I love you, Daisy."

"And I love you. That's what kills me. I spent half my life trying to be different than my mother. And now, look at me. I fell in love with a rodeo cowboy. Just. Like. Her."

"Jesus, Daisy. She didn't love Rusty. It's not the same thing."

"Isn't it? I've loved you for so long that maybe I idealized you. You're not this perfect man."

"Sweetheart, nobody is."

"That's not what I meant. But it's just I didn't let myself think about the life you led before. I'm a pretty blank slate, and you're…you're…"

"*Not* a blank slate."

"There's lots of different kinds of cowboys in the rodeo circuit. Some men bring along their wives, girlfriends, families. Others are loners too intent on the win to be distracted. And others are like Rusty, having a good time with every buckle bunny they could find." She took a breath. "Which one were you?"

"Do you really have to ask? I'm the *loner*."

He'd been the cowboy too intent on winning to be distracted by anyone. Except for that last event. He'd lost his concentration and now he understood why. He'd still been grieving for his mother, and the fact was that rather than face his grief, he'd run from Stone Ridge. Run hard, and fast, and far from reminders of what he'd really lost. Everything that mattered.

He'd lost his focus and paid for it dearly.

"Wade, you had a reputation. I wouldn't listen to the rumors, but maybe I just didn't want to believe them. Those rumors about my mother turned out to be true. Secrets don't work. They come out eventually and destroy lives."

"We don't have any secrets. If you want to know whether I was a monk, then no, I wasn't. But I was no *Rusty Jones*."

"I want to believe that." She gnawed on her lower lip and tears sprung to her eyes.

His heart cracked open like a walnut. "But bottom line, you don't."

"Wade, I'm sorry. I don't know if I can do this—"

"No need." He held up a palm. "Don't be sorry. If you don't trust me, we have nothing. I think we're done here."

With that he turned, and hopped in his truck, salvaging a little slice of his pride.

He drove away without looking back, leaving his sore and bleeding heart on the Double C Ranch.

# CHAPTER 21

*P*lans with Daisy for an all-night tree trimming on Christmas Eve gone, Wade had nothing to do. He'd been invited to the Henderson ranch for brunch, along with nearly everyone else who didn't have other plans, but that wasn't until tomorrow morning.

Merry Christmas to him.

The stupid, sappy—both literally and figuratively—tree stood in the corner. Naked. Lights and ornaments Daisy had brought over lay in a box under the tree. He could trim the tree by himself, of course, but there was no point to that. He'd avoided this ritual for a damn good reason.

Whenever he got himself home in time for Christmas, he'd decorate the tree for his mother. *Her way.* She'd cook a roast and serve him spiked eggnog while she barked directions. They'd argue, eat, drink, and laugh the entire time. Lights went on the way she wanted, meticulously, on every bough. The ornaments one inch apart. He took care of the tree topper. Even he, over six feet, required a ladder. She'd always wanted to get the tallest tree in all the land. The pine needles brushed the top of their ceiling. Ridiculous.

*Lord, he missed her.*

Wade grabbed a cold beer from the fridge and eyed a casserole he'd defrosted to have food available. For *Daisy.* And man, he *hated* casseroles. Every single blessed one. He hated everything they represented. Condolences issued by way of comfort food. Food that can be easily frozen and served later. Food for the grieving because apparently everyone forgot how to cook when they lost a loved one. Well, this was the last straw. This was final. No more casseroles in his house!

He viciously pulled the covered enchilada dish out of the fridge and emptied it into the trash can. Cheese, tortillas, chili peppers, corn, and meat mushed together in the trash, smelled like day-old tacos, and made his stomach roil and pitch.

*Go talk to your horse. You always feel better afterwards.*

Wade made his way to the stables and brushed Dante, then took him for a ride around the property. The day was cold and crisp and clear, helping his mood. The cattle grazing in the pasture cheered him even more, and he decided then and there that he would have more horses as soon as financially feasible. ATVs were great, and far cheaper, but there was joy in the majestic animals. And he wouldn't deprive himself of that connection to his past.

Also, he was going to give lessons. Barrel racing, bull riding, lassoing. Teenagers and young kids. He wouldn't push the younger ones like his father had pushed him. He'd let the love of the sport grow naturally. His focus would be one of safety, since he could serve as a cautionary tale.

Maybe Linc would want to be involved and help get this started. After the holidays, he'd give Kari Lynn a call, see if she still wanted his advice. He loved the rodeo, and just because he couldn't participate anymore didn't mean he couldn't help others. There was joy in the competition, and not only in the winning. It would be another way of giving back to the community that he had loved so much. He had a new sense of community.

Different, but still important. Yeah, he was back to stay. Even without Daisy. This was his land. It was no longer simply dirt, and he understood his mother's connection. It was more than land. This was generational. A strong heritage of hardworking folks. Stone Ridge was his town. His mother's home, and now his. Again.

Yeah, he could keep busy. Plenty to do.

Outside the new barn, he spied the Model T where they'd left it. Daisy had worked hard on that car, had it running at one time for a couple of minutes. The girl had talent. And for more than one thing. Not just cars, but also slipping inside a man's heart when he wasn't looking.

Wade slid his hand down the hood, trying to understand the fascination. Seeing this car through her eyes, instead of his father's, he no longer saw a wasted investment but a link to the past. So many people ran from their pasts, but Daisy had chosen to embrace hers. No more secrets, she'd said. He admired the hell out of that.

Wade had always been less of a car person than he was a horse person, but necessity had forced him to learn a few things. And he had the tools. Polishing the beast that had survived a roof falling on it would give him something to do for the rest of the day. Keep his mind off Daisy. He snorted. *That* was a joke. He'd begun to think of this as *Daisy's* car. As he dusted and polished, he had a brilliant idea.

Yes. This would work.

"I finally outsmarted you, old man."

A few hours later, Wade was nearly done with part one of his master plan when a truck pulled up. *Lincoln.* Well, Wade should have expected this visit. He wiped the oil off his hands and walked to meet him.

His oldest friend looked pale, and stunned, and Wade's gut clenched with worry. As an only child, Wade couldn't imagine the shock of finding that someone you'd grown up with as a sibling wasn't fully related to you by blood.

"I guess you heard," Wade said.

"Yeah." Lincoln dragged a hand down his face. "And I had to get away. All the crying, the hugging, the kissing. I've had enough. Time for a break."

"How's Hank doing with the news?"

"Better than I thought he would. Maybe he was prepared. Same with Mima and Jackson. It's not like any of us hadn't considered this could be a possibility. We just didn't want to believe it and now we have to accept this." Lincoln hesitated for a beat. "Hey, I wanted to thank you for being there for Daisy. It makes sense that she wanted someone who wasn't as connected to the outcome."

Wade liked to think it had been more than that, but he'd recently been humbled. Not everyone believed Wade Cruz was the best thing since Texas became a state. The woman he loved, for instance. Turned out he was right in the first place. He wasn't good enough for her.

"I was honored to help."

Lincoln clapped Wade's back, and they walked toward the new barn. "What are you up to? Take my mind off my family mess."

"Lots of planning," Wade said. "I wanted to talk to you about starting up a clinic to teach rodeo, right here in town. On my land."

"Yeah?"

"Finally got over myself. It would sure supplement my income while I get the cattle ranch profitable. You know what they say, those who can, do. Those who can't, teach."

"Proving once again that those who teach are often the best at what they do."

Wade chuckled at the underhanded compliment. "While I can no longer participate, I can certainly teach the sport."

"That's a great idea, actually."

"Glad you think so. I'm going to need your help getting this clinic started."

"Count on it, buddy. Whatever you need. I'm there."

For the next hour, they were two old friends again. Former rodeo cowboys, arms spread over the fenced corral. Heads bent, making plans. The possibilities of a new future opened up to Wade and some of the weight of losing Daisy lightened. Not all. No, he expected he would carry that for the rest of his life and love her for just as long. He would not be one of those men who married someone other than the one woman who had his whole heart. Hank had shown him what a disaster that could be. Better to wind up alone.

Lincoln walked to his truck. "Guess we'll see you at the family dinner tomorrow?"

"She didn't tell you?"

"Tell me what?"

"We broke up."

"What? Why didn't you *say* something?"

"It didn't come up."

"It didn't come up! What do you mean it didn't come *up*? Shit fire, what did you *do*, Wade?"

"What did *I* do?"

"You must have done *something* to screw this up! She's loved you for half of her life."

"She wanted some 'distance' and 'time.'" He held up finger quotes. "Doesn't know if she can do this. She has this strange idea that because she fell in love with a rodeo cowboy she's following in your mother's wayward footsteps."

Lincoln narrowed his eyes. "What? That's crazy!"

"I agree, but if that's what she thinks, I have to let her go.

She doesn't trust me, bottom line, mostly because of Rusty, I imagine. That man keeps ruining our lives just by existing."

"Damn it, Wade! Did it ever occur to you that someone who's been abandoned by both parents might just want a man who will never let her go?"

*No. It hadn't.*

He was a certified jackass. He'd let his own foolish pride cloud his judgment.

"Shit fire!" Wade threw his hat to the ground. He'd done that only once before, when he'd lost a tournament because of one bad call. "Why didn't I think of that?"

"I'd call you a dimwit, but this is something I would do. Sometimes, when you're too close to the situation, you just can't see it." Lincoln pointed. "And ego gets in the way. You have to fix this. Just because she's gone off plan and she's a little bit confused, that doesn't mean you give up on her. You love her, right?"

"I want to *marry* her, that's how much I love her."

Lincoln let out a low whistle. "Never thought I'd hear *you* say you want to get hitched."

"Same, buddy. Same. And now look at you. I never wanted to get hitched, because I'd never been with Daisy. She changed everything for me. I love her."

"Give her some time and she'll come around. And for the love of God, don't you ever give up on her."


*Dear Albert,*

*Earlier today, Daisy came by to give me the news. She's not Hank's biological daughter.*

*Merry Christmas!*

*Here's the thing. I was foolish enough to believe that nothing would ever hurt as much as this news. I thought everything in our lives would change. I don't know why. Because suddenly I looked at this beautiful girl whom I've raised since she was a toddler, and I knew the truth in an instant. Nothing has really changed. Nothing at all. And it never will, as we belong to each other in a way that DNA can't create. We're a family and that's much harder to accomplish than mixing up a bunch of genes while having yourself a bit of fun. If you catch my drift.*

*All of us gathered together and Daisy told us the truth. We cried, we hugged, we gave assurance of our love. Daisy, my little spitfire, in the center of all this devotion, understanding that this didn't matter to any of us. She has proven to us, time and again, that she's a Carver through and through, biology be damned!*

*And with that, I wash my hands of this matchmaking business. I'm an old lady and plum tuckered out. Daisy will love who she loves and choose whomever she chooses. Her heart may be broken a time or two, whether by a bright and shiny rodeo cowboy, or simply a rancher's son. Either way. Shit happens, as the cowboys these days are saying.*

*As long as my darling girl is happy in the end, I don't care who she winds up marrying. And, of course, I have given her my approval of Wade. You would have been proud. He's Rose's boy, and as you said, she raised him right. It's true that he's bright and shiny and oh-so-handsome but something in the way he looks at Daisy shows me that this is different. I think he loves her, Albert. Really loves her.*

*And, I've chosen to have faith.*

DAISY CRIED ALL DAY. Hank held her in his arms first, then Brenda. Next, Lincoln, Jackson, Sadie, and Eve. Finally, even Sammy got in there with a sweet baby hug.

This was tough enough to endure without a cracked heart, but Daisy had one of those, too.

She hadn't pictured breaking it off with Wade on Christmas Eve but maybe it had been for the best. Rumors often contained at least a seed of truth, and plenty of women referred to Wade as a commitment-phobe. Not marriage material. She'd disagreed, of course, but simply because she'd refused to believe otherwise. Clearly, the name "Wild Wade" wasn't just about his fearlessness on the circuit. He was a rodeo cowboy and with his looks, it was entirely possible that years from now, a child or two would show up on his doorstep, wanting a DNA test.

The services at Trinity Church that night were a blur for Daisy. Pastor June went on and on about gifts. And about unconditional love. Love was patient. Kind. Not rude or prideful, not easily angered. *Keeps no record of wrongs.*

Daisy slunk lower and lower on the bench pew as she listened to words surely meant for her. Guilt spiked like a painful prick. She'd never judged Wade before. Never painted him with the bold, broad brush that some others had. Because she loved him. Always had. Maybe she always would. But at least she'd spare herself from the heartache of losing him to another woman someday.

She wondered if Linc already knew about her and Wade, as he'd disappeared for a few hours, and gave her strange looks during dinner.

She didn't want to talk about Wade. Her heart ached like someone had pierced her chest with an ice pick. Love wasn't supposed to *hurt* like this. She was so tired of losing the people she loved. And she'd loved Maggie with all her heart. Daisy remembered that much. She remembered how Maggie was once Daisy's entire world. Her sun, her moon, her stars.

Someone else had now taken that place in her heart and it wasn't whom she'd expected.

*Wade.*

Tonight they were supposed to trim the Christmas tree. It was to have been an all-night thing, probably ending by making love under the tree. She wondered what he was doing tonight instead and whether it was possible that he was hurting as much. He had no family and was trying to rebuild a ranch on his own. Her heart ached remembering the look in his eyes when she'd told him that she had doubts about him. It was not what he'd expected from her. She'd hurt him.

But he'd hurt her, too, by so quickly breaking it off and walking away. She might have liked to see him fight for her, for them. The same way he fought for anything that truly mattered to him.

For his mother. For the rodeo. For his ranch.

He hadn't fought for her.

And still, she loved him.

She'd been sliding down a mountain, with no one there to catch her when she landed. Wade had. He'd been there for her and held her for hours while she'd cried every last tear. Another guy would have cut and run. Not Wade.

It was late on Christmas Eve, but still, Daisy picked up the landline in her bedroom and dialed the number on the business card. "Hello, Mr. Jones? This is Daisy. I've given this a lot of thought. And I do want my part of the inheritance."

"What made you change your mind?"

"Someone very special to me needs the money. A retired and injured rodeo cowboy. You can tell Rusty that he's going to help restore an old cattle ranch."

"That's great, Daisy. It's good to know he'll be helping someone, especially a rodeo cowboy. He's going to love that. And thank you for coming by to see him. It meant a lot."

"I'm sorry I wasn't kinder. What happened wasn't entirely his fault and I understand that."

"That's generous of you. I will tell him you said that. Merry Christmas."

Feeling just a little bit better, Daisy hung up and steered her thoughts away from Wade. Sweet memories of reaching for him. His constant and solid presence like an anchor in her life.

"Daisy?" Mima hollered from the kitchen. "Are you asleep?"

Well, had she been asleep she wouldn't be *now*. But she wasn't in bed and likely wouldn't be till late tonight. She couldn't stop thinking about Wade and what she'd done. She'd allowed him to believe she didn't think him good enough for her. This was so far from the truth it was laughable, but she'd practically spelled it out for him.

*Love is patient. Love is kind.*
*Believes all things.*
*Endures all things.*

"I'm not sleepy." Daisy stood under the archway of the entrance to the kitchen. "Do you need something?"

"This is just like when you were little and couldn't fall asleep waiting for Santa Claus." Holding a plate of cookies, Mima tipped her chin toward the table.

Daisy hated to break it to her, but this wasn't at all like waiting up for Santa filled with the wide-eyed excitement of a young child. This was insomnia because her world had been torpedoed. Then she'd blown up the rest of her life and now didn't quite know how to move past this ache.

"I don't need any more cookies. They make me thirsty." But Daisy took a seat anyway.

"Just indulge me one last time."

Tentacles of fear spread through Daisy's heart. "What do you *mean* one last time?"

She waved a hand dismissively. "I'm not dyin'. But I will, someday. It's inevitable, sugar. How much longer can I possibly live? We're not meant to live forever on earth. I'll be joinin' my Albert in heaven someday."

Daisy didn't want to think about Mima being gone, but it did give some comfort to think of them together again. And

Daisy could almost picture her grandfather right now, standing in the kitchen as he so often had, watching Mima cook.

*"You smell like gravy, woman,"* he'd say, sniffing her neck.

*Mima would raise her wooden spoon to him. "How dare you!"*

*"And I love gravy."* Pop would then grab Mima, spin her around, and kiss her.

She would giggle, muss his hair, and call him *"old man"* with a deep affection.

"Do you miss him?"

"My goodness, of course I do. He was the love of my life."

"You never missed the bright and shiny rodeo cowboy, did you?"

Mima took a bite of the gingerbread man, then chewed thoughtfully. "Well, no, but maybe that's because it wasn't really love. More like infatuation. Albert was the one for me."

People used to tell Daisy that she was infatuated with Wade. A crush. And the worst of them all: just puppy love. Won't last. Will fade with time. But it hadn't faded. If anything, her feelings for him grew deeper and stronger with every passing year. Every now and again, she'd prayed for her feelings to go away because it was too painful to love someone who was always gone and so far out of her reach.

"How do you know it's really love? True love?" Daisy played with a cookie in the shape of a Christmas tree.

"When you can't stop thinking about them. When life without them is unthinkable. When you can't stand the thought of them being in pain or hurting."

Daisy felt all these things, but also a bone-deep disappointment that he'd given up too easily. Too soon.

"And what if they disappoint you?"

"True love has nothing to do with that. People will forever disappoint you. That's our human nature. What matters is if the one you love can be loyal to you. Committed to you. If he'll stick around when things get rough." She took a breath. "And if you can do the same for him. Also, it doesn't hurt if your heart speeds up when he walks into a room."

Daisy's heart had done that for Wade for as long as she could remember. Whenever she'd see him with Lincoln and he'd grin and say, "Hiya, Peanut" she couldn't help but think he meant more than that. Even those two words had always felt like love. In her heart, every time he said those two words, she'd heard, "Love you."

"That's how you feel about Wade, isn't it?" Mima prompted.

"Yes. But I don't want to."

"Why?"

"I thought he was right for me, but maybe you were right all along."

"This is hard for me to say, but I wasn't right at all. Albert made me realize…um, what I mean is, I suddenly came to my senses about all this. The shiny rodeo cowboy in my past had blinded me again. Daisy, not all rodeo cowboys are the same. You can't picture them all as Rusty."

"Actually, Rusty told me that, too. Some cowboys bring their families along on the circuit. Others are the serious kind that have to win every time. And the rest are a lot like Rusty."

"Yes, and Wade was the serious one intent on winning."

"Why do you say that?"

"Oh, sugar. I'm sorry I didn't tell you this sooner, but it really wasn't my story to tell."

"What does that mean?"

"Well, Wade's father liked to gamble. That *isn't* a rumor."

"Yes, that's how they kept Rose alive and paid for her cancer treatment."

Mima shook her head. "No, Jorge left nothing besides a heavily mortgaged ranch."

"And the classic vintage car Wade couldn't sell," she muttered.

No *wonder* he hated that car. It was everything he needed and nothing he could have. Not Wade. He wouldn't break his promise. Wade was a man of his word. That told her everything she ever needed to know about him.

"Most people think Wade should have a lot of money from all his years in the rodeo. Only a few of us know the truth. We keep quiet about it because Rose asked us to. She didn't want to humiliate her family, or Wade. But his father gambled all the money away. Wade *had* to win. He didn't just have to win for the classic ol' rodeo ego, or for the thrill. He won to save his mother. To save the ranch. So, I have no doubt he was serious and determined to win."

"He *had* to win."

"And there were all those times he worked for Hank during the off-season. Did you think he did that simply to flirt with you?"

"No," she squeaked.

Wade's flirting, the way he couldn't seem to say no to a woman, all those things led one to believe something else entirely about "Wild Wade." That he was *exactly* like Rusty.

*But I should have known better. I did know better. This is my fault.*

She'd let fear stop her again when she'd promised to be done playing it safe.

"I was right about him all along. Except there at the end, I let fear cloud my vision. I let this thing with Rusty confuse me just because I so desperately didn't want to be like Maggie. I've tried to be the opposite of her all my life."

"No one blames you. This whole paternity thing threw you for a loop. It must have felt like your whole world was imploding."

"Wade was so understanding and supportive. He doesn't

judge me for being the love child of a rodeo cowboy and a buckle bunny. I didn't want to be this walking cliché. And I didn't want to be *anything* like her."

"Well, sugar, a lot of good women have fallen for a cowboy." Mima patted Daisy's hand gently. "That's why I wanted to have this talk. Ever since your mother left, I've tried to do nothing but protect you. Maybe I went too far. I thought you should have someone like my Albert. Someone who offered you love, safety, and security. I didn't see Wade as safe or secure. The poor lamb has been through so much and I honestly didn't see him staying. And I know you need someone who won't ever let you go."

And Wade had let her go too easily. Yes, she'd been the one to voice her doubts. To define him by two words: *rodeo cowboy* when he'd been so kind to her. He should have argued with her. Fought. And still…

"I do love him. It seems I always have."

"Rose was right about the two of you."

"Rose?"

"Until the day she died, she believed you and Wade were meant to be. That someday the two of you would be together. It was written in the stars, don't you know."

"What? Why didn't I hear about this?"

"Honestly? None of us believed it. It seemed so unlikely. Wade was gone so much, always taking risks, and you were the girl afraid of your own shadow. We all loved Rose but thought maybe she was a little fanciful. But she was a sweetheart, and Lord, how I miss her. I should have encouraged you and Wade, but I had to think of you first before I encouraged what Rose wanted."

Daisy thought back to the night at the Shady Grind when Lenny had said, "You mean Rose was right?" About that time, Wade had done his best to distract her by challenging her to a pool game. Of course, he probably knew what his mother believed but maybe he'd never taken her seriously, either.

"If you love him, take the risk. I took a risk, too, after having my own heart broken. And I found true love with a rancher. It will be different for you. But I swore to Albert that I'm out of this matchmaking business. So, this is entirely up to you. I didn't think it was fair not to mention it since I've not been Wade's greatest fan. That wasn't fair of me. It's Christmas, for cryin' out loud. And I'm going to choose love over fear. Maybe you could do the same."

DAISY WOKE on Christmas morning with dried tears on her cheeks.

She'd fallen asleep with thoughts of Wade. With memories of him from long ago, when they'd been kids. And of the past two weeks as she'd gotten to know and love him so deeply.

Daisy hadn't fallen for a rodeo cowboy. Years ago, she'd loved a beautiful boy with all her heart. That boy had tried everything to please his father, adored his mother, was her brother's best friend, kind and loving, and the only son of a woman whom Daisy loved.

She couldn't wait until after Christmas Day to fix this.

He was the best thing to ever happen to her and she'd been right about him all along. Only fear had stopped her from moving forward. Unfounded fear.

Daisy woke and careened down the hallway to the kitchen, half dressed. "Mima!"

Her socks had her sliding and nearly falling until she righted herself by pressing her palm against the wall.

"Good Lord, child! Don't scare me like that." Mima held a hand to her neck, her gaze dropping to Daisy's half-dressed state. "What is this mess?"

"I have to miss the gift giving this morning. My presents are all wrapped and under my bed. But I need to find Wade. I have to fix this. The thing is, I broke up with him because I made the mistake of thinking he was a rodeo cowboy."

"Well, he *was*. He retired." Mima cocked her head as if dealing with someone who'd taken a knock to the head and forgotten a few days in there.

"That's not the point! He's the 'serious loner intent on winning.' Why did I ever doubt him?"

Mima slowly shook her head. "I don't know why either of us did, sweetheart. He's Rose's boy."

"He is, and I love him so much. I hurt him, and I have to make it all up to him. Even if it takes me the rest of my life."

"I'm sure you will but I do hope it won't take *that* long."

"Is it too early to go over there? What am I saying? He's always up early. He works so hard on the ranch, on everything."

She glanced outside to judge the weather when she saw the glistening chrome of the Model T. It was parked just outside their home, by the barn.

And had a big red bow on it.

"What is it? You've been standing there for a whole minute. Did it snow or something?" Mima joined Daisy at the window. "Well, son of a biscuit eater, what in tarnation is that?"

"It's a vintage classic car."

"Well, I can see it's a car, Daisy. I'm not *blind*. What is Wade's car doing on my land?"

"I don't know but I'm going to find out." She threw open the front door.

"Now, young lady, not without proper clothe—"

Daisy didn't hear the end of that sentence. She grabbed her boots by the front door and tugged them on, running outside in her long T-shirt.

The Model T had been polished and gleamed to a shine and there was a note taped to the front shield.

*He never said I couldn't give this away.*
*~ Wade*
*P.S. Merry Christmas*

The keys were in the ignition.

It was, by far, the best Christmas present she'd ever had, from the most honorable man she'd ever known.

Mima had followed her outside, a coat thrown over her shoulders. By then, Daisy had jumped behind the wheel of the car.

"This is a classic," she said. "They don't make them like this anymore."

"You and your cars."

"His father wouldn't let him sell this car."

"That sounds just like him. Idiot man. Leave your son a ranch in need of a major overhaul and don't give him any help in raising the money."

"This is a gift. You don't sell a gift. If anything, you give it away." She smiled. "It's called regifting."

Like her inheritance, a gift from a man who owed her something. A gift of which she would give every penny to Wade.

"Very generous of Wade to give you this car. I think you better take it for a spin. Go thank him. But try to be back in time for gift giving."

After running back inside to change into her jeans and a warmer outfit, Daisy started up the antique and waved to Mima.

Daisy made it three feet before the car stalled.

She got out, looked under the hood, shook her fist, and

begged the car gods for assistance. "Don't prove me wrong. I worked so hard on you!"

"Daisy, sugar, *cars* can't hear you," Mima said patiently. "I've told you that since you were a little girl."

"But I can hear me," Daisy muttered as she tinkered under the hood and found the problem. Within minutes, she had the car humming again. She patted the roof of the car and gave Mima a triumphant smile.

"Let's face it. I have a gift. Machines fear me."

But this Model T didn't fear her enough. Not enough to go over twenty-five miles an hour.

"C'mon!" She hit the steering wheel. "I would like to get there before tomorrow."

Thankfully, traffic would be extra light today, not that it was a freeway thoroughfare at any other time. But today, everyone would be curled under a warm blanket still in bed, or maybe already opening presents with their young children. Or with their lovers.

And she was driving a vintage car down the highway, except she thought the word "driving" might be a little generous. She was more or less limping down the road.

Speaking of limping, there was a golf cart right behind her. Driven by Lenny, who didn't understand two words: day off.

"Hiya, Missy. What's doin'?" Lenny called out as he passed her. "Out for a leisurely drive there?"

Riding next to him was Maybelle, Beulah's sister, who lived alone on the dairy farm not far from here.

"Merry Christmas, Lenny," Daisy said, not wanting to be impolite. She nodded. "Miss Maybelle."

"What kind of car is that?" Lenny said. "It looks like an antique."

"It is. Very special." Daisy kept her eyes on the road, for

what she had no idea. She'd have plenty of time to brake were a turtle to cross.

This was torture. She wanted to get to Wade and apologize. Kiss him and ask him to forgive her for jumping to the wrong conclusion. It might be faster to walk there.

"Lenny, don't you ever take a day off?"

"This *is* my day off," Lenny said. "We're goin' to brunch over at the Henderson ranch. Winona invited us."

Were they on a date? *Lenny and Maybelle?*

Hey, why not? Love at any age. And with any luck, she'd get to Wade before *she* was sixty.

"I'm on my way to Wade's so maybe I'll see y'all later. Go on ahead of me, Lenny. I think your golf cart might be faster."

"No question there. What if I push you?"

"I would like to get there in time to set up my punch," Maybelle said. "You know how Winona loves my punch. I'm sorry, young lady."

"Y'all go on ahead. I'll get there."

Lenny went ahead, Maybelle sending Daisy a wave and blowing a kiss. She mouthed, "Thank you" and winked.

Before long, they were a dot in the distance.

Daisy petted the dashboard. "Don't you worry, you're special. So what if you're not particularly fast? Maybe *fast* is overrated."

Wade had taken pains to clean her up. He might have spent all night doing it. Her heart ached and swelled picturing him slaving over the car he hated. *For her.*

Finally, she arrived at the Cruz ranch. Another twenty or so minutes—when she was tempted to get out and push —and she was down the dirt road to the main house. She didn't see any sign of Wade, but his truck was near the barn.

She parked and looked up to find Wade standing on the

porch, eyes narrowed. Was he still angry? The gift implied he wasn't, but his tight jaw said something else.

"You drove the car here?" he said, sounding incredulous.

"Yes, why? Didn't you drive it to me?"

"*Drive* it to you? I thought it didn't run for longer than a couple of minutes!"

"Then how did you…" She turned to the car, waving her arms in a flourish.

"Riggs and I used a trailer to haul it over to you." He walked down the steps, slowly. "You drove it here, Peanut?"

*Peanut.* The nickname that put distance between them, that made it clear they were again nothing more than friends. She had hoped that it had become his affectionate pet name for her. Now, the wary look in his eyes made her wonder if he'd ever forgive her for being an idiot.

"Um, machines fear me. But don't get too excited. She doesn't want to go above twenty-five miles an hour." Slowly and deliberately, she walked toward him until she was only inches away. "Thank you for my gift. I particularly liked the note. It's…everything."

Dear Lord, he still hadn't said anything. Just studied her from under those hooded eyes.

"Oh, Wade. Please forgive me. You can't be reduced down to two words. You're not just a 'rodeo cowboy.' You're the boy that I've loved half my life and still love. I've been through so much lately that I got confused. I lied to you. Of *course* I trust you. I know you. You're my whole heart."

He stared at her, unblinking, without saying a word. She was so nervous that she kept talking.

"I want to go inside with you and decorate that tree if you haven't already. I just want to pick up where we left off."

He still hadn't moved from the step where he'd been standing. Well, that was it. Other than throwing herself into his arms—which she briefly considered—she didn't know how else to make this up to him. She'd made a mistake from a knee-jerk reaction. Fear, her nemesis. If he couldn't forgive her, then…

Should she tell him about the money? No, she'd surprise him with that later.

"Okay, well." She gnawed at her lower lip. "I guess I'll be going. Merry Christmas."

"Wait a second." Wade came slowly down the rest of the steps.

"Yes?" She closed the distance between them.

"This is my fault. Lincoln reminded me that if I love you, I'm not allowed to just give up. Believe it or not, I didn't." He reached for her hand and brushed a kiss across her knuckles. "It took me less than a day to get over myself. I was just going to give you a little time before I came after you, guns blazin'. I love you, Daisy. With all my heart."

Oh, yes! Her heart was finally full again.

"I didn't know that your mother always saw us being together. You could have told me that."

Wade cleared his throat. "She saw it in a dream and wouldn't stop talking about it. Said that if I didn't get my head out of my butt, I would someday lose you to some other guy."

"That would never happen." She pulled back to meet his eyes. "Actually, it *didn't* happen, and there were several years in there where it could have."

"Meant to be, I guess. That's what my mother said." He lowered his head and gave her a deep kiss. "Thank you for waiting for me."

"I love you, Wade. And there's no way we're not going to spend Christmas together."

"Christmas or Labor Day, you're never gettin' away from me again."

"Please promise me that. Don't ever let me go. Even

though I hope we've been through the worst, you never know."

"I promise I won't let my stupid pride get in the way again if you promise you won't believe every foolish rumor about me."

Daisy made the motion of a cross against her heart.

"I've got a gift of my own coming to you. I accepted Mr. Jones's inheritance, and I want you to have it when the time comes. From one old rodeo cowboy to another, one who's a far better man. I like the serendipity of that. Full circle. You deserve it, Wade. You gave up all that money the show offered you to be with me. And I want you to have the ranch working again, back to what it used to be. And I don't want you to break your back doin' it." She smiled what she hoped was a wicked and knowing smile. "I have plans for that back of yours. I need for it to last several more years."

Wade chuckled, wrapped his arms around her waist, and pulled her tight against him. "It sounds like we both found a way to accept a gift we didn't want, so long as we found a way to give it away to someone we love."

"I think that's perfect."

# EPILOGUE

*Six months later*

*D*ear Rose,
    *Well, I write letters to Albert. Why not also to you, my dear friend? I hope you know that I miss you dearly, and your boy is doing just fine. We're taking good care of him, yes, we are. We weren't at all sure he'd be okay, what with the injury, and the grief he couldn't bring himself to acknowledge. Daisy has been so good for him, and he for her. You were right about those two. I don't know why I didn't see it.*

*Sometimes love can happen between the two most unlikely of people, I guess. Especially when they're bound together by the common threads of family, home, and friendship. I don't know why I never saw it before, dear friend. You're right. They're perfect together.*

*Oh, and the wedding was beautiful! Rather quick, some thought, but why waste time when you know it's right? All us*

Carvers were present when Wade went down on bended knee after Sunday night dinner at our home. Sadie, Eve, Brenda, and I were sobbing by the end of his heartfelt proposal. I never would have thought those sweet words would have come straight out of "Wild Wade's" lips. What a fine man you raised, Rose. What a fine man.

Daisy almost didn't allow him to finish before she jumped into his arms and said yes. Loudly! She'd been waiting a long time for that moment. In a way, I know you have, too.

The wedding was at Trinity Church, of course, the place that has unfortunately been the site of far too many of our runaway brides. No one was even slightly worried about my Daisy, of course. She nearly flew to the altar. You would be surprised to see how lovely she looked in a white dress with flowing train and sweetheart collar. The girl who loves her jeans and flannel certainly looked like a young Grace Kelly on that auspicious day.

Then again, Wade filled out a tuxedo like a movie star himself. And to think they almost talked him into the dating reality show. Offered him money and still he turned it all down for true love!

Beulah still hasn't given up on Mr. Cowboy, bless her heart. What am I to do? All of mine are hitched and happy so they can roll in more women if they like. There are plenty of men here in need of a good woman. And we are certainly running out of them.

But don't you worry, Rose, your boy has one of the best of our women. Daisy will never stop loving him. And I'm sure babies are coming along, lickety split! If we are lucky enough to get a girl, I will be campaigning for your namesake, a "little Rose."

Well, I best sign off now. Daisy and Wade have invited us all over to the opening of his new rodeo clinic. That poor man, Rusty, died a few months ago and left some money to his daughters. That helped Wade and Daisy to start the clinic, where Wade will be teaching some of his skills. Lincoln will be lending a hand, teaching roping among other things.

. . .

*I* REMAIN YOUR OLDEST FRIEND, *in death as in life. Keep a light on for me, dear Rose.*

*Kisses and hugs,*
*~ Lillian Carver*

## ABOUT THE AUTHOR

Born in Tuscaloosa, Alabama Heatherly lost her accent by the time she was two. Her grandmother, Mima, kept both the accent and spirit of the southern woman alive for decades.

After leaving Alabama, Heatherly lived with her family in Puerto Rico and Maryland before being transplanted kicking and screaming to the California Bay Area.

She now loves it here, she swears. Except the traffic.

ALSO BY HEATHERLY BELL

Lucky Cowboy

Nashville Cowboy

Built like a Cowboy

Grand Prize Cowboy

Winning Mr. Charming

The Accidental Kiss

COMING SOON:

The Charming Checklist

The Trouble with a Kiss

Mr. Cowboy

For a complete book catalog, please check the author's website:
heatherlybell.com